last of four novels that preceded Machado Assis's famous trilogy of realistic master-ces, *Iaiá Garcia* belongs to what critics have ed the Brazilian author's "romantic" phase. . it is far more than that implies. Like his er early works, *Iaiá Garcia* foreshadows the mes and characters of Assis's most masterful vels.

Iaiá Garcia intertwines the lives of three aracters in a subtly and wryly developing ationship. While the youthful Iaiá is growing o womanhood, a tentative love affair occurs tween the aristocratic Jorge and the prideful tela. This affair is afflicted by ironic shifts of tune and in time the maturing Iaiá becomes rival for Jorge's attentions. Assis's portrayal the relationship among these three characters a perceptive study of uncompromising pride, warted love, jealousy, misunderstanding, be-lderment, and attainment.

As the translator, Albert I. Bagby, Jr., con-nds, the story of Iaiá, Jorge, and Estela re-ects the formula that Assis saw as fundamen-l to human life: "Will and ambition, when ey truly dominate, can struggle with other elings, but they are the weapons of the rong, and victory belongs to the strong." In ssis's view success comes to the strong and ilure to the weak. But both inhabit a world at is neutral—neither helping one nor hin-ering the other. The outcome of events in *Iaiá Garcia* may not seem entirely optimistic, but either is it pessimistic. And Mr. Bagby con-ludes, "Perhaps to understand the optimism of Assis one needs only to be . . . a hard, prag-natic realist. . . ."

Whether hard realists or unregenerate roman-ics, readers of this novel will find it a com-elling tale of love lost and won. Like his earli

[CONTINUED ON BACK FLAP]

a of Assis's *The Hand & the Glove*, y's English rendering of *Iaiá Garcia* original Portuguese is done with both nd sensitivity.

The Translator

Bagby, Jr., was born in Pôrto Alegre, an American mother and a Brazilian the age of eighteen he came to the ates, where he studied at Baylor, Mis-rth Carolina, and Vanderbilt univer-received a Ph.D. in Spanish literature University of Kentucky in 1968. Pres-s an associate professor of Portuguese sh at the University of Texas at El

Machado de Assis

IAIÁ GARCIA

Translated by
ALBERT I. BAGBY, JR.

THE UNIVERSITY PRESS OF KENTUCKY

ISBN: 0-8131-1353-9

Library of Congress Catalog Card Number: 76-24338

Copyright © 1977 by The University Press of Kentucky

A statewide cooperative scholarly publishing agency
serving Berea College, Centre College of Kentucky,
Eastern Kentucky University, The Filson Club,
Georgetown College, Kentucky Historical Society,
Kentucky State University, Morehead State University,
Murray State University, Northern Kentucky University,
Transylvania University, University of Kentucky,
University of Louisville, and Western Kentucky University.

Editorial and Sales Offices: Lexington, Kentucky 40506

Preface

Without the help of a number of people, this translation could not have been done. But before I acknowledge my debt to friends and family, I wish to discuss the general philosophy behind the translation. It has been my intention to find that always-elusive middle ground between literal interpretation and paraphrase which would best convey the distinctive flavor of the author's original words. For the sake of his genius and his readers, I hope that I have succeeded. At times it seemed best to leave the original Portuguese word or phrase—when there was no adequate alternative in English—as, for example, in the case of the name "Iaiá." In such instances, I have provided explanatory footnotes.

It is my further hope that the introduction which follows, along with the bibliography and textual notes, will provide further aids to the study and understanding of Assis.

To Massaud Moisés I am indebted for some of his notes and for the edition (São Paulo: Editora Cultrix, 1967) from which I translated. On a more personal note, I wish to express deep gratitude to my wife Nancy for her constant and careful editing of the manuscript, and to Professor Albert I. Bagby, my father, for his attentive proofreading of the entire manuscript. A profound debt is owed to the University of Texas-El Paso, and to Beverly Ryan, without whose assistance this book would not be published. Finally, special thanks also must go to Professor John Esten Keller, for his recognition of and interest in the dissemination of Assisian literature in the United States of America.

ALBERT I. BAGBY, JR.

Introduction

THE LIFE OF MACHADO DE ASSIS

Time and some painstaking research over the last two decades have served to clarify a number of misconceptions—some malicious, some romantic—about the childhood of Joaquim Maria Machado de Assis. Born June 21 and baptized November 13, 1839, he was the son of Francisco Jose de Assis and Maria Leopoldina Machado de Assis. His paternal grandparents were freed slaves, mulattoes, natives of Rio; his maternal grandparents were born in Portugal and presumably were white. Assis's mother was a native of one of the Azores. When the boy was ten she passed away, and five years later his father remarried.

Assis was born in a humble neighborhood of Rio called the Morro do Livramento and spent his childhood there. He attended public school until the eighth grade, and from an early age he manifested an interest in a literary career. His mother was literate, and if his childhood was humble, it was not uncultured. Friends attested to his refined manner, his unwillingness to participate in rowdy drinking or bawdy storytelling, his singleminded devotion to letters. A young man who, from ages fifteen to eighteen, was writing poetry, polemics, librettos for opera, and was translating French into Portuguese, could not have come from an environment of total illiteracy.

There is evidence that between ages fifteen and thirty Assis held a variety of jobs: typesetter, proofreader, editor, staff writer, and clerk. There is also evidence that he took part in numerous social and artistic ventures, was involved in the theater, and frequently went to the opera. His life was a busy one, and his friends moved in literary circles. He had also found time for romance before he met and married Carolina Xavier de Novais.

During a period of employment with the Paula Brito Bookstore, his literary ambitions found opportunity for development, and his first work, published in 1855, was the poem "Ela." In 1856 he went to work as a typesetter's apprentice for the Tipografia Nacional, today known as the Imprensa Nacional. Reportedly he was a dreamer and hence a worker who needed prodding; but the director understood his inclinations and encouraged him in his literary ambitions.

After two years there he began work on the *Correio Mercantil*, where, as an assistant and reviewer, he began to climb out of obscurity, exercising his talents in poetry and the theater. From 1860 to 1867 he worked for the *Diário do Rio de Janeiro*, and from 1867 to 1875 he wrote for the *Semana Ilustrada*. As a journalist he expressed his opinions frequently on political matters.[1] While critics have pointed to his neglect of the political scene in his fiction, to say that the omission proves disinterest is clearly an exaggeration. If Assis's novels are not primarily political, they do reflect an awareness of the world about him, as Miécio Tati points out.[2]

Assis's first volume of poetry, *Crisálidas*, was published in 1864, and his efforts over the next decade were divided among poetry, theater, and journalism. His financial status improved considerably during the sixties and seventies, and his various publications brought him some fame in literary and artistic circles.

In 1867, at the age of twenty-eight, Assis met Carolina Xavier de Novais, a refined, mature, and attractive young Portuguese woman who had just arrived in Brazil. Assis met her apparently through her brother, Faustino Xavier de Novais, his friend and a Portuguese poet. He seemed to find in this woman a tender, understanding spirit, a woman whose love and dedication and whose appreciation of his work would serve as a complement to his life. He described her as a rare combination of sentiment and intelligence—one with the capacity both to feel and to think. The marriage had Faustino's blessing, though he died three months before the wedding actually took place (November 12, 1869).

Assis began the decade of the seventies a married man. That period of conjugal happiness lasted thirty-five years. Unfortunately, we know little about the relationship of Assis and Carolina, as the author took great care to protect the privacy of their personal lives. The little evidence we do have—a poem, a novelette, a few letters—indicates that theirs was a strong, mature, loving relationship.

---

1. Miécio Tati, *O mundo de Machado de Assis* (Rio de Janeiro: Livraria São José, 1961), p. 63.
2. Ibid., p. 64.

In 1872 and 1874 respectively, Assis published his first two romances, *Ressurreição* and *A mão e a luva*. His appointment to the position of first officer of the State Secretariat of the Ministry of Agriculture, Commerce, and Public Works in 1873 gave him an income that permitted him to further his writing. But the pressures of his job, added to his efforts to complete *Iaiá Garcia* in 1878, demanded that he rest; and he took a leave from his post at the secretariat. Accompanying his physical exhaustion were worsening attacks of epilepsy from which, along with various intestinal disorders, he had long suffered.

In the mountains of the state of Rio, Carolina became at once a wife, a mother, and a nurse to the convalescing Machado. Without doubt, these three months in Nova Friburgo—one of the rare occasions on which Assis left the city of Rio—gave the author a different and more mature perspective, a maturity reflected almost immediately thereafter in his writing.

With his return to Rio began the richest period of his literary production. Although Assis continued to be plagued by epilepsy and myopia, he did publish in 1881 in volume form the novel *Memórias póstumas de Braz Cubas*. He was also excelling in his civil duties, and in 1889 he was promoted to head of the Directory of Commerce. In 1892 came another novel of the first order, *Quincas Borba*, and nine years after that, *Dom Casmurro*. He was now famous.

Despite problems with his health, Assis led an active social life, belonging to the Association of Brazilian Men of Letters and the Society of Letters and Arts. As a crowning accomplishment to his desire to see born an organization which would provide order and prestige to the literary life of Rio, he was the first president of the Brazilian Academy of Letters, and he remained in that office until his death.

Assis's prestige was well established, but his time was short. Carolina became seriously ill and a trip to Nova Friburgo for recuperation was in vain. When she died on October 20, 1904, Machado de Assis, profoundly feeling the loss of his strength and companion, began his own slow decline. His last novel, the short work *Memorial de Aires*, published in 1908, is Assis's rendering of the memories of his wife. The pessimism which many a critic has noted and will insist is a mainstay of Assis's works is not present in this novelette, though its tone is melancholy.

Machado de Assis died on September 29, 1908, surrounded by some of his closest friends and highest representatives of Brazilian letters—

José Veríssimo, Euclides da Cunha, and Coelho Neto—and knowing the heritage which he himself had left behind was enduring. Already one of the highest expressions of Brazilian literary achievement, he would become in time one of the most important literary figures of his hemisphere, with his works translated into several languages.

A complex personality like Machado de Assis is always of some curiosity to readers. As characters in novels take on real life, so authors also begin to live and breathe. So that we have more than our own imaginations to build on, let us listen to the description recorded by Francisca de Basto Cordeiro, who knew both Assis and Carolina:

He was of medium height, with lightly wavy, sleek, black hair, a sparse beard, and a moustache of flat hairs spaced as though they had been implanted . . . his complexion, bronze. On myopic and dark eyes he wore a *pince-nez* of golden circles with a black ribbon so that it would not fall. He spoke in a low voice, seldom and haltingly. He always dressed in black and wore a bowler hat; the archetype of the civil servant, correct and discreet. . . . An obscure and mediocre figure, he was at once saturnine and delicate, simple and reserved, grumpy and suspicious. He was not very expansive but sure about his friends, irritable and affectionate. He had the apparent inconsistencies of a nature that was exaggeratedly vibrant and concealed; a tender and delicate soul. His character was upright and honest. He inspired few friendships but knew how to make friends and retain them. He was endowed with a singular talent for investigating mediocre souls. A strange and complex spirit, he slowly elicited public admiration, creating the immortal works which went beyond the borders of Brazil. He was a Janus of double personality under the buckled mask of an indecipherable temperament, racial complex, and pride in the value he recognized in himself.[3]

A LITERARY ANALYSIS AND PLOT SUMMARY OF *IAIÁ GARCIA*

Critics in Brazil and the United States continue to evaluate Assis on the basis of those novels at the forefront of his creative endeavor: *Braz Cubas, Quincas Borba*, and *Dom Casmurro*. This trilogy of masterpieces—all from the author's so-called realistic phase—is preceded by

---

3. Francisca de Basto Cordeiro, *Machado de Assis que eu vi* (Rio de Janeiro: Livraria São José, 1961), pp. 13-14. Translation mine.

Iaiá Garcia, the last in the series of four novels normally judged as belonging to the author's earlier "romantic" phase.

However, Assis's early works—*Contos Fluminenses, Histórias de Meia-Noite*, and the novel *Ressurreição*—are crucial to an understanding of Assis's literary and artistic development; *Ressurreição* in particular has long been underrated.[4] Really a better novel than *A mão e a luva*, *Ressurreição* is—like *Iaiá Garcia*—important for its emphasis on themes which later are developed more fully.

In this introduction it is my purpose to discover whether the psychological probings and the longer, more dramatic, descriptive passages of *Iaiá Garcia* already embody the transformation in spirit and technique ordinarily attributed to *Braz Cubas*. In order to aid this purpose I have provided a brief summary of the plot; to do so seems indispensable to a lucid commentary and analysis. Therefore, those who wish to read the work without being told of the outcome stand forewarned.

The story revolves mainly around the lives, ambitions, and aspirations of three people—Iaiá, Estela, and Jorge—whom the author reveals fully. While the supposed main character of the novel, Iaiá, is still developing into womanhood, a love affair between slightly older Jorge and Estela is being born. It is quickly snuffed out, however, by Estela, whose pride will not allow her to endure the differences in their social classes, despite Jorge's willingness.

It is while Jorge labors to understand and overcome the obstacles that thwart his and Estela's possible love affair that a determined Iaiá enters the stage. Having fallen in love with Jorge, she carefully maneuvers him into reciprocating. Whether he does fall in love with her is not quite evident or important. What is important is that an unlikely candidate becomes a likely one because of her strength of character and ambition, while an apparently likely choice is deprived of happiness because of her excessive pride and her lover's unwillingness to conquer that pride. (The novel is in part a profound study of the strength nature gives woman for the sustenance of her pride.)

Although the ending is a happy one for Iaiá and Jorge, the reader is left with a feeling of bewilderment: Did the author intend for Iaiá to

---

4. Machado de Assis, *Iaiá Garcia*, ed. Ivan Cavalcanti Proença (Rio de Janeiro: Tecnoprint Gráfica Editôra, 1970), pp. vi-vii.

triumph under the guise of a princess? It is ironic that, although the book is named for Iaiá, the true protagonist—or at least the most important character in the novel—is, to my mind, not Iaiá but Estela.

In the introduction to his edition of *Iaiá Garcia*, Ivan Cavalcanti Proença sees in the novel the style and elements which will come to fruition in *Dom Casmurro* and *Quincas Borba*. He speaks of *Iaiá* as a bridge between the romantic and realistic phases, yet sees *Iaiá* as more romantic than realistic or psychological.

Arguments like Proença's are typical of those who make sharp divisions between the romantic and realistic phases of Assis's pessimism. Those who have seen a great transformation between novels four and five explain it as having occurred during a three-month period (December, 1878 to March, 1879) which the author spent in the hills of Nova Friburgo recovering from a serious illness. If change occurred at all, I see it not as a move from flighty romanticism to hardened, practical realism, but rather, as a move from a less artistic to a more artistic style of writing. That is, I see in the later novels only what one might expect—the marked improvement in literary style that comes with practice and maturity. Helen Caldwell saw this when she said:

[Assis] considered . . . his later books, improvements on the earlier ones. . . . each novel was an artistic experiment never repeated, which in one respect or another represented an advance over its immediate predecessor. That is not to say, of course, that the last novel was the "best" or the "greatest" or the "most powerful." It was, however, a new triumph. . . .[5]

Originally my greatest concern with assertions of rank pessimism was that, in almost every case, proponents of this theory have made use of only the five novels belonging to Assis's "second phase"—granted, his most important works. I am moved to reassert my position for two reasons: first, because I note that criticism continues to see Assis as a permanently eclipsed sun;[6] and second, because there continues to be

---

5. Helen Caldwell, *Machado de Assis*, p. 219.

6. Among the specialists on Assis who continue to depict him as pessimistic, particularly in articles, essays, and introductions to new editions of his works, are Afrânio Coutinho, Eugênio Gomes, Edson Prata, Ivan Cavalcanti Proença, and M. Cavalcanti Proença. Helen Caldwell is a notable exception, as can be seen in her recent study of Assis's novels. Among the lesser-known evaluators of Assis as

no detailed evaluation of the novels of the first phase—too long over-looked because of an assumed lack of literary merit.[7]

Let me first make clear that it is not my intention to argue that there is no foundation for the position taken by the vast number of critics who regard Assis's world as somber. It is, in fact, easy to see what inspires this understanding of Assis in his trilogy of masterpieces— *Memórias póstumas de Braz Cubas, Quincas Borba*, and *Dom Casmurro*. It is equally true that there is little in the plots or denouements of those novels which makes us celebrate man's nature. Machado de Assis lays bare the souls of men, most of which are quite ugly to look upon.

Further, because critics are usually concerned not only with labeling, but also with explaining authors and their works, endless attempts have been made to explain Assis's somber novelistic world through what is known or thought about his life.[8]

Actually, as Helen Caldwell points out, much that has been accepted traditionally as fact has been offset recently by an equal amount of contrary data. While Assis stuttered, was near-sighted, suffered from epilepsy, and was of mixed racial origins, he also came from a more or less cultured if humble environment, was sociable and charming, helped lead more than one academy to literary prominence, and was deeply loved and respected.[9]

According to the author himself, knowledge of his life was not essential to an understanding of his fiction. It must be recognized that there is no overwhelming evidence to the contrary. Only his last novel, which testifies to Carolina's influence, could be considered autobiographical.[10]

Granted that Assis's pessimism is indisputable, what is important is that we consider whether critics have given us the whole picture, or

---

pessimist are Gondín da Fonseca and Expedito Teles, who is extreme in his depiction of Assis's pessimism.

7. Even the well-known critic Massaud Moisés, in his excellent editions of Assis's works (Editora Cultrix), provides us with little more than some brief paragraphs of commentary in his introductions to Assis's early novels. Again, Helen Caldwell's seems to be the only study which examines the first four novels in any detail.

8. Caldwell collates and adds to the recent corrected information about Assis's life in the early chapters of her *Machado de Assis*.

9. Helen Caldwell, *Machado de Assis*, pp. 3-4.

10. Ibid., p. 4.

whether perhaps they have been myopic in their vision of his world—especially the world of his first four novels.

Let us then quote the formula on which *A mão e a luva* was based and which is indispensable to a total comprehension of the writings of Assis: "Will and ambition, when they truly dominate, can struggle with other feelings, but they are the weapons of the strong, and victory belongs to the strong."[11]

In capsule, Assis's formula is *success for the strong* (the ambitious and well organized, who aspire and who know how to fulfill their aspirations) and *failure for the weak* (the timid, the uncertain, and the insecure, who cannot control their passions and emotions or who simply have none). This formula may be observed implicitly in *Ressurreição* and *Helena* and quite explicitly in *A mão e a luva* and *Iaiá Garcia*. In the latter two the proof resides in the characters and in the outcome of the plots. However, let us complete the formula before scrutinizing the novels. Those who are victorious, as well as those who are not, function within a world or an ambient which is totally indifferent. That is to say, the world is neutral toward them and therefore neither helps nor hinders them in whatever they seek to accomplish. Assis's world is not adverse, negative, unsympathetic, or, as some have thought, even sadistic; it is neutral.

Assis's stage is peopled by characters each of whom is striving in his own way for improvement, accomplishment, success.[12] Yet for Assis there is no middle road, no half success; only complete success is really success. A partial success is the equivalent of failure, and it is for this reason that his neutral or indifferent ambient often seems adverse.

A case in point is that of Félix in *Ressurreição*. In order to succeed in life Félix must contend, not with an adverse ambient, but only with himself—his skepticism of any goodness or nobility in other human beings. A sad case indeed, for none of the social, ethnic, or caste problems which afflict characters in other Assis novels exists between Félix and his intended, the beautiful and kind Livia. He loves and is well loved in return, but the wedding never materializes because of Félix's distrust.

---

11. Machado de Assis, *The Hand and the Glove*, trans. Albert I. Bagby, Jr. (Lexington: University Press of Kentucky, 1970), p. 102.

12. For an interesting article on the various female types which Assis created consult Maria de Lourdes Teixeira, "As Mulheres Machadianas," *Revista Brasili-*

Félix is a loser in Assis's game of life, for he does not possess the skill at human relationships—the ability to trust and share—which is required to live happily and fully in a highly complex world. In consequence we have, not a tragic ending, but a foolish one—foolish because, with everything perfectly provided to make happiness possible, Félix lacks only the strength of will to see it through.

To me Assis seems to be saying, not "This is life; isn't it awful?" but "This is life; it is neither good nor bad—it simply is. Those who make it, make it; those who don't, don't; and theirs," he might have added in later life, "is the more interesting story."

A quick look at the character list of Assis's novels would show us a startling variety of failures—victims who either did not know how to triumph, or who, tragically, were unable to do so because, although they themselves possessed the necessary attributes, they could not find a partner able to complement their efforts in the struggle to conquer an indifferent world. Among these could be included Félix and Livia, Estêvão and Jorge of *A mão e a luva*, Helena of *Helena*, Estela of *Iaiá Garcia*, Rubião of *Quincas Borba*, and Capitú and Bento of *Dom Casmurro*—virtually every principal character in the second phase of Assis's career. In addition, many of these characters go beyond simple weakness or disorganization to a state of mind which is sick, dangerously confused, or immoral—characters out of naturalistic novels, were they not creations of an author so openly against *tremendismo*.

But even though it is easy to understand why Assis's vision of reality is so often seen as dismal, it should be equally possible to understand where he allows for a less bleak interpretation. Let us consider *A mão e a luva* for a moment. Guiomar, a beautiful "hand," finds for herself the perfect "glove," the ambitious and talented Luis Alves. Vanquished are Estêvão, a weak, romantic young man lacking in self-confidence, and Jorge, a superficial, indecisive fop.

The final dialogue between the two "winners," Guiomar and Luis, is a sample of Assian "optimism":

"I saw that you were a man with a resolute mind," said the girl to Luis Alves who, seated, was listening to her.

---

ense (São Paulo) 4 (março-abril, 1956), pp. 65-75. The author picks Livia as the ideal Assis woman and Sofia (of *Quincas Borba*) as perhaps the most well rounded and complete creation. Ironically, critics have seen not one of the author's female characters as ideal as Assis's own beloved wife Carolina appeared to be.

"Resolute and ambitious," added Luis Alves, smiling. "You must have perceived that I am one and the other as well."

"Ambition is no defect."

"On the contrary, it is a virtue; I feel that I have it and that I am sure to make it succeed. . . ."

Guiomar, who was standing before him, her hands locked in his, let herself slide slowly down upon her husband's knees, and the two ambitions exchanged an affectionate kiss. Both settled down as if that glove had been made for that hand.[13]

The appearance of *Helena* in 1876 marks a schism between the first two and second two novels of Assis's so-called first creative phase. In novels three and four, *Helena* and *Iaiá Garcia*, we are no longer being shown merely the "inside" from the "outside," as in the previous works; instead, we now begin to penetrate, with Assis, the souls of the characters. Everything seems more real because even the plots—while not necessarily more possible than the previous ones—are interestingly graced with more gravity and realism. Both Estácio and Helena seem to be real, struggling souls, as do Jorge, Estela, and Iaiá in the next novel. *Helena* offers its readers real dramatic possibilities, situations which border on tragedy without ever crossing the line.[14]

The story concerns a case of probable incest, a theme Assis used in some of his short stories.[15] Helena is the supposedly illegitimate daughter of a prestigious aristocrat who, upon dying, directs in his will that she be brought to the family estate and treated as a full daughter.

Estácio, the man's son and heir, is an eligible young man with a mind of his own, warm, sensitive, and naive. Overwhelmed by Helena's femininity and beauty, he becomes obsessed with her. Helena returns his love, and knows (as the reader does not at this time) that no incest is involved.

When it is discovered that incest is not a problem, the marriage is held up only by two factors: social convention and Helena herself. Estácio has the ingredients of the winner, as he shows by rejecting social convention. But he does not have the power to convince Helena, and little by little she is dragged under by the current of adverse circumstances and her own unwillingness to fight the tide.

---

13. Machado de Assis, *The Hand and the Glove*, pp. 116-17.
14. See Caldwell's opinion, *Machado de Assis*, pp. 49, 58-60.
15. Ibid., pp. 52-54.

With incest not a part of the picture, there is no reason why Helena must die in this work, unless one considers the formula of victory versus defeat.[16] Again the author has shown us two individuals in an amorous struggle which demands adjusting to and overcoming the problems of the world they live in.

Let us now approach *Iaiá Garcia*, whose theme is similar, though the outcome is different. The Estela-Jorge relationship is similar to that of Helena and Estácio, where a great love in the process of unfolding is obstructed and ended by adverse circumstances, or, by lack of strength and spirit of one of the characters. The result is never in doubt for those aware of the Machadian formula: Iaiá wins because the ambitious (those who know what they want and how to get it) are always the winners. Estela cannot win because she is a stoic, because she does not possess the passion to overcome her pride or the ambition to defy social convention. She loves, and sincerely, but she cannot receive the prize because she is not willing to work actively to secure it. Iaiá, on the other hand, *is* willing, and her conquest of Jorge and of the difficult situation in which she sees herself parallels the victory of Guiomar and Luis Alves. Estela, on the other hand, must adjust to a life of resignation—in Assisian words, one which is neither sad nor bad, but just as certainly not happy.

What is interesting in this novel is the number of passages in which the author expresses the formula. All of these passages, naturally, are associated with interpretations of the character of Iaiá. Speaking of nature and her milieu, the young woman describes to Jorge the conflicts taking place within her, and explains to him her way of dealing with doubts and uncertainties. First, she tells him, it is necessary that one understand the world one lives in before one can conquer it. Her method of doing this is slow, deliberate, and determined where discovering the truth is concerned. Jorge is pleased to find himself in possession of no less a conquest than Iaiá, with her "natureza original, moralmente exuberante e forte."

Note the similarity of Guiomar/Luis Alves's attitude toward ambition to that of Iaiá/Jorge's:

---

16. Caldwell sees a "house of Usher" type of doom creeping into the walls of Vale's mansion. This could certainly explain the otherwise illogical and forced ending, but I in no way see that Assis has given us an "atmosphere novel" in *Helena*.

It was possible that all . . . [Iaiá's] daring disguised a plan—an ambitious plan which might be an attempt to exchange beauty for the advantages of an ostensible and superior position. When that suspicion took root in his mind, Jorge did not feel his admiration or esteem diminish, since the ambition, if there was ambition, seemed to be well bred.   (p. 128)

Assis never faults ambition when it is realistic in its aims.

However, it was less ambition for social advancement that drove Iaiá to pursue Jorge than a desire to protect her father by inserting herself as a barrier between Estela and Jorge.

It was to combat this silent enemy that she threw into the field of battle that portion of shrewdness which nature had given her, her facial charms, and her spiritual acumen.   (p. 135)

It has been noted that Assis, in his early novels, spoke often of conquest of the ambient because he himself was bent on conquering the social and literary worlds of his day. Ambition and social ascendancy, of paramount importance in the early works, became less dominant as Assis ascended the ladder. While this conjecture is of some interest, it is less important to an understanding of Assis's realism than is his admiration for strength and determination.

Other pieces of evidence weight the scales in favor of realism over romanticism in this novel. Each of the characters bears a depth of character and strength typical of the realist. Jorge, now in his twenties, has lost the passion of his youth. Mellower, he looks for a "love with its eyes open," and counsels Iaiá along these lines:

"Allow a little of the poetic in life, but don't fall into the trap of the romantic; the romantic is perfidious. . . . It's not enough for the heart to say, 'Love this one.' It's necessary for the eyes to approve the heart's choice."   (p. 125)

Assis explains, "he was trying to temper the romantic in her with a dose of reality" (p. 130).

The scene which ultimately convinces us that Iaiá will conquer is the one in which Maria das Dores, her invalid friend, questions her about who Jorge is. When Maria asks if he is her fiancé, Iaiá lies that he is.

"When is the wedding?"
"I don't know the day. . . . But that it will take place is certain. Or I am not who I am."   (p. 127)

This dialogue occurs only a short time after the author has called our attention to the "indifferent firmament that witnesses the struggle": "This immense, taciturn being has eyes with which to see, but no ears with which to listen" (p. 115).
Assis also points out the nature of life's struggles:

Of the qualities necessary for playing chess Iaiá possessed the two essential ones: a quick eye and benedictine patience—qualities precious in life itself, which is also a game of chess, with its problems and games, some won, some lost, others neither.   (p. 102)

The ambient is as neutral as the chess pieces, as indifferent as any sport. As in all games, it is the players who make the difference; and Iaiá has the qualities to win. There is no hint of bitterness or pessimism here; only the simple statement.

Iaiá Garcia stands as a companion to *A mão e a luva* as regards Assis's theme of victory to the strong. Despite nature's indifference to man's strivings in Assis's world, these two novels do offer the insightful reader examples of man's triumph over adversity, and his consequent happiness as a result of his determination and strength. Note Assis's description of the victorious Iaiá: "[Iaiá] found untold happiness in marriage. Society did not deny her affection and respect" (p. 165).

With all of this, we cannot say that Assis offers his readers only two choices—strength and ambition, or sentiment, beautiful but weak—and that either one or the other triumphs. For he will give neither side free passage without a bittersweet departure. Thus, despite all our study suggests, we cannot be certain, when we reach the final page of the novel, where the author's sympathies lay or what he wanted the reader to feel.

If Jorge and Iaiá are realistic in their ambitions, Estela even more so reflects an understanding of her ambient. As a young girl she had learned to rein in her feelings, to slow them to the pace of her own proud nature and the nature of the world around her. Faced with having to explain to Iaiá her feelings for Jorge, she says:

"There existed between us a great chasm, very broad. . . . I was humble and obscure, he distinguished and esteemed, a difference which might have disappeared if nature had given me a different type of heart. I took the full measure of the distance which separated us and decided simply to avoid it. . . . Marriage between us was impossible . . . because

I would have considered it a type of favor and I hold myself in very high regard." (p. 159)

And of her own marriage to Iaiá's father:

"I found all the joys of marriage at your father's feet. We didn't marry for love. It was a choice of the mind, and for that reason it was right."
(p. 159)

Estela saw in life a certain bitterness which she avoided by a realistic view of her world—one dominated by class and personal pride. And while we lament the possible loss of mutual love, we must admire the realism of one who says, "I know who I am and what I can accept." Estela, at the novel's end, must set out to establish a new life for herself—alone—with only her pride to arm her against an indifferent ambient. When she returns to the city at intervals to place flowers on her husband's grave, Assis's only and final comment on her is the last line of the novel: "Something . . . is salvaged from the shipwreck of our illusions." How can the reader feel happiness over the success of Iaiá when he must greet with sadness the defeat of the proud but beautiful Estela!

Rather than see, then, an Assis whose physical, environmental, and racial disadvantages led him to a pessimistic view of the world, why can we not see an Assis whose struggles to overcome, whose feverish ambition, whose success in nearly every literary effort he undertook, led him to see life as belonging to the strong? Such a vision was his right; had he not earned it?

If some would not call this optimism, it is at least not pessimism. Rather, it may be an objective view of life which few have because few are able to achieve what Assis (and Iaiá, Jorge, Luis Alves, and Guiomar) achieved. Few of us have the strength of will—or perhaps the social necessity—to conquer the ambient. Perhaps few of us have had to struggle to lead a comfortable life, and perhaps most of us settle for that. Thus while we admire the strong and the ambitious, we have a certain envy of them which makes us like them less; hence we rationalize their strength as cold, unfeeling haughtiness. Perhaps to understand the optimism of Assis one needs only to be a realist, a hard, pragmatic realist—for that is what is required to appreciate the Iaiás and to reject the Estelas.

IAIÁ GARCIA

Chapter One

Luís Garcia had just moved through the doorway on his way out, when a servant appeared and handed him the following letter:

October 5th, 1866

Mr. Luís Garcia:

Please do me the favor of coming to see me today, between one and two in the afternoon. I need your advice, and perhaps some favors.

Valéria

"Tell her I'll go. Is Madam here on the hill?"

"No, sir, she is on Inválidos Street."

Luís Garcia was a civil servant. In 1860 he had chosen a modest house in a sparsely populated spot in Santa Teresa, where he had since lived as a widower. He wasn't a friar, but like them, he wanted solitude and tranquility. The seclusion wasn't complete nor the tranquility uninterrupted, but they were always greater and more attainable here than down below. Because of the superficial life of the city, the friars had lodged themselves on the other hills but came down often, i.e., whenever the sacred ministry demanded it, or when the government was in need of the canonic sword; and the occasions were not rare. But generally the voice of secular strife did not resound around their houses. Luís Garcia could say the same, and, since no apostolic calling ever incited him to open the doors of his refuge to others, it could be said that he had founded a monastery in which he was almost the entire community, from prior to novice.

At the time this narrative begins, Luís Garcia was forty-one. He was tall and slender, clean-shaven, with incipient baldness and a circumspect air about him. His manner was cold, modest, and courteous; his facial expression, a little sad. A careful observer would have been able to

1

detect behind that apparent or assumed impassivity the ruins of a disillusioned heart. Such was the case; his experiences in life had left Luís Garcia prematurely in a state of apathy and skepticism, with vestiges of disdain. The disdain was not something that revealed itself in any outward expression; it was to be found in the ironic quality of his heart. Outwardly there was only an immovable mask, slowness of gestures, and a tranquil attitude. Some might fear him, others detest him, without his deserving either execration or fear. He was inoffensive by nature and by method. Like a typical clergyman, he figured that an ounce of peace was worth more than a pound of victory. Few people really loved him, and those who did, made poor use of their affection, an affection never returned in equal measure—*with but two exceptions*. But this did not keep him from rendering favors. Luís Garcia loved the species but spurned the individual. Whoever called upon him for favors rarely went unrewarded. He rendered assistance without zeal, but with efficacy, and it was in his nature to forget the benefit rendered before the recipient had done so.

Luís Garcia's life was like his personality, taciturn and withdrawn. He neither visited nor received guests. His house had few friends; there reigned within it the melancholy of solitude. There was only one place that could be called cheerful; it was a few feet of garden space which Luís Garcia surveyed and watered every morning. He would rise with the sun, take the watering pot and give the flowers and plants a drink; then he would withdraw to do some work before breakfast, which was at eight o'clock. After his breakfast he would take a leisurely walk to the administrative branch where he worked, and if he had a little time he paged through the daily newspapers rapidly. He worked silently, with a cold serenity of method. At closing time he returned home immediately, rarely stopping on the way. When he arrived, the Negro servant, Raimundo, had the table set for him—a table which measured about four to five spans—upon which he served dinner, limited in variety of courses and average in quality, but abundant and tasty enough for a stomach with no demands or cravings. From there he would go to see his plants and reread some worn-out volume until nightfall. Then he would sit down to work until nine, which was tea time.

It was not only his life-style which was so conventional; the house reflected the same formality. Each piece of furniture, every object— even the most commonplace—seemed to have become petrified. The drapes, which were ordinarily drawn at a specific hour, seemed to become annoyed if the air and light were not allowed to sift through them at the usual time; the same windows were always opened and never others. Regularity was the common rule, and if the man molded things to suit his manner, it is no surprise *that his manner also molded the man himself.*

Raimundo seemed expressly made to serve Luís Garcia. He was a Negro of about fifty, of medium stature, strong in spite of his years, a type of African that was submissive and dedicated. He was a slave though free. When Luís Garcia inherited him from his father, he did not count him as part of the spoils but immediately gave him a writ of freedom. Raimundo, nine years older than his master, had carried the latter in his arms and awakened him in the morning as though he were his own son. Finding himself free, he felt that his freedom was a way of being expelled from the home; and he experienced a daring though generous impulse: he made a gesture as though to tear up the enfranchisement. But he repented in time. Luís Garcia noticed only the magnanimity, not the boldness. He was touched by the slave's affection and understood his sincerity completely. Between the two a closer tie was woven which united them forever.

"You're free," said Luís Garcia; "you may live with me as long as you like."

From then on Raimundo was like an external soul of his master. He thought for him, and reflected for him his very thoughts.

In all of his actions he was no less silent than punctual. Luís Garcia never gave any orders; he had everything he needed at the right time and in the proper place. Although he was the only servant in the house, there was time left over in the afternoon for him to talk with his former master in the little garden as night descended. There they spoke of their small world, of unusual everyday occurrences, of what the weather would be like the following day, of this and that outward circumstance. When night had completely fallen, and the city was opening its "gas" eyes, they would return to the house, walking slowly side by side.

"I'm going to play for you today, aren't I?" the Negro sometimes said.

"Whenever you like, *meu velho.*"[1]

---

1. The expression *meu velho* as used here by Assis carries the approximate meaning of "my dear old man." Currently it might mean the same as "old man."

Raimundo would light the candles, get the marimba,[2] and walk to the garden where he would sit down to play and hum some African tune in a low tone—faint memories of the tribe in which he had been born. The black man's chanting was not one of homesickness; none of his tunes were played in mournful tone. They were happy, warlike, enthusiastic. Finally he would grow silent. His thoughts, instead of returning to the African crib, would climb through the window of the room in which Luís Garcia worked and would settle upon him like a protective fetish. Whatever the social and natural differences between the two, domestic relations had made friends of them. Nevertheless, of Luís Garcia's two favorites, Raimundo was only the second. The first was a daughter.

As the garden was the most pleasing part of the house, Sunday was the most festive day of the week. On Saturday afternoon, after dinner, Raimundo would go down to the Rua dos Arcos to get *sinhá moça,* who was being educated in a *colegio.*[3] Luís Garcia awaited them sitting at the door or leaning against the window, when he was not hidden in some corner of the house to make the little one laugh. If the girl didn't see him at the window or door, she realized he had hidden and would run through the house, where it was not hard to find him because there weren't many nooks to hide in. They would then fall into each other's arms, and Luís Garcia would take her and place her on his knees. Then he would kiss her and take off the little hat which covered her light brown hair and part of the rosy and delicate forehead; he would kiss her again, this time on her hair and eyes—eyes which were clear and emitted an insinuating and curious light.

She was eleven years old and her name was Lina. Her nickname was Iaiá. At school, since the other girls called her this, and since there were more than one with the same name, they would add the family

---

2. A modern marimba is a musical instrument somewhat like a xylophone, consisting of a series of hard wooden bars, usually with resonators beneath; it is played by being struck with small hammers. The one Assis mentions was probably slightly different, since it seems to have been easily portable.

3. *Sinhá moça* is a Brazilian colloquialism that may be translated "miss" or "missy." As used here, *colégio* probably means a private elementary school for girls, which Lina was attending. It is a very general term which could mean simply school, elementary school, secondary school, academy, or even junior college, depending upon what parallel one wishes to draw between Brazilian and United States education.

surname. Thus she was Iaiá Garcia. She was tall, slender, and mischievous; she possessed the quick and unpredictable movements of the swallow. Her lips parted easily into smiles—smiles which the pretenses of life had not yet clouded nor the ironies of years dulled. The kisses exchanged with her father were tender and plentiful. Luís Garcia would place her on the ground, then again lift her to his knees, until he could finally consent to pull himself away from her for a few moments and Iaiá would go to the *preto*.[4]

"Raimundo, what do you have for me?"

"I've got something," he would answer, smiling. "Iaiá won't be able to guess what it is."

"It's a fruit."

"No, it isn't."

"A bird?"

"Wrong again."

"A piece of candy."

"What kind of candy is it?"

"I don't know. Give it to me."

Raimundo would tantalize her a little longer but would finally give up the gift he was holding. Sometimes it was something sweet; sometimes fruit, a curious insect, a bouquet of flowers. Iaiá jubilantly acknowledged the slave's gift with little leaps of happiness and gratitude. Raimundo would look at her, drinking in the happiness which streamed from her eyes like a torrent of pure water. When the gift was fruit or candy, the girl would quickly take a bite, looking and laughing at the *preto,* gesticulating and interrupting herself from time to time:

"Very well! Raimundo is Iaiá's friend. Hurrah for Raimundo!"

And from there she would go to change her clothes and visit the rest of the house and garden. In the garden she would find her father already seated on his usual bench, his legs crossed, his hands folded on his knee. She would go to him, sit down, get up, pick a flower, chase insects.

At night there was no work for Luís Garcia; like Sundays, nighttime was completely devoted to the child. Iaiá would tell her father anecdotes about school, trivialities worth neither more nor less than those

---

4. An endearing reference to Raimundo, which means literally "the black man."

5

of adults—little, insignificant intrigues, misdemeanors which amounted to nothing. Luís Garcia would listen to her with the same attention he would give a great historical narrative. His thin, austere face would lose its coldness and indifference. Leaning over the table with his arms outstretched, his daughter's hands in his, he considered himself the most fortunate of men. The little girl's narrative was as children's usually are: disjointed and abbreviated, but filled with a glow of their own. He would listen to her without interrupting; he corrected, to be sure, some mistake of pronunciation or some less accurate expression; aside from that, he only listened.

A little after dawn all three were up. The sun over Santa Teresa was the same as that over the Rua dos Arcos. Nevertheless, Iaiá saw in it something more or better when she saw it come into the room through the Venetian blinds. She would go to the window which opened onto a part of the garden and would see her father drinking the cup of coffee which, on Sundays, preceded his brunch.[5] Sometimes she would go to him; other times he would walk toward the window, and, with the window sill between them, they would exchange affectionate greetings. Throughout the day, Iaiá filled the house with her vibrant gaiety. Luís

---

5. A difference of opinion exists as to the meaning of *almôço* as it was used in Assis's day. Helen Caldwell feels that at that time this word was taken to mean breakfast, not lunch as we think of the noon meal. Caldwell offers the example of Kidder, Fletcher, and Ewbank (Anglo visitors to nineteenth-century Brazil), who described Brazilian meals then as follows: strong coffee at sunrise (*café*), a substantial meal later in the morning (*almôço*), dinner at 1 or 2 P.M. (*jantar*), tea at 9 P.M. (*chá*).

This description may have been generally true, but it fails to take into account individual custom, social class, and Assis's own arbitrary use of the term (i.e., his use of it to refer to different meals). For example, in two of his masterpieces, *Memórias póstumas de Braz Cubas* and *Quincas Borba,* meals as a vehicle for social interaction form a strong leitmotif. In both works, especially the latter, Rubião frequently invites friends for meals at his home (*venha almoçar*) at around the noon hour. The mention of wines, cooked meats, and after-meal coffee would contradict the notion of an 8 A.M. *café* or a 10 A.M. brunch.

Custom probably did not change significantly from 1890 to 1930, when the *Pequeno dicionário brasileiro da língua portuguesa* defined *almôço* thus: "the first of the two substantial meals of the day," or, the noon meal (translation mine). Certainly "lunch or luncheon" is the current meaning of *almôço* (cf. the *New Appleton Dictionary of the English and Portuguese Languages,* 1967).

In this work Luís Garcia has *almôço* at 8 A.M.; Procópio Dias and Jorge have *almôço* at 10 A.M. (see pp. 61-62). And we shall translate *café* or *almôço* according to the particular experience the context suggests is taking place.

Garcia's face would light up with the reflection of youth which dispersed the accumulated shadows of time; Raimundo lived off of the happiness of both of them. It was Sunday for all three, and the master and his former slave were as much like school children as the girl.

"Raimundo," the girl would say, "do you like saints that are meant to be eaten?"[6]

Raimundo would straighten out his body, begin to smile, and, giving his hips and torso the movement of his African dances he would answer, crooning:

"Pretty saint! Delicious saint!"

"And a working saint?"

Raimundo, who was already expecting that question, would stop suddenly, place his head between his hands, and move away muttering with terror:

"Oh, oh . . . don't talk about that saint, Iaiá, don't talk about that saint!"

"And what about a saint that's for eating?"

"Pretty saint! Delicious saint!"

And the *preto* would repeat the first stanza, then the second, until Iaiá became weary and would move on to something else.

Play wasn't all there was. A small part of the day—a little more than an hour—was devoted to an examination of what Iaiá had learned at school during the preceding days. Luís Garcia asked questions; made her read, count, and draw something. The girl's docility captivated the father's soul. There was no uncertainty or hesitation; she would answer, read or draw, according to what she was told or asked to do.

"Do you want to hear me play the piano?" she asked one day. "Look, like this."

And with her fingers on the edge of the table, she "played" a musical passage on nonexistent keys. Luís Garcia smiled, but a veil fell over his eyes. Iaiá had no piano! It was necessary to give her one, though it would mean a sacrifice. If she was learning at school, was it not in order to play at home someday? This thought lodged in his mind and disturbed his rest for the day. The following day Luís Garcia gathered courage, took his savings account booklet, and went to with-

---

6. The meaning here is unclear, but it seems to be a reference to a candy image of a saint.

draw the money necessary to buy a piano. The little savings he had accumulated were for his daughter; the piano was likewise for her. Her inheritance was not being diminished.

When on the following Saturday Iaiá saw the piano which her father had bought for her, her happiness was intense but short-lived. Her father had opened it; she awakened the sleeping notes to life on the large piece of furniture with her little hands, which were still uncertain and weak. Standing beside the instrument, his eyes on her, Luís Garcia was repaid for his sacrifice, contemplating his daughter's delight. It was over soon. Between two notes, Iaiá stopped, looked at her father, at the piano, at the other pieces of furniture; then her expression changed; she said she felt dizzy. Luís Garcia became frightened, took hold of her, and called Raimundo; the child insisted that she was better, and finally that the dizzy spell had passed altogether. Luís Garcia breathed in relief. But Iaiá's eyes did not become happier, nor was she as mischievous as she had been earlier.

The cause of the change, unknown to Luís Garcia, was the insight that was dawning in the girl's mind. She had suddenly remembered her words and the gesture she had made the Sunday before; it was those words that explained the purchase of the piano. She compared it, its new and shiny look, with the other furnishings of the house—modest, used, dingy—the soiled straw of the chairs, and the old rug gnawed by time and use, a contemporary of the sofa. From this comparison she became conscious of the sacrifice her father must have made in order to comply with her wish—an idea that made her sad, though not for long, as so often happens with a child's sadness. Not only was insight dawning, but moral pain was also causing an eruption within her soul, free until now from the dictates of fortune.

It was over now! Very soon the sounds of the piano merged with Iaiá's trills and with the slave's and the master's smiles. The piano furnished one more Sunday entertainment. One day Iaiá confided to her father the idea she had of becoming a piano teacher. Luís Garcia smiled at these childhood plans, as fragile and fugitive as their impressions. He had also had them at ten. What remained of those early ambitions? A fragment, and nothing more. But just as the aspirations of those times had made him happy, it was right not to discourage his daughter from this innocent and modest ambition. May she never have higher ones! Furthermore, what could he desire for her if not that which would make her independent and self-supporting? Iaiá had a beauty and education of her own. But they might not be sufficient to give her a good marriage and family. An honest profession could prevent the possible blows of adversity. It could not be said that Iaiá had musical talent; what did that matter? In order to teach the grammar of art it was sufficient to know it.

It remains to be said that there was yet a third attachment in Iaiá's life; it was Maria das Dores, the nurse who had reared her, a poor *catarinense* for whom there were but two objects of religious devotion capable of conducting a soul to heaven: the Virgin Mary and the daughter of Luís Garcia.[7] She would go to the girl's house from time to time, on those days when it was certain the girl would be there. She went from S. Cristóvão where she lived, but she was not happy until she had rented a shack in Santa Teresa in order to be nearer her "adopted" child.[8] A brother of hers, an old quartermaster who had been involved in the campaign against Rosas, was her working companion.[9]

Such was the unvaried and placid life of Luís Garcia. No ambition, greed, or struggle was there to becloud the serenity of his soul. The last serious pain he had had was the death of his wife, which occurred in 1859, months before he had gone into hiding in Santa Teresa. Time, that invisible chemistry which dissolves, restores, extracts, and transforms all moral substances, eventually killed in the widower's heart, not the memory of his wife, but the pain of having lost her. It is important to say that the tears shed on that occasion honored the deceased wife, since they represented conquest. Luís Garcia had married neither for love nor profit; he had married because he was loved. It was a generous move. The woman was not of the same nature as he; their personalities originated at different points on the horizon. But the devotion and love of his wife opened up in him a fountain of high regard. When she died,

---

7. *Catarinense* refers to a person from the southern state of Santa Catarina, often satirized for its backwardness. It has a scant population composed largely of Slavic and Germanic immigrants.

8. *Filha de criação,* for which there is no exact English equivalent, means literally "a daughter by virtue of rearing," that is, an adopted daughter in the sense that the child was entirely cared for by a woman who otherwise bore no blood relation to her.

9. Manuel Ortiz de Rosas was an Argentine dictator who contemplated adding the area of Paraguay and Uruguay to his own country in the early 1850s. He unfortunately provoked Brazil, which moved against him under the command of the Duke of Caxias. The Brazilian army liberated Montevideo and finally defeated Rosas at the Battle of Monte-Caseros. The dictator fled to England.

Luís Garcia realized that he had lost an unselfish and devoted soul; the hope that his daughter had inherited something from her consoled him.

Thus lived this skeptical, austere, and honorable man, oblivious to external things, . . . when the letter of October 5, 1866, summoned him to the drama which this book intends to narrate.

Chapter Two

The time designated was not convenient for Luís Garcia, whose work hours did not easily allow for interruption. Nevertheless, he went to the Rua dos Inválidos.

Valéria Gomes was the widow of an appeals court judge who had died two years earlier and with whom Luís Garcia's father had exchanged some favors. There were not constant and close relations between Luís Garcia and the widow, but she and her deceased husband had always held him in high esteem and treated him with much affection. After the judge's death, Valéria had appealed to Luís Garcia two or three times for assistance; nevertheless, it was the first time she had done so with such formality.

She received him affectionately, extending to him her hand, still youthful despite the years, which exceeded forty-eight. She was tall and stout. Her head, proud and erect, seemed in its lofty attitude to protest the drabness and sadness of her eyes. They were dark, her eyebrows heavy, her hair abundant and streaked with silver strands. She had not been happy of late, but on that day she was unusually worried. As soon as they had entered the living room she fell into an armchair, leaned back, and remained silent for a few moments. Luís Garcia seated himself tranquilly in the chair she indicated to him.

"Luís Garcia," said the widow, "this Paraguayan war has been long and no one knows when it will end. Did any news come today?"

"Not that I know of."

"Yesterday's did not encourage me at all," continued the widow after a moment. "I don't believe in the peace López has proposed.[1] I am afraid this will end badly."

---

1. Solano López was a Paraguayan dictator who sought to dominate the Rio de la Plata zone in order to form a great empire. Brazil, Argentina, and Uruguay, becoming directly involved, allied themselves against him. The ensuing war lasted from 1864 to 1870.

"That may be; but since it doesn't depend on us. . . ."

"Why doesn't it? I believe the moment has arrived when all mothers should make a great effort to set examples of courage which will not be forgotten. As for my part I am working on my own Jorge to enlist as a volunteer. We could get him a rank of first or second lieutenant; he'll return a major or colonel. However, he resists to this day. It is not a lack of courage or patriotism; I know he has generous sentiments. Nevertheless, he resists. . . ."

"What reason does he give?"

"He says he doesn't want to leave me."

"That's a good reason."

"Yes, because the separation would be trying on me, too. But it is not a matter of what he or I may feel. It is a matter of something graver—our country, which is more important than self."

Valéria spoke these words with a certain air which seemed to Luís Garcia more affected than sincere. He did not believe in the motive she gave. The interest the widow was now showing in relation to the outcome of the campaign was entirely new to him. The public motive excluded, there must be one which she had not wanted to, or could not, reveal.

Could he justify such a conclusion? He did not dare put in words his suspicion and doubt; he only allowed himself to dissuade her, saying that an average man would count for little or nothing on the scales of destiny. And since her son opposed the separation, it was more prudent not to insist.

To all these reflections Valéria retorted with some general ideas about mothers setting good examples. When it became necessary to vary her answers, she admitted that a small element of personal interest entered into the project.

"Jorge has graduated," she said, "but he hasn't the inclination for the legal profession nor for that of judge. For the time being he enjoys life; but the days are flying by and indolence becomes a way of life in time. I would like to give him an illustrious name. If he goes to war he may return a colonel, come to appreciate military life, follow it, and thereby honor his father's name."

"Very well; but let's consider another possibility. What if he dies?"

Valéria grew pale and was quiet for a moment while Luís Garcia looked at her to see if he could discern the inner workings of her mind, forgetting that the idea of a possible disaster had probably occurred to her a long time back, and that if she had not hesitated in the face of it, it was because her resolution was unshakable.

"I thought of death," said Valéria after a little time had elapsed; "and, of course, my son's obscurity would be better than a disaster . . . but I rejected that idea. The more important consideration, of which I was speaking, must take precedence over any other."

Immediately, as if to prevent him from insisting upon the considerations previously presented, she told him bluntly that if Jorge refused, she was counting on the influence of his advice.

"You are our friend," she explained; "your father was also our friend. You know that both you and he always enjoyed our respect. In any case, I would not wish to call upon anyone else."

Luís Garcia did not answer right away; he was not inclined to accept the responsibility, and he did not wish to refuse openly; he was looking for a way to avoid answering. Valéria insisted so strongly that it was impossible to remain silent any longer.

"What you ask of me is very serious," he said; "if Jorge gives some weight to my advice and goes to war, I assume a portion of the responsibility, which will not only put a burden on my conscience, but will also alter our relations and will perhaps diminish the warm friendship I have always enjoyed in this house. The favor you are now asking of me—who knows but that you may someday throw it in my face as an act of imprudence?"

"Never."

"On such a day," observed Luís Garcia, "you will surely be as sincere as you are today."

"Oh, such dark thoughts! I don't believe in death; I believe only in life and in glory. The war has just begun and there are already so many heroes. My son shall be one of them."

"I don't believe in premonitions."

"Are you refusing?"

"I can't risk accepting."

Valéria was depressed with the answer. After a few moments of silence she got up and went to get the handkerchief she had left on a table when she entered the living room. She wiped her face and continued looking at the floor, one of her arms drooping in a pensive attitude. Luís Garcia began to think about how to dissuade her effectively. His skepticism did not make him immune to the sufferings of others, and Valéria did seem to be suffering at that moment, whether

her assertions were sincere or not. He wanted to find a means of reconciling the widow's desires with his own neutral position—something that was plainly difficult.

"Your son isn't a child," he said. "He is twenty-four years old; he can decide for himself, and he of course will tell me just that. . . . Furthermore, it is doubtful that he will let himself be influenced by my suggestions, after resisting his mother's wishes."

"He respects you a great deal."

"Respect" was not the right verb. "Listen to" would have been more appropriate because it expressed the true nature of the relations between the two of them. But the widow was using every possible means to gain assurance from Luís Garcia that he would help her in persuading her son. When he told her once again that he could not accept the responsibility, he saw her bite her lip in a gesture of resentment. So Luís Garcia followed a middle course.

"I promise you one thing," he said. "I will sound him out, discuss with him the pros and cons of your plan, and if I find him more disposed. . . ."

Valéria shook her head.

"Don't do that; I can already tell you that it will be a waste of time. Jorge is sure to give you the same reasons he gave me, and you will accept them as natural. If in your estimation I deserve anything, if the friendship which linked you to our family has not died, I ask that you, with your authority, help me in this effort. Enter into this as I myself would, ready to convince and win him. Will you do me this favor?"

Luís Garcia thought for a moment.

"Yes, I will," he said feebly.

Valéria seemed to revive with the answer. She told him to come for dinner that same day or the next. He refused twice, but he could not hold out against her entreaties, and promised to come the next day. The promise was a means not only of ending the widow's insistence, but also of learning what the secret explanation of that lady's action was. The honor of the nation was certainly the noble and august mask for personal rather than public motive. Luís Garcia opened up the channels of reflection and did some conjecturing. In the end he didn't doubt Valéria's patriotic intention, but he asked himself if she hoped to gain some personal advantage from the move she was going to make.

The human heart is the region of the unexpected, the skeptic said to himself as he climbed the stairs to the office.

14

At the office he learned that some bad news had arrived from Paraguay. The allies had attacked Curupaití and had retreated with great losses; the enemy seemed stronger than ever.[2] It was even supposed that the peace proposals had been no more than a ruse to strengthen the defense. Thus, military fate had come at the right moment to reenforce Valéria's arguments. Luís Garcia imagined all that she would say to him the following day.

The next day he went to Inválidos Street for dinner. He found the widow less upset than she might have been in view of the news of the day before, if, in fact, the outcome of the war concerned her as much as she said it did. She even seemed to Luís Garcia more serene. She came and went with a satisfied and determined air. She had a smile for everything she heard, a tenderness, an informality, the desire to please and captivate, all of which Luís Garcia studied with the keen, sharp eyes of suspicion.

Jorge, on the other hand, seemed reticent and silent. At the dinner table Luís Garcia furtively examined the expression in his sad eyes and the frown on his forehead, a look which indicated the resentment and irritation in him. In reality, it was hard to send to war one of the most beautiful ornaments of peace. Sadness didn't usually reside in those eyes; they were ordinarily bland and peaceful. A thick, black mustache, product of nature and the barber, covered his lip and lent to his face a virile expression which it did not otherwise have. His slender and graceful carriage was the only aspect about him that could definitely be military. Elegant, Jorge occupied one of the top places among the dandies of the Rua do Ouvidor.[3] He could have been born there; he could probably die there. . . .

Valéria was right when she said that she could find in her son no love for the legal profession. Jorge remembered much of what he had learned; he possessed a ready intelligence, rapid comprehension, and an extremely alert memory. He was not deep; he had surveyed more than he had assimilated. Above all, his was a theoretical intelligence; to him the formalist was the same as the barbarian. Having the material assets which allowed him to live well, he spent a small portion of his time

---

2. Curupaití was the location of one of the battles of the Paraguayan War, which took place on September 22, 1866, and in which the allies were defeated.
3. Literally, "Street of the Hearer," one of the most important avenues in Rio de Janeiro, especially in Assis's day. It was on this street that "things happened."

practicing law—as little as he could—just enough to have his name on the door of his office and in Laemmert's *Almanac*.[4] No experience contradicted in him the impulses of youth and the raptures of the imagination. Imagination was his weak side; in him it was not creative and pure but vague, tumultuous, and sterile. He was generous and good, but suffered a little from pride, which diminished his natural goodness. There was in him the embryo of a future man, waiting for the years, whose movement is slow, opportune and inevitable, to give stability to his character and virility to his intellect.

Dinner was neither happy nor lively. They talked at first of unimportant things. Then Valéria directed the conversation to the latest news from Paraguay. Luís Garcia remarked that it didn't seem as bad to him as the newspapers said, without, on the other hand, denying that it was a matter of a serious setback.

"It's a six-month war," he concluded.

"Is that all?"

That was the first question from Jorge, who until then had done nothing but listen and eat. Valéria picked up the other end of the dialogue, and corroborated Luís Garcia's opinion. But her son continued not to interfere. When dinner was over, Valéria rose; Luís Garcia did the same. The widow, resting her hand on his shoulder, said in a familiar and deliberate tone:

"Don't stand on ceremony; I'll be right back."

Once the two men were alone, Luís Garcia thought it a good idea to go straight to the heart of the subject which had brought them together.

"Don't *you* want to go to Paraguay?" he asked as soon as Valéria had disappeared down the corridor.

"Not at all. Nevertheless, I'll wind up around there."

"Really?"

"Mother desires nothing but that, and I know you yourself, sir, share her opinion."

A negative response brushed the lips of Luís Garcia; but he checked it in time, confirming by his silence Valéria's pious deception. He had in his hands the means of annulling the effect of the mistake—by showing himself indifferent. Jorge amused himself, balancing a toothpick on the

---

4. A *Who's Who* of people in the legal and other professions.

edge of a wineglass; and after looking at him, Luís Garcia finally broke the long silence:

"But why are you giving in now after refusing for so long?"

Jorge raised his eyes, motioned to him; and they went out onto the terrace.

"You are an old friend of the family," he said; "I can confide in you. Mother wants to send me to war because she cannot restrain the feelings of my heart."

"Some love affair," Luís Garcia concluded half-heartedly.

"A passionate one."

"Are you sure of what you're saying?"

"Yes, I am."

"I don't believe it," Luís Garcia replied after a moment.

"Why not? She is counting on distance and time to suppress a love which she assumes has not grown deep roots."

Luís Garcia had taken a few steps, accompanied by Valéria's son; he stopped for a moment. Then the two continued to stroll back and forth. The former was reflecting upon Jorge's explanation, which seemed to him truthful *if* the boy's love was unworthy of his name. Such a question he did not have the courage to ask; but he searched for a circuitous path by which to arrive at it.

"A trip to Europe," Luís Garcia observed after a short silence, "would produce the same result with no further risk than. . . ."

"I turned down the trip; it was then that she thought of the war."

"But if she wanted to go to Europe, would you refuse to accompany her?"

"No, but Mother hates the sea; she would never go. It is possible that, if I held out to the end in relation to the war, she might conquer her aversion to the sea, and the two of us would go. . . ."

"And why didn't you hold out?"

"First of all, because I was tired of refusing. This fight between us has been going for a month and a half. Today, because of the news from the south, she spoke to me so insistently that I gave in once and for all. The second reason was a bad but justifiable sentiment. I chose the war so that if something should happen to me, she would feel remorse for having lost me."

Luís Garcia stopped and faced the young man silently.

"I know what that look means," continued the latter. "You find me cruel, and I am only normal. The resentment lasted only a moment. It passed, and a shadow of remorse remained. I'm not blaming Mother; I know the tears our separation will cost her. . . ."

"There is still time to refuse."

"What is done is done," said Jorge, shrugging his shoulders.

"Do you know something? I think it is poor taste to give this business an epiclike outcome. What does the Paraguayan War have to do with this affair? I am going to suggest to her a way of settling things. Give in only half way; go to Europe alone; come back after two or three years. . . ."

Jorge smiled contemptuously.

"Your advice shows the difference in our ages," he said. "If I went to Europe, what sacrifice would I be making for the person I love? On the contrary, she would be the one sacrificed. I would be going to have a good time, to stroll around, to see new things, maybe to find new loves. If I go to war it's different; I sacrifice my well-being and risk my life; I will have something. Although we are still separated, she will not deny me her regard. . . ."

"Her regard?" said Luís Garcia, astonished.

He didn't continue; but Jorge understood, through that word alone, the kind of woman Luís Garcia supposed the chosen one of his heart was. He made a gesture; he didn't venture to say anything. He regretted having said so much. Without daring to recommend silence, Jorge began to suggest it subtly—an unnecessary tactic, because Luís Garcia was not the kind of man who would reveal what had been entrusted to him, and a dangerous one, because it made the mystery grow in proportion. Luís Garcia smiled covertly on sensing Jorge's cautious manner; and when it became annoying to him:

"Don't worry," he said; "you needn't fear that I shall make your love life public. I repeat my advice to you: don't jump into a senseless adventure with your eyes closed. Going to war is very noble, but one should go for other reasons. A disagreement because of a love affair concerns neither Pôrto Alegre nor Polidoro.[5] A priest should be the one to put a stop to it."

Jorge smiled in a friendly spirit and bid Luís Garcia farewell; from

---

5. Brazilian generals of the war with Paraguay. The Count of Pôrto Alegre commanded the Second Brazilian Corps; Polidoro substituted for General Osorio, who had fallen ill.

there he went to dress for the theater. Luís Garcia was more than ever resolved to let things take a free course without intervening. As soon as Jorge had left, he prepared to do the same, bidding Valéria a good evening. The latter accompanied him to the door of the living room.

"Won't you tell me anything?" she asked when she saw him about to go through the door.

"What shall I tell you?"

"Did you speak to my son?"

"I did."

"Did you find him willing?"

"I can't say he wasn't."

"But reluctant?"

"I can't say he was."

Valéria smiled with a tinge of resentment. "I can see that this subject irritates you."

Luís Garcia denied it. Valéria leaned against the doorpost.

"No one," she exclaimed. "I don't have anyone on my side. I'm alone; I'll remain alone."

"Let's be frank," Luís Garcia said. "Your son is giving in, but he is doing so under constraint, and I do not see that he can be made into a hero. What motive can be so strong that you are obliged to require of that young man more of a sacrifice than he can make?"

Valéria didn't answer.

"I know your motive," he said after an instant.

"You do?"

"I suspect it; and if you will allow me to be frank, I must say that I find it peculiar; at least there is no balance between cause and effect. Your son is in love. Is it a matter of its being a woman of a certain kind? His are youthful escapades, and not, I think, the kind to cause a scandal. Is it a matter of some young lady whose attachment to Jorge is not acceptable to you? I shall say nothing in this respect; but think, first, before sending him to Paraguay."

Valéria took Luís Garcia's right hand between her own hands. She thought a long time, then said in a faint voice:

"Suppose . . . that it had to do with . . . a married woman?"

Luís Garcia lowered his head in a gesture of assent. Since his eyes went all the way to the floor he did not notice in the widow's face a quick flush that deepened and then disappeared. If he had seen it, if he had looked at her imperiously, perhaps the widow would have lowered her eyes, ashamed at having lied. Luís Garcia saw nothing. He remained silent, gave his approval, and promised to help her.

It was nighttime when Luís Garcia left Valéria's house. He left annoyed about everything—the mother and the son, his relations in that house, the circumstances into which he had gotten himself. Climbing the slope on foot, pausing from time to time to look down, he was moving along as if apprehensive about the future, superstitious, seized by intermittent and inexplicable fears. It was not long before the light of the house became visible to him, and in a little while he could hear the lonely chanting of the slave and the primitive notes of the marimba. They were the voices of peace; he quickened his pace and sought refuge in solitude.

Chapter Three

Luís Garcia had little effect on Jorge's spirits. Once he had declared his intentions, the youth no longer faltered. He did not ignore the fact that the undertaking to which he had set himself was beset with difficulties. The war, especially after the Curupaití disaster, promised to last a long time; no one was discouraged, and the government was effectively backed by the people. Jorge obtained the title of "captain of the volunteers."

Twenty days after the conversation on the terrace of Inválidos Street, Jorge appeared at Santa Teresa, in uniform and ready, in such a way, however, that it was still difficult to distinguish the man of fashion from the military man. The same skill which had tailored his formal attire had fashioned his captain's uniform. Around his waist he sported a red sash, whose tips hung gracefully at his side. He was wearing shiny boots, over which his trousers of fine cloth were fitted. His cap, tilting slightly to the right, did not muss his hair, which was combed in the style of the day; his mustache had the same long, pointed, and lustrous tips.

On seeing him enter in full uniform and about to leave for the south, Luís Garcia was not able to escape a feeling of pity. It seemed to him that he could see behind the youth the foreboding of death, with its eternal, lifeless smile. But the feeling of compassion passed; he reminded himself immediately of the widow's last words and couldn't keep from condemning the boy. He even saw with certain aversion a twenty-four-year-old man who was going to risk his own life, and perhaps that of his mother, to avoid giving up an unworthy passion.

"Do I meet with your approval?" asked Jorge with an air of benevolent irony.

"You will look better after the war, 'General,' " the other answered.

" 'General'? Maybe."

Saying this, Jorge started talking about his hopes and his future. His imagination was beginning to disperse his melancholy. He could already see in the undertaking a romantic and mysterious adventure; he felt himself a medieval knight, come to life to do battle for the love of his damsel, an opulent and beautiful chatelaine, who would be waiting for him on a Gothic balcony, her soul in her eyes and her eyes on the drawbridge. The thought of death or mutilation did not come to agitate its pale and bloody wings in his face. What he had before him were infinite vistas of hope. Nevertheless, it was a serious moment, and only with difficulty could his spirit avoid recurring reflection. Furthermore, Jorge had gone up to Santa Teresa resolved to tell Luís Garcia everything, in order to leave behind the only serious confidant of his love life; but he just couldn't utter the words. Either Luís Garcia's age or the nature of their relationship hindered this intimate confidence—more than for any other reason because of the singularly preoccupied and cold manner of Luís Garcia at that moment. Jorge took it upon himself to get the matter under way.

"Give me that goodbye hug," he said; "I'm sailing tomorrow."

"Already?"

"I came to say goodbye."

Luís Garcia looked at him silently for two or three minutes, then grasped his hands.

"Go," he said; "work for your country; don't fail in your responsibilities and don't for one day forget your mother."

Jorge left and walked down, taking long and shaky steps in the direction of Dona Luisa Street. When he was halfway there he stopped, as though he wanted to turn in another direction; he shrugged his shoulders and went on. He went along submerged in his own thoughts and only came to his senses when he stopped in front of one of the houses on that street.

Before entering, let us find out who the dwellers were.

Valéria's deceased husband, when he was practicing law, had a clerk who, even more than clerk, was his confidant. His name was Mr. Antunes. It was services of a certain kind that brought them together more intimately. Fortune sometimes changes nature's plans, but the two went hand in hand in that man, born and reared for subordinate assignments. Familiar with all forms of adulation, Mr. Antunes would go from hyperbolic flattery to opportune silence. In a short time he became not only a hard-working and punctual clerk but also, and above all, a factotum of the judge—his right arm—from electoral responsibilities to domestic purchases, a vast scale in which the role of confidant of amorous enterprises was a part, so that he never lacked for the judge's protection. He saw his salary grow and his gratuities multiply. He was even allowed at times to eat at the house, on ordinary days when there were no important guests; on more solemn occasions he would be the first to decline. At the end of three years of acquaintance, he had absolute control of the situation.

Precisely at that time it happened that his wife died, leaving him with a ten-year-old daughter, an interesting girl, who had sometimes visited the judge's house. The judge took care of Mrs. Antunes's funeral arrangements and paid for the daughter's and father's mourning apparel. Mr. Antunes was not a man of extreme opinions. He had the conviction that not all is vanity under the sun, as Ecclesiastes suggests, nor all perfection, as Dr. Pangloss opines.[1] He felt that there is a loose balance of good and evil, and that the art of living consists in getting the greatest good out of the greatest evil. After his wife's death he managed to get from the judge a complete wardrobe for his daughter in order to get her into a school, since until then she had not learned anything and, with things as they were now, he couldn't leave her at home alone. The judge had supplied the wardrobe; sometimes he paid for the schooling; the visits became more frequent. The child, who was pretty and well behaved, gradually made her way into Valéria's heart; and on the day that the little girl finished her schooling, Valéria took her into her home.

Estela—that was her name—was at that time sixteen years old. When the judge passed away, Mr. Antunes suffered two blows instead of one: that of seeing him die, and that of seeing him fail to make out a will. Aneurisms bring about such unexpected afflictions.[2] In order to lend fortune a hand, Estela's father bestowed upon the widow the attention he had formerly dispensed both her and her husband—a moral obligation he owed the judge's family. Estela owed that family her education and affection; she might come to owe it a dowry, a husband,

---

1. Ecclesiastes is a book of the Old Testament which is based on the words of the preacher: "Vanity of vanities, all is vanity." Dr. Pangloss is a character in Voltaire's *Candide* (1759).

2. An aneurism is a sac formed by local enlargement of the wall of an artery, caused by disease or injury. This was evidently the cause of the judge's death.

and deep gratitude. Who could tell? Perhaps Jorge's heart would even unite the two families. Such an ambition was something that Mr. Antunes nourished in the deepest recesses of his soul.

Jorge was about to complete his studies in São Paulo; he was halfway through the fourth year.[3] Coming to the capital during his vacation, he found himself confronted with an unexpected situation; his mother had contrived a marriage plan for him. The chosen was even a distant relative of Jorge's. Her name was Eulália. She was nineteen years of age according to her baptismal certificate, and thirty in mental development. She was a young lady without illusions or vanity, perhaps without passions, endowed with sound judgment and a simple heart and, above all, a beauty without blemish and an elegance without ostentation. "A pearl," Valéria would say when she hinted to her son the wisdom of marrying Eulália.

The pearl, nevertheless, did not seem anxious to ornament anyone's forehead. When Valéria first probed the heart of her young relative, she found there tranquil water, without either the ebb or flow of the tide. She tried to discover whether some breeze had aroused the girl's interest, and she learned that it hadn't; so she resorted to more drastic means.[4] It was not difficult for Eulália to perceive what the widow's wishes were, nor did she resist when she knew. Reason told her that the marriage was acceptable; she waited. Valéria was satisfied with the results, and hurried to probe Jorge's inclination when he returned at the end of the year.

Owing to her ability in uncovering others' desires, Valéria managed to get from her son a conditional answer. That was something, at least. The reasons for the widow's insistence were complex: the qualities of the relative, the great affection she had for her, the fear of dying suddenly, and her confidence in herself as a good judge of character. During his last year at the university Jorge had thought a few times about marriage as one thinks about a remote project; but as time ran on his heart became reserved and fearful. Once he had graduated he gave

---

3. In Brazil the fourth year of study constituted the last for graduation from the university.

4. The text here literally says, "She summoned the *sirocco* and the *pampero* to her aid." The *sirocco* is a hot wind from the southeast which blows over the Mediterranean, while the *pampero* is a strong wind that blows from the southwest, in Brazil originating in the Argentine pampas.

up the idea. He wasn't frank enough to tell his mother, and Valéria waited confidently for her son to say in another language that which she had already told him in hers.

In order to understand exactly the reason for Jorge's aversion to a young lady whose qualities would tempt any other, one must not forget that these qualities were precisely those most objectionable to his nature. It was not enough that she was elegant and pretty, discreet and gentle. Something else was necessary, something that corresponded exactly to his imagination; she lacked a touch of the romantic.

To this attitude was added a new one, which took possession of him at the end of three weeks after his arrival in Rio de Janeiro. The daily sight of Estela produced a strong impression on Jorge. Despite the fact that they lived in the same house, it was difficult for them to be alone together because the clerk's daughter spent all her time following the widow around—a situation which did not have the positive effect of altering the course of events. Not being able to move from general to intimate conversation, Jorge spoke to her with his eyes—a language the girl either did not or pretended not to understand. Estela's imperturbable seriousness was just another irritant, no less cruel than the gentle manner and resolute air which showed in her pale, quiet face.

Pale she was, but without any note of ascetic melancholy. She had large dark eyes, with an expression of moral strength which was the principal characteristic of her beauty. Taken one by one, the girl's features were refined and delicate, but the impression left overall was one far from the natural tenderness of the female sex. Usually she wore black, a color she preferred above all others. Free of adornments, her dress emphasized her graceful, lofty, and lissome form. Nor was she accustomed to dressing any other way, except for some trinket or piece of lace which the widow gave her from time to time. Of her own volition she refused every kind of embellishment, accepting neither ruffles nor earrings nor rings. At first glance one would have called her a feminine Diogenes whose threadbare cape left visible the vanity of a beauty that wished to assert itself just as it was, without any other artifice.[5] But, given the girl's character, one might guess two motives—a natural inclination toward simplicity, and, even more, the consideration

---

5. Agrippino Grieco, in his *Machado de Assis* (2d ed.; Rio de Janeiro: Conquista, 1960), affirms that it is really a matter of Antistenes and not Diogenes;

that her father's means did not allow for expensive furbishings and that therefore it was not wise for her to become attached to luxury.

"Why don't you put on the earrings Mother gave you last week?" Jorge asked Estela one day when there were guests for dinner.

"The most beloved gifts are put aside," she answered, looking at the widow.

Valéria pressed the edge of the girl's chin between her thumb and forefinger: "How poetic!" she exclaimed, smiling. "You don't need earrings to be pretty, but go put them on; they suit you well."

It was the first and last time that Estela put them on. Her intention was too obvious not to be noticed, and Jorge did not forget either the girl's answer or the constraint with which she obeyed. He could not believe she was ungrateful, because he noticed the affection with which Estela treated his mother. There did not seem to be a similar regard for him; there was certainly respect and consideration, but seldom familiarity, and even when there was, it was a formal familiarity as one might have for a casual visitor.

Jorge began to find the house a more pleasant place to be than the street; and at night, when there were no guests, he spent his time at a table reading, or playing cards with the two of them, or watching them work while he told them tales of school or read the news from Paraguay and Buenos Aires or simply some page out of a novel. In that more or less patriarchal atmosphere the hours passed quickly, so quickly he was unaware of time. After five or six weeks spent thus, he made himself his own confessor, examined his conscience, and discovered within it something that was not the sensuous fantasy of the first moment; and, far from absolving himself, he sentenced himself to the hard penance of abstention. He returned to old habits and abandoned domestic get-togethers. But the application of medicine, no matter how sincere it might be, could no longer do much against the progress of the disease. Estela was often obstinately in his mind; and on the street, in the theater, in the gatherings he attended, the serious profile of the girl crept in between him and reality. If he could avoid seeing her, a cure would not be impossible; but how could one escape the memory of a woman whose image appeared before him several hours of each day?

Antistenes (413-323 B.C.), scorning convention and riches, was the first to wear the beggar's cloak and carry the staff as a symbol of philosophy (see pp. 39-46).

Furthermore, his daydreaming aided the fatality of circumstance. After a month the nature of the sentiment had changed: it was purer. But the sentiment did not seem willing to vanish: it was more violent than ever.

Since Mr. Antunes was taking his daughter to visit a friend of his one evening, Jorge took advantage of the situation to hint to Valéria the propriety of returning Estela to her father.

"Why?" asked the widow.

"Having a stranger among us is always a hindrance," answered Jorge. "I don't deny that she has good qualities, but she is an outsider."

"What does that matter, if I get along well with her? I have known her since she was small; she is a better companion than any other. But why do you bring this up now?"

"I have been thinking of the responsibility that weighs upon us. If she were a relative of ours, all right, we would have an obligation; but this not being the case, I feel it would be better for us to free ourselves."

"Don't worry; when the time is right I'll arrange a marriage for her. But I will not accept a mediocre husband. He must be a person who deserves her. You don't know how valuable that girl is. She is not only good; she has a certain elevation of sentiment; she has never neglected me and never flattered me either."

Jorge agreed with a nod of his head and said nothing more. What he had just made was a sincere but weak attempt to remove Estela from the house; it was the tax paid to conscience. This done, he let nature take its course, convincing himself that the danger was not so great nor the remedy so urgent, and that, after all, he was a man.

In the midst of this situation, what did Estela feel or think? Estela loved him. The moment she discovered that feeling in herself, it seemed to her that the future was opening up before her spacious and bright; but it was only for that instant. As soon as she discovered the feeling, she tried to suppress it or hide it—lock it up, at least, in the most secluded recesses of her heart, as if it were something to be ashamed of, or a sin.

Never! she swore to herself.

Estela was the living opposite of her father; she valued her soul above her destiny. She was proud, so proud that she even made inferiority appear as a halo. But her pride did not emanate from impotent envy or sterile ambition; it was a force, not a vice; it was her buckler of diamonds—that which preserved her from ills, as that of Tasso's angel who defended chaste and saintly cities.[6] It was this feeling that made her turn a deaf ear to her father's suggestions. As a simple addition or favored protégée, she did not consider herself as having the right to dream of some higher and more independent position; and even if it were possible to attain to such a position, we may venture to say that she would refuse, because in her eyes it would be a favor granted and her cup of gratitude was full. Valéria, who was proud herself, had discovered this quality in her, and did not dislike her for it; on the contrary, she came to appreciate her all the more.

Estela's pride not only silenced her heart, it instilled within her the necessary moral confidence to live peacefully even in the midst of danger. Jorge had never perceived the feelings he had inspired; and, on the other hand, he never envisioned the possibility of some day inspiring them. Estela manifested to him only cold respect and cold dignity.

One day, when one of Valéria's houses in Tijuca became vacant, the widow decided to examine it before renting it out again.[7] She was accompanied by her son and Estela. They left early and the trip was a happy one for the girl, who was visiting that suburb for the first time. When the carriage stopped, Estela felt as if it had barely had time to leave Inválidos Street.

The house needed some repairs. A master carpenter, who was already there, followed the family from one room to another. Only Valéria and he spoke; Estela had no voice in the matter and Jorge was indifferent. What did he care about the plastering of a wall or the repairing of a floor? He joked, laughed, or whispered into Estela's ear a witticism about the master carpenter, whose remarks were execrable. Estela, who was smiling with him, nevertheless kept a straight face at the epigrams.

As they went from room to room they came to a small veranda, where a new situation detained them for a while. At one end of the veranda was an old dovecote, where they found, forgotten or abandoned, a pair of doves. The two birds, after twenty-four hours of

---

6. Torquato Tasso (1544-1595), one of the most eminent Italian poets of his time and the author of a long poem of religious inspiration written in keeping with the spirit of the Counter-Reformation, "Jerusalem Liberated" (1580).

7. Tijuca was a lower-middle to middle-class suburb on the northeastern edge of Rio de Janeiro.

solitude, seemed to want to greet the people that suddenly appeared there.

"Poor little things!" said Estela as soon as she entered the veranda.

Valéria watched for a minute, maybe half a minute, and went on to see the rest of the house. Estela remained to look at the two doves and did not see her leave.

"Do you want to take them?" said Jorge's voice.

The girl turned around and answered no.

"However," she continued, "it would be nice to give them to someone so they won't starve to death. They are so pretty!"

"But why don't you take them yourself?"

"I'll ask the carpenter to take them out of there," she said, taking a step toward the inside.

"That's not necessary; I'll take them out."

Estela refused the favor, but the young man had made up his mind that he was going to satisfy the girl's wish himself. The dovecote was not within reach; it was necessary to climb on the parapet of the veranda, stand on tiptoes, and stretch out an arm. Even then, he would have to count on the good will of the doves. Jorge climbed on the parapet. If he lost his balance he could fall to the ground; to avoid that, Jorge grasped with his left hand an iron bar which was on the corner pillar and which held him up; then he stretched his body and reached the dovecote with his hand. One of the doves was easily caught; the other, at first elusive, was captured after a little effort. Estela took them; Jorge jumped to the ground.

"If Dona Valéria saw this, she would certainly scold," said Estela.

"A great achievement!" answered Jorge, brushing his hands and the lapel of his cutaway with his handkerchief.

"You could have fallen."

"But I didn't; the risk is over. The little things are pretty, aren't they?" he continued, pointing to the doves which Estela held in her hands.

The girl responded with a nod and moved a few steps as if to go to the widow. Jorge detained her, placing himself between her and the door.

"Don't leave," he said.

"What is it?" asked Estela, calmly raising her large, limpid eyes.

"Don't pretend!"

Estela lowered her head silently and tried to turn in another direction to go into the adjoining room. Jorge again blocked her path.

"Let me pass," she said without anger or pleading.

Jorge had moved back to the door, the only one of the three that was open. What he was doing was risky; but, besides the fact that Valéria and the carpenter were on the floor above—he could hear their steps—he had at that moment lost all presence of mind. The place was deserted, and naturally the time which he could count on to tell her everything was ample. But his lips remained sealed for a few moments while his eyes bespoke the eloquence of a passion which was ill controlled and about to explode.

Estela did not insist, but she remained in front of him, quiet and without arrogance, as if expecting to be obeyed. Jorge would have wished her suppliant or confused; her composure wounded his self-esteem, making him see that there was no danger, and revealing, in any case, the greatest indifference. Who was she to affront him this way? It was the second time he had asked that question; he had done so when he was first attracted to her. This time the answer was deplorable. Fastening his eyes on Estela, he said in a tremulous but imperious voice:

"You will not leave without telling me if you like me. Come on; answer! Don't you know what such silence can cost you?"

Not receiving an answer, he continued after a brief pause: "You are brave! I want you to know that I can come to hate you . . . perhaps I already do; know too that I can take vengeance on your disdain, and I will even become cruel if it becomes necessary."

Estela only sighed and went over to lean against the parapet and look at the grounds. It was her intention not to irritate him with the cold and mean answer which her heart dictated, and to wait for Valéria to come down. However, her back was turned to Jorge, a situation which was not intentional but which seemed to the latter a simple means of conveying her scorn for him. Jorge's irritation was great. After about two or three minutes of silence, he walked in the direction of the parapet where Estela, her head bent down, was kissing the heads of the doves which were leaning against her breast. He paused while the girl remained motionless. He contemplated her yet for a moment, and if Estela had looked at him she would have noticed that the expression in his eyes was one of respectful tenderness and nothing else.

This was a fleeting moment, however, as was the sentiment. Leaning toward the girl, Jorge spoke in a manner that neither refinement nor character but only resentment could explain:

"Why are you wasting your kisses on those birds when they can better be employed?"

Estela trembled all over and raised to the young man a pair of eyes that flashed with indignation. She was no longer pale but livid. Stunned, she didn't know what to say or do, and unfortunately, neither did she know that Jorge's question, as offensive as it seemed to her, was not yet the greatest insult. Jorge had before him a cloud through which he could see neither his own personal demeanor nor the dignity of the woman he loved; he saw only the indifferent woman. He took her face between his hands, pulled her to him, and before she could pull away or cry out, he covered her mouth with kisses.

Freed during the tussle, the doves flew off over the heads of both of them and lighted again upon their little wooden house, where no moral fate consigned them to that love without hope, that agony without dignity.

Estela smothered a groan and covered her face with her hands. The voices of Valéria and the carpenter, who were approaching, could be heard. Jorge experienced a moment of uncertainty and hesitancy; but the reaction had taken place and, besides, it was necessary to erase the effects of that scene so that the widow would not notice them.

"Here comes Mother," he said quietly to Estela; "I am not to blame for what I did, because I am very fond of you."

Estela turned around and wiped her eyes. In a moment Valéria and the carpenter came in. The latter left right away, having agreed upon the repairs which were indispensable to the house. Valéria, irritated with the sight of the damage she found, was criticizing the negligence of the tenants. Only after a few moments did she notice that neither of the two had responded. Jorge seemed timid and Estela sad. As she had wiped away her tears, Estela's face was smeared and her beautiful eyes seemed faded. Jorge didn't dare to look at his mother or Estela; he looked at the tips of his boots, where a little of the plaster from the parapet remained. His hands were behind his back, and he was leaning against a doorpost. Valéria noticed the attitudes of the two; but since she was able to dissimulate her impression, she altered neither her manner nor her voice. But her eyes never again left them.

In no time at all they were in the carriage. It was late. The trip was made almost entirely in silence; at least, only Valéria said a few words.

By the time they reached Inválidos Street, the widow suspected that there was something between the two and that it was serious. Throughout the day she tried to think of a way of learning the nature and details of the situation, but could find nothing better than to question one of them directly. Jorge had left the house immediately afterwards and did not return for dinner; Estela did not smile the entire day and said almost nothing.

It was not necessary to question her. As soon as she had risen the following morning, Estela went into Valéria's bedroom and asked for a few minutes of her time. She explained to her the necessity of returning home. She was a young woman; she should render her father the services he would need from someone, and which he had the right to expect from his daughter. It was not a matter of ingratitude, she added; she would take from there an unforgettable memory; she would return often and would always be obedient and grateful. She was only giving in to the obligation of being with her father. This request confirmed Valéria's suspicion but clarified only half of the situation. Was Estela's withdrawal a means of avoiding Jorge or of being able to speak to him more freely? Valéria tried to sound out the girl's heart, telling her that the reason given was insufficient and that some hidden cause was moving her. Then she reminded her of the love she had for her, and that Estela should not fail her in the confidence she owed her.

"Come now," she said; "tell me everything."

Estela asserted that there was nothing more; but as the widow insisted, she answered by lowering her head, which was worth half a confession. Valéria struggled on yet a long time; she employed both sweetness and intimidation, but the girl gave in no farther.

"Very well," said the widow, "have your way."

Thus it was that Estela, at the end of a short period of residence in Valéria's home, returned to her father's house on Dona Luisa Street. Mr. Antunes was disconcerted with the news; he said he was getting along perfectly well alone, he thought Estela's behavior was neither commendable nor fair to the judge's widow. His praises of the widow availed him not at all because Estela would not back down from her resolution, nor did the widow try to dissuade her.

The separation accomplished nothing; worse yet, it intensified Jorge's love for the very reason that the distance between them only spurred his imagination. Two forces contended within the young man's heart: the barrier, which made the love more intense, and the regret, which made him more respectful. There remained in him no resentment of Estela's decision; he felt guilty, and even more, he felt himself a victim of the girl's flight. Not all of this was the result of his love alone; part of the effect was due to Estela's austere behavior, which eventually instilled in Jorge's mind a different idea from that which he had had of her. Valéria discovered little by little the inefficacy of the remedy she had accepted. She was certain about her son's romantic attachment, and she could see that, far from dying out its life was just beginning, less imprudent perhaps, but none the less sincere and profound. She learned that Jorge often visited the house on Dona Luisa Street; she trembled over the future, and pondered about how to destroy the budding hopes.

Either she already loves him, or she can come to love him, she would say to herself.

Valéria was facing the two possible outcomes of the situation in the event that the girl came to love her son: either the degrading of Estela, whom the widow loved very much, or an alliance of the two, a solution which was repugnant to her sensibilities, ideas, and plans. She would never consent to such an alliance. A quick solution was urgently needed.

She returned energetically to the project of marrying her son to Eulália, and strongly suggested to him that he obey her. Jorge began by resisting and wound up pretending, but the trick didn't fool his mother. Valéria immediately called to her aid her young relative. Eulália, who had had time to reflect, told her frankly that she was not willing to become her daughter-in-law because Jorge would never come to love her; and, not believing there could ever be any romance in the marriage, she felt that aversion or total indifference was the weakest of conjugal ties.

Unaided from this source, the widow then thought of the trip to Europe; and, when he refused her on that count, she resorted to the Paraguayan War. It was not without its cost that she resorted to this means, violent for both of them; but, once adopted, its advantages seemed brighter to her than the danger seemed dark. Thus it was that from a comparatively insignificant incident, a serious outcome resulted, and from a domestic matter, a patriotic action emerged.

Chapter Four

It was completely dark when Jorge arrived at Estela's house. Mr. Antunes was at the door and might have been expecting him; he received the visitor with some agitation and sadness.

Four months had passed since the scene at Tijuca, and during that time Jorge had gone many times to the house on Dona Luisa Street. Estela had neither avoided nor mistreated him; she was as serene and cool as always, speaking very little to him, it is true, but with such freedom that it seemed there had not been the slightest misunderstanding between them.

For his own part, Jorge endeavored to erase the memory of that episode, behaving with the respect and propriety which seemed to him sufficient to redeem the lost esteem. Sometimes they remained alone together in the living room. Mr. Antunes would devise some scheme that would oblige him to be absent for a while—with the only purpose, he would say to himself, of helping nature. But especially on such occasions, otherwise propitious, Jorge would not cross the line he had drawn for himself. He didn't murmur so much as one amorous word to her; he gave her no look that could make her blush or otherwise react. Any allusion to the scene at Tijuca, even a yielding look, would be harmful to Jorge's cause; he avoided that trivial error, saying nothing that could closely or remotely remind the girl of it. They spoke little and of unimportant things, as people who didn't know each other well.

It was only when he had completely lost the hope of winning her over by ordinary means that he accepted the proposal of enlisting in the army. The day he broke the news to them, the effect on both father and daughter was profound, but different for each, because the father was completely aghast and became inert, while the daughter felt her soul breathe freely; and if a secret and frightening voice seemed to say to her *don't let him go,* another more dominant and strong thundered that the departure meant liberty and peace. The trip, the distance, time,

34

and the nature of military responsibilities should wrest from him a feeling which Estela felt was causing domestic dissension and which, in any case, lessened her in her own eyes.

"So it's tomorrow then?"

"Tomorrow."

Estela received him as usual, despite her father, who seemed determined to make those last moments unpleasant for him.[1] Mr. Antunes's sadness was intense. He belonged to that order of souls who, through the years and even during the winter frosts, continue to wear the short pants of a tender age, and for whom life always has the aspect of castles made of cards carried over from childhood. Once the idea of marrying his daughter to the graduate had taken root, he lived off of it as though it were a *fait accompli*. The war incident did not awaken him to the reality of the situation, but it seemed to him that it was postponing his wish, and that was enough to worry him. Now that he saw Valéria's son in uniform, about to depart the next day, he fully realized that the separation was taking place. After a half hour of conversation, Mr. Antunes withdrew from the living room for a few minutes; he went for some cigars.

"Take one of mine," said Jorge.

"Never; yours are too strong."

Never before had Jorge's cigars suffered a complaint from Mr. Antunes, who smoked them as regularly as he had smoked his father's. Estela felt humiliated by the answer and the action. Jorge, who was standing next to a table, saw Estela's father leave, and remained there looking at the floor. Estela buried her eyes in the work she was doing.

Jorge finally raised his eyes and focused them on the girl, whose beauty seemed to him that night even brighter and more ethereal than ever, precisely because he was beginning to see her through the nimbus of nostalgic distance. She was concentrating on her work with labored silence. Her hands, which rivaled the purest, moved the needles without visible commotion or trembling. This indifferent and dignified aspect no longer offended the young man; he could gauge the difference in the situations—something accomplished since his first ideas about Estela. But time was running out, and the silence was making him increasingly

---

1. The indirect object pronoun here does not make it clear whether the reference is to *him* (Jorge) or to *her* (Estela). From the sense of the paragraph, it could be either.

shy; finally he decided to break it, and break it in such a way as to allow himself to gain at that moment either release from or destruction in the life he was about to engage in. He took two steps toward Estela.

"Perhaps we won't see each other again," he said.

"Why not?" said Estela without raising her eyes.

"I may remain buried in Paraguay."

"Your mother wouldn't like to hear you say that. . . ."

Another two minutes went by. Jorge, putting his entire soul in his words, said in a low, sad voice:

"I am sailing south tomorrow. It isn't patriotism that is taking me; it is the love I feel for you, a love great and sincere, which no one can take from my heart. If I die, you will be my last thought; if I live, I want no other glory than that of feeling loved. Both depend entirely upon you. Tell me, should I live or die?"

Estela had raised her head; when he finished, she was standing. She gazed at him for a few moments with a neutral and expressionless look. Womanly vanity might have been satisfied with the solemn amends made and forgiven; but Estela's pride won out and she did not give in to any feeling of fairness or humanity. An ironic smirk brushed her lips from whence sprang these unkind and disdainful words:

"You are a fool."

When her father returned to the living room moments later, Jorge had one of his hands on the back of a chair and was as pale as a corpse. Estela had gone to the door of the living room alcove, resolved to lock herself in.

Mr. Antunes had seen nothing; but upon observing the faces of the two, it was not very difficult to guess that something had happened between them. He guessed it; nevertheless, he hadn't quite grasped what it might be, whether a painful farewell scene, or something less favorable to his calculations. He went to the young captain and asked him to be seated, but Jorge declared that he was leaving and excused himself. Without looking at Estela he stretched his hand out to her, which she took with the most tranquil air in the world. Her father was hoping to see a furtive tear, a feigned gesture, anything that might speak in favor of his hopes. There was nothing. Estela neither lowered her face nor hid her eyes. Jorge, yes; despite the effort he was making, his hand shook when he grasped the clerk's.

Mr. Antunes saw him to the door. There, before opening it, he wanted to hug the young officer.

"Allow me this sad honor," he said. "These are a friend's arms, believe me."

Jorge consented without enthusiasm; but when he came in contact with the body of Estela's father, it seemed to him that he was hugging a part of the girl, and he embraced him tightly. This demonstration flattered the other man extremely; it even moved him.

"You can count on me," he whispered; "I'll stay here to help you."

Jorge heard him, grasped his hands mechanically, accepted a last hug, and moved abruptly toward the street.

Unbearable is the pain which denies one the right to question fortune. The most difficult of sacrifices is that which cannot be consoled by conscience. Jorge suffered the pain, but the sacrifice was going to destroy him.

He didn't go home from there; he wouldn't dare face his mother. During the first hour which followed his leaving Estela's house, he was unable to control his thoughts; they raced through his brain unabated and without direction. His heart was beating hard in his chest; from time to time his body was seized by shivers. He was walking along feeling scorned, humiliated, and with a tinge of remorse in his heart. He would have wanted to erase the scene of that night with one stroke, at least to blot it out of his mind. Estela's words resounded in his ears like the hissing of an angry wind; he carried in his mind the scornful picture of the young woman, her manner without tenderness, her eyes without mercy. At the same time he remembered the Tijuca scene, and something told him that that night was the revenge of that morning. One moment he felt hateful; the next, ridiculous.

Your mother is right, cried an inner voice; *you were going to stoop to an alliance unworthy of you; and if you didn't know how to respect either your own person or your parents' name, it is right that you pay for your mistake by having to gamble in war. Life is not a Virgilian eclogue; it is a natural agreement, which is neither accepted with reservation nor violated without penalty. There are two natures in society, and the social nature is as genuine and imperious as the other. They do not contradict each other; they are complementary—that is, they are the two halves of man—and you were going to give in to the first and not respect the rightful laws of the second.*

You are right, an opposing voice told him, *because that woman is worth more than your destiny, and the law of the heart precedes and is superior to other laws. You weren't going to step down; you were going to allow her to step up; you were going to correct fortune's mistake. Listen to God's voice and leave to men that which they have brought on themselves.*

Jorge walked along, thus torn by opposite sensations, until he heard it strike midnight and he walked home, tired and oppressed. Valéria was waiting for him, not having gone to bed. That silent devotion—common to mothers and to be expected on the eve of a harsh and lengthy separation—was like a balm to the boy's wounded heart. It also caused remorse. It pricked his conscience to see that he had wasted several hours away from the creature whom he was going to leave truly longing for him, the only person who would intercede before God for him. Valéria had guessed where her son might be, and trembled with fear as the hours went by, apprehensive that, Estela loving him as she did, the two might have stolen away from the bondage of social conventions, seeking refuge in some secret retreat. She first thought this, but changed her mind, doubtful of herself and of the integrity of her actions. She didn't doubt the nature of the wrong; but didn't the remedy chosen exceed the wrong? Supposing that such a thought was her first punishment, she nevertheless reacted with determination, assembling her faint and scattered energies, and became again the woman she was, with all her strong natural or assumed qualities. Besides, what good was repentance if it was too late?

Her son came in, his features composed but sad. Valéria received him without any expression of censure or grief. She said nothing to him; he spoke little and they bade each other a simple farewell on that last night in which the young man would be sleeping under his parent's roof.

The night was a troubled and sad one for him. He wasted almost all of it, taking inventory of a life which was going to end—looking through papers, burning friends' letters, giving away a few belongings, and finally, writing some testamentary instructions and letters to intimate friends. When it was nearly four o'clock in the morning he lay down; at seven he was up. Valéria was up before him. A few people came to say farewell and to be with his mother at the solemn moment of parting. Among these was Estela's father, whose visible sadness, sincere as it truly was, veiled an even deeper sadness.

Finally, the moment of separation came. Valéria had controlled herself as long as she could; but the last moment brought so much pain that it was impossible for her to hold up. The widow's moral constitution was strong, but her self-control had lasted long and her will had worn itself out in the daily effort. When the last moment of separation came, the tears burst from her eyes, not tumultuous nor interrupted by sounds and moans, but of the other kind, that lacerate faces silently, remnants of a dignity that succumbs to the law of nature only with difficulty. She stretched out her still beautiful arms and placed them on her son's shoulders; in that posture she contemplated him for some time. Then she kissed him and pulled him tightly to her heart.

"Go, my son," she said in a firm voice. "I'll pray to God for you; God is good and will return you to my arms. Serve your country, and remember your mother!"

They were her last words. Jorge didn't hear them. His soul was prostrate and deaf. He wept also, less silently than Valéria, but the same tears of distress.

"Goodbye, Mother dear!" he said, finally tearing himself from her arms.

He left. Valéria didn't see him leave; she had turned her back to everyone, and went to her bedroom to grieve over her self-imposed misfortune.

A short time later, his native city passing out of view, Jorge felt that he had turned the first page of his destiny and was about to begin another, written in blood. The spectacle of the sea depressed him even more; solitude spread out before him infinitely. He spent the few days of the trip in that mental debility which follows misfortune. Finally, he disembarked at Montevideo, going on to Paraguay from there.

The second lap of the journey, the strange people, new things, the agitation in the theater of war—all this produced in him a wholesome transformation. His flexible and mobile spirit shook loose the shadows of grief which darkened it, and, once his face was turned in danger's direction, he began to visualize, not obscure or even glorious death, but triumph and laureate return. Having imbibed the initial portion of the campaign, Jorge felt himself a man. The time for frivolities had ended; the time for austere and long-lasting sacrifice had begun. He was going to face unknown problems, expose himself to unforeseen dangers; but he was going resolute and firm, with his mind serene and clear, and the flame of confidence aglow in his heart.

Chapter Five

Jorge's first letters were all to his mother. They were long and effusive, enthusiastic, careful, and even childish. Discounting the scant portion of truth there might have been in them, enough remained that Valéria's heart understood; it was a sweetening balm to her in his absence, dispelling her apprehensions.

Jorge soon familiarized himself with military life. The army, en-camped at Tuiuti, was not beginning any new operations; it was a matter of gathering the necessary elements in order to continue the campaign in a sure and decisive manner. Since there was no important action in which he could test his strength and become skilled, Jorge looked for situations with some danger, risky assignments whose success might depend upon a daring spirit, sagacity, and patience. That desire won for him the approval of his immediate superiors.

His commanding colonel became especially observant of him; he sensed Jorge's youthful spirit in his gentle and quiet look. At the same time he observed that, amid the easy and various pleasures of the encampment, converted by inactivity into a village of amusement, Jorge maintained a monastic reserve, a chaste horror of anything that might divert him from caring for, or even thinking about, military obligations.

The colonel was typical of his profession; he loved war for war's sake. He would probably have died of nostalgia under the shelter of peace. He was brave and gruff mannered. In the beginning what he disliked about Jorge was his neatness and the remnant of his ballroom manners. Jorge, nevertheless, without forsaking immediately the ways of civilian life, developed in time a soldier's mettle. His desire to work, to risk his life, to temper his spirit in the fire of danger changed the feelings of the colonel, who now saw in him a good companion at arms; after a short time, he sought to promote him.

Although Jorge spoke of the colonel in the letters he wrote to his mother, he didn't speak of him as a friend, nor did he have friends in the encampment, or if he had them he didn't consider them as such. He listened to the confidences of many, brightened the hopes of some, comforted the sorrows of others; he never, however, opened the door of his heart to passing curiosity. One page, nevertheless, of his life as a military man—youthful, attractive, well off, who attended neither the theater nor the entertainment of the camp, who laughed but little and badly, who spoke only of war when he spoke of anything—would have been of great interest.

One day, a major from Ceará found him sitting on the discarded piece of a gun carriage cast in a secluded place, looking one moment at the horizon, the next moment tracing a star in the dirt with the point of his sword.

"Captain," said the major, "it seems you are seeing stars at noon." Jorge smiled at the joke but did not, on subsequent days, leave off drawing stars on the ground or looking for them in the fields of heaven. The officers, drawn to him by their approval, did not become bound to him through close contact. Jorge was not only taciturn, but variable— sometimes docile, other times harsh, often absent-minded and introspective. He was especially absent-minded when he received letters from Rio de Janeiro, among which it seldom happened that there was not one from Mr. Antunes. Estela's father watered with the brackish water of his style the hope he had not lost. His letters were veiled nuptial poems. He talked a great deal about himself and a lot more about his daughter, whose soul, he said, was singularly sad and distressed. Jorge resisted the desire of also talking about Estela. More than once her name would almost fall from the point of the pen; he would immediately mark through it, just as he would erase any phrase that might seem to allude to his feelings. The sentences he wrote to the girl's father were dry, without any special interest, polished and cold.

One day, however, before the middle of the year 1867, he was not able to resist the need of entrusting the secret of his love to someone or of declaring it to the four corners of the earth. There was no one near who deserved the confidence. Jorge searched his brain and remembered Luís Garcia, the only outsider to whom he had confided half the secret he had taken to war. Discreet hearts are rare; a majority of them are not falcons who, though wounded, fly silent, as the ballad says; a majority are magpies, who tell all or almost all.

By that time Jorge's heart had already undergone a great transformation. The nature of his love had changed without lessening in intensity, converting itself into a sort of mystical adoration, a profound and strong sentiment that seemed to breathe a higher atmosphere than did the rest of creation. He spoke of it so himself in the letter to Luís Garcia, without divulging the name of the person nor any circumstance that could put him on the track of the truth; he required absolute silence of him and related what he felt:

> It is not important to know who it is—what is essential is to know that I love the most noble creature in the world, and the sad part is that, not only am I not loved, but I am even sure that I am detested.
>
> My mother was mistaken when she felt that my love had found an echo in another heart. Perhaps she would have given up sending me to Paraguay if she had known that this unrequited love would be my punishment. It was; it no longer is. This intense feeling came with me, despite what I heard her say on the eve of my sailing; and if it didn't grow, it is because it couldn't grow. But it changed from the child that it was and became a man of wisdom. A crucial event, distance between us, and the intervening months were enough to accomplish the miracle.
>
> I don't know if I will ever see her again, for a bullet can bring my life to an end when I least expect it. If I see her, I don't know how she will feel about me. But one way or the other, this love will die with me, and her name will be the last to leave my lips.
>
> The love I feel no longer knows the meaning of impatience, jealousy, or exclusivism; it is a religious faith that can live whole in many hearts. Perhaps you don't understand me. Serious men are deaf to these subtleties of the heart. Frivolous men don't understand them. I myself don't know how to explain what I feel, but I feel something new, a longing without hope but also without despair. That is enough for me.

Jorge reread what had been written and found it at times too clear, at other times too obscure. He hesitated yet awhile; finally, he folded the letter, sealed it, and sent it to Rio de Janeiro.

When the answer reached his hands, the army was preparing to leave

Tuiuti. Jorge was completely absorbed in matters of war, dreaming of battles, mentally stabbing López's soldiers. Luís Garcia's letter said little or nothing about the subject of Jorge's letter; it was almost entirely composed of advice and reflections, given in a sober and measured language, reflections and advice almost exclusively relating to the duties of men and soldiers.

Jorge expected just that; he knew, even if only slightly, the dry and cold personality of Luís Garcia. Nevertheless, he was momentarily disappointed and sad. Was it true that no one sympathized with his secret misfortunes or his lonely ventures? At the end of long months of separation, not even Estela would be thinking about him, nor did he find anyone with whom he might break the bread of longing, the last nutriment for an unrequited love. The consciousness of spiritual solitude depressed him for a moment; all the strength accumulated during those months vanished, and his soul fell prostrate.

A few days later the march from Tuiuti to Tuiu-Cue took place, followed by a series of encounters and movements in which there was much of Plutarch.[1] Only then was Jorge able to confront the true face of the war, whose beginnings he had not attended; he stood out in more than one heroic expedition; he took risks, showed himself brave and patient. The colonel idolized him; he felt himself caught up in admiration of that youth, who fought during the battle and remained silent after the victory, who communicated ardor to the soldiers, retreated from no enterprise, even the most risky, and whom some star seemed to protect with its wings of light.

He once noticed in one of the deadly battles of December of 1868, a year and a half after Luís Garcia's letter, that the youth's boldness seemed to extend beyond the customary, and that instead of a man who was battling, he was a man who wanted to die. Fortune saved him. The battle over, the wounded gathered up, the dead buried, the colonel went to him in the tent and found him sadly silent, his eyes swollen and still. The colonel didn't notice; he went in to congratulate him for his conduct, even if it had been a little excessive. Jorge had risen respectfully and was looking at the colonel without saying a word. The latter looked at him and saw in him signs of depression.

"What in the devil is the matter with you, Captain?"

---

1. Plutarch was a historian and moralist famous for his *Life of Illustrious Men of Greece and Rome*, also called *Parallel Lives*.

"Nothing," answered the youth.

"Did you receive letters from Rio de Janeiro yesterday?"

"One, from my mother."

"Is she well?"

"In perfect health."

"In that case. . . ."

The colonel stopped and reflected, then continued:

"I know what it is."

"What it is?" exclaimed Jorge, trying to smile.

"It will be done," continued the colonel. "The thing is on its way, it will be done; I won't tell you any more."

And he gripped him on the shoulder, with a gesture that could just as well mean "Relax, Captain," as it could "Congratulations, Major." Jorge understood that gesticulated play on words and grasped the colonel's hands, thanking him not for the rank he was announcing to him, but for the esteem he had for him. The colonel looked at him for a few minutes in a paternal way.

To ascend! They dream of nothing else, he growled to himself, and left.

Jorge remained alone. He lit a cigarette which he was not able to finish. Then he sat down, unbuttoned his uniform, took out a letter, opened it, and reread a few lines at the end. The letter was from Luís Garcia. He gave him news of his mother, who, because of illness, had gone to Minas for the waters; and he concluded with these amazing words:

> . . . it remains for me to tell you, if in any way my life can be of interest to you, that last Saturday I was remarried. My wife is the daughter of Mr. Antunes. Your mother served as our matron of honor.

With his eyes fixed on those few lines, Jorge seemed oblivious to all else. The paper, received the day before, was crumpled as though it had been in his hands for a year. He would look, reread, and wouldn't understand; when he did come to understand, he could not believe it. Estela's wedding was, in his eyes, an absurdity; but, after the intervals of doubt, the truth took hold of him. Reason told him that such news had to be correct. After two days he understood something about his mother's silence: the reason, no doubt, was the same that had caused her to send him to Paraguay. She never spoke to him of Estela nor of Luís Garcia's marriage, a silence calculated to completely extinguish in his heart the final murmurs of a love without echo.

Jorge then felt an emotion peculiar to such crises—a feeling of hatred for the entire human species, from his mother to his enemy. He became discourteous, violent, deliberately cruel: a temporary effect, which was succeeded by a profound depression. Wounded a few days later at Lomas Valentinas, he left the army (whose operations only continued after the middle of the next year) for a few months. Jorge took part in the campaigns of Pirebebuí and Campo Grande, no longer as a captain but as a major, the rank bestowed upon him after Lomas Valentinas. At the end of the year he was a lieutenant-colonel, was in command of a battalion, and was receiving the embraces of his old commandant, who was happy to see him acclaimed a hero.

Just after March of 1870 when, the war over, he was in Asunción, yet another unexpected and disastrous event occurred to grieve him deeply. Valéria died. Luís Garcia gave him the sad piece of news, which he guessed before reading it, since the last letters had already predicted the dismal outcome. Jorge adored his mother.

Although it was true that he had come to war against his will, it was nonetheless true that it had covered him with laurels, and that he would have wanted to place them in Valéria's lap. Destiny decided otherwise, as if it wanted to counteract each one of his accomplishments, making his heart bleed.

At the end of October he returned to Rio de Janeiro. Exactly four years had passed. Entering the channel and seeing his native city come into view, Jorge compared the time, the anguish, and the hopes of his departure with the glory and the weariness of his return.

He felt neither happy nor unhappy, but in that intermediate state which is the normal condition of human life. He compared himself to the morning sea, neither stormy nor calm but lightly whitecapped and rough, as much at the point of dropping as of rising and hurling itself at the beach. What drowsy breeze or destructive typhoon might come to sweep its invisible wings over him? Jorge didn't probe it. He had his eyes on the past and present; he left matters of the future to time.

Chapter Six

Before going directly to the heart of the action, let us see through what turn of destiny Estela's marriage came about.

Few could have guessed toward the end of 1866 that the campaign would last for another four years. General Mitre's calculation with regard to the three months from Buenos Aires to Asunción had, to be sure, already fallen into the abyss of historic illusions.[1] Proclamations are like lotteries; fortune makes them sublime or vain. Nevertheless, that of the Argentine general, which was already an erroneous assertion, expressed the conviction of three nations at the time. From the first confrontation with the enemy, it was seen that the campaign would be difficult and drawn out. The illusion evaporated; the reality remained. Even then, we were not alarmed. Nevertheless, it was difficult to presume, in October of 1866, that the war would continue until March of 1870. It was felt that a diligent effort would be sufficient to make up for Curupaití, to knock over Humaitá, and to defeat the dictator—not in General Mitre's three months, but in a lot less time than would in reality be the case.

Considering all this, it is no surprise that Valéria feared at every moment the end of the war and the early return of her son. If that happened, she would have struck a useless blow, and the fire of the scarcely extinguished ashes could reignite. Valéria preferred radical solutions. Once her son had been removed, she saw the necessity of annihilating whatever hope remained, and the surest way was to marry off Estela. Proceeding thus, she would also be doing justice to the affection she had for the girl, an affection which had never diminished. She knew that between Estela and her father there were moral differences that were difficult to reconcile. The two spoke a different

---

1. Mitre, one of the most important Argentine generals of the Paraguayan War, later became the president of Argentina.

language; they could never understand each other, especially (she would say to herself) in the choice of a mate.

Two months after Jorge sailed, Valéria invited Mr. Antunes to Santa Teresa, where she had a summer house. The message was written, a circumstance which lent it a kind of dignity. Never before had the widow written him. Mr. Antunes read and reread the note, showed it two or three times to his daughter, and was tempted to show it to the neighbor across the street. While he dressed, he placed it on the table, casting his eyes on it furtively, weighing its courteous expressions from memory, searching them, dissecting them. When he was dressed, he put it away carefully in his wallet. On the street he escaped from some importune individual by stating emphatically where he was going. As to the motive of the message, he couldn't guess what it might be, nor did he have much time for that. He contemplated it, though, and supposed that it concerned some favor she was going to ask of him.

It was a favor, and the widow was not asking it of him; she was doing it for him, and didn't delay in telling him so. After ten words she asked his permission to give Estela a dowry.

"I wouldn't want to do it without your consent," she concluded. "That's why I sent for you."

No matter how vile a man may become, nature can dignify him, even if only for a minute. Estela's father experienced that minute. Paralyzed and speechless at first, later still speechless but no longer paralyzed, Mr. Antunes revealed in his otherwise common face a dignified emotion. The dignity, however, disappeared with the silence. When he opened his mouth to thank the widow for the proof of affection she was giving his daughter, his soul regained its customary manner. Valéria interrupted his speech with such superior art that Estela's father felt it better than he understood it. The widow possessed that genuine kind of generosity which consists less in doing the favor than in disguising it; she told him that, in giving Estela a dowry, she was fulfilling a wish of the judge's and, without waiting for the elegy which Mr. Antunes would probably have recited, she made a long and affectionate inventory of the girl's qualities.

"She is a very good daughter," concluded the widow. "She has qualities worthy of the highest esteem, and, above all, I am her friend."

"That, madam, is the greatest fortune that could befall her. As for her being a good daughter, it isn't vanity that makes me say it, but I believe madam is right. She is like her mother, who was a saintly soul."

"Estela is no less so. And she is pretty! In the end she'll come to love someone, don't you think?"

"Yes, she will, she will," agreed Mr. Antunes. "In fact, I'm not sure she's not already in love. She is so quiet! Lately she has seemed . . . sad."

"Sad?"

"Distracted . . . like a person whose mind isn't at peace. I don't know whether it's love or sickness. I don't believe it's sickness because she is strong and looks well. Poor little thing! But she's always happy . . . that is, I mean, not happy. . . . I mean to say, she's not always sad . . . or. . . ."

Valéria smiled mentally at Mr. Antunes's confusion, which she attributed to the excitement the news of the dowry had produced in him; she interrupted him, telling him to bring his daughter to see her.

Half an hour later Estela heard the news about the widow's generosity, which her father hastened to give her, and contrary to his expectation, she received it quietly and gravely. Not finding the explosion of happiness which he was expecting, Mr. Antunes shook his head in discouragement.

"I don't understand you, daughter!" he responded. "You must tell me what it is you want to be in this world. You're not wealthy—even less than that. You haven't the slightest hope for the future. I can't leave you anything because I have nothing. Here is a lady who loves you, who is doing you a favor, and you receive it as though it were an injury."

The father's observation brought the daughter to the reality of the situation.

"You know I'm not given much to laughter, Father," she said. "You may rest assured that the news you've given me has made me very happy."

It didn't make her happy at all. Never had the inescapability of the position she was in weighed so heavily upon her. After the Tijuca episode, this favor seemed to her a sort of damages which Jorge's mother was liberally paying her, a cleansing water which would wash from her lips the kisses she was making an effort to extinguish, like Lady Macbeth with her bloodstain: "Out, damned spot!"[2] That was

---

2. In Shakespeare's play these words are uttered by Lady Macbeth in act V as she tries to eradicate the bloodstains caused by the murder of Duncan.

her estimation of the situation; it was also her grief. The haughtiness with which she had behaved since that morning somehow had augmented the pride which Jorge's inconsiderate act had for a moment humbled. But no matter how spontaneous the widow's gesture may have been, in the girl's eyes it seemed to emanate from the same place as the affront. Estela didn't differentiate between the assets of the mother and son. It was all one and the same purse, and that was where her dowry was coming from.

With that oppressive thought she entered the home of the widow, whose reception relieved her mind of its deepest worries. Valéria kissed her with a more maternal than protective gesture. She didn't even let her finish her speech of gratitude; she interrupted her with a caress. Then she spoke to her of beauty, of her affairs, of a hundred things alien to the purpose that brought them together—a generous pretense which Estela understood because she also knew the secret of that moral finesse.

Fifteen or twenty days later, Valéria questioned Estela directly, and the answer she received was contrary to her expectations.

"I love no one," said the girl, "and I probably never will."

"Why?" asked the widow eagerly.

Estela smiled.

"I could tell you that I don't have a heart," she answered.

"That wouldn't be true. But you are probably going to say that a good husband isn't easy to find."

"That's it."

"You're right, to a point. Of all the rare creatures, the rarest is a good husband; but what is difficult to find is not impossible. I've gotten it into my head that I'm going to find you a jewel. If I find one, what will you do?"

"I'll accept," said the girl after a moment.

"Not that way; I don't want you to accept against your will; you must accept with love . . . because I don't believe you don't have a heart; what you have is a pretty girl's vanity. Let me see," continued the widow, placing her hand on Estela's chest. "You do, oh! You have a heart that seems to want to tear your chest out. Estela, you're ill!"

"Imagine!" exclaimed the girl laughing. "Why, I have health to spare! I'm not sick, I'm moved. Let's talk about my fiancé. Don't ask me to love him passionately, because I wasn't born for that. I am reserved by nature. But a little affection, a certain amount of interest. . . ."

"Precisely: the seed of love. Time will take charge of producing the tree."

For three months they didn't discuss the subject. At the end of that time, Valéria having come down from Santa Teresa, Estela went to spend a few weeks on Inválidos Street. "Nothing yet?" asked the widow as soon as she saw her. "Nothing at all," was the answer. Given their situation, it wasn't easy for Valéria to find her the desired fiancé, unless the girl herself designated him, and that was the most improbable of all hypotheses.

Nevertheless, family life renewed some of the old habits between them. Valéria came again to feel the necessity of having her companionship, of conversing with her, of entrusting her with her ideas and migraines. Estela offered all the advantages of an old friend, in addition to being young and, even more, being pretty, a quality the widow appreciated since she was one of the most beautiful women of her day. Nothing kept them from completely restoring the situation that had existed before, except the memory of the recent past. It was this that had left between them a certain caution, a certain distance, which Mr. Antunes sometimes actually suspected without being able to understand. They didn't speak of Jorge or the war, or of anything that might revive the memory of the past.

When the summer of 1867 began, Valéria moved to Santa Teresa, where Estela sometimes went. On one of those occasions, she found there Luís Garcia's daughter, who was almost thirteen and was finishing her studies at the *colégio*. There was a moment of hesitation between the two; Iaiá, who was as mischievous and spirited as ever, felt shy in the face of Estela's seriousness; but that moment was short and their affection immediate. The summer over, the widow decided not to return to Inválidos Street; and, with the pretext or motive that in Santa Teresa she was more alone, she managed to get Estela to go there for a time. Estela went up in March.

By then Iaiá had already become a part of the intimacy of the home, less for what there could be that was appealing and attractive about her—and there was—than because of her own effort. The girl's sagacity was her supreme quality: she quickly understood what was most undesirable, how to avoid it and, what is more, did so. That quality had taught her the syntax of life, while others never get beyond the alphabet, where they often reach their peak. Having obtained the key to Valéria's personality, Iaiá opened the door with little effort.

She went there almost every Sunday, in the afternoons and sometimes in the morning, despite the resistance of her father, for whom Sundays were golden days, but only when exclusive. Luís Garcia gave in, not because of the widow, but to please his daughter, who seemed to derive pleasure from visiting the house. *She's still a child,* he thought. *It's wise to humor her.* When Iaiá dined at Valéria's, Luís Garcia would either dine there also, or would come back for her at night, and would take her home after an hour of conversation. Estela's presence made those visits even more enjoyable for the girl, and, in a short time, it was Estela's affection which most occupied her heart.

It was the law of contrasts that had united these two creatures, because Luís Garcia's daughter was as bold and youthful as Mr. Antunes's daughter was reflective and placid. One was looking toward the future while the other was coming from the past; and if Estela needed to temper her moral ambient with a ray of Iaiá's adolescence, Iaiá felt instinctively that there was in Estela something to heal or console.

One day Iaiá found Estela beside a table with a photograph album opened before her. The young woman was so engrossed that she only became aware of Iaiá's presence when the latter stopped on the other side of the table and focused her eyes on the album. Estela was slightly startled but immediately composed herself.

"Your father has the look of a kind-hearted man," she said.

"He does, doesn't he?" answered the girl with enthusiasm.

Actually, one of the pages in the album did have a picture of Luís Garcia; but on the other page was Jorge's picture, one of the three or four in the widow's collection. Iaiá, who adored her father, thought Estela's observation the most natural thing in the world, and didn't even look at the other photograph. Estela closed the album quickly with a shaky hand and was hardly able to smile at the insistence with which Iaiá returned to the subject. Her chest was heaving and her look vague and remote, vanquished by the campaigns of the south. Her heart was beating violently. But the commotion lasted no more than three or four minutes.

"You could marry Daddy," said the girl, after looking at Estela for awhile.

Estela was again startled, but this time it was only surprise. Since Iaiá was hugging her around the waist, she leaned close to the girl and asked, smiling:

"Would you like very much to be my step-daughter?"

"Yes, I would."

Estela shook her head, not in a negative gesture, but in disbelief. She already knew something of Luís Garcia's character; strictly speaking he was an acceptable husband. She saw in him a man of placid, mediocre, but sincere affection. She saw him respectful without abasement; polished without affection; speaking little but with some depth—in any case, at the right moment; living, finally, for himself and for his daughter. From everything she had observed, she concluded that sobriety was this man's moral law, and that from the chalice of life he asked no more than a few sips, very few. What did it matter? Conjugal love is strictly a chronicle; fidelity and a little style is enough for it. While there were some similarities between them, there were also differences, but Estela could gamble on time to adjust their differences. However, although the husband was acceptable, the marriage didn't seem possible. His exterior sobriety more or less surrounded him in an impenetrable atmosphere.

Iaiá didn't insist; but two or three Sundays later, everyone being at the *chácara*, she interrupted the general conversation to ask Estela if she really felt affection for her.[3]

"I've already said I do," replied Estela promptly.

"But do you like me very much?"

"Very much," repeated Estela, prolonging the first syllable.

"Why don't you come live with me?"

The others laughed; Estela kissed her on the forehead. The widow and Estela remained to play a game of cards, but they played without giving it their attention; then they had tea, but without appetite; finally they slept, but without being sleepy. Perhaps the same thought worried them. The next day Estela asked the widow, smiling:

"What if I told you that I have found a prospect for a husband?"

"Who?"

"Luís Garcia."

Valéria grasped her hands.

"An excellent man," she said; "a worthy and capable husband. I have known him for many years, and he was never unworthy of our esteem. And . . . do you love each other?"

"Now that is more complicated," replied Estela. "I can't say that I love him; nevertheless, I would like to be his wife. He may not want to

---

3. A *chácara* is a country estate.

be my husband, but that's the very reason I'm consulting you, and I ask you to tell me, since you approve of the choice, if I can expect reciprocation and if I should. . . ."

"You should do nothing; I will take care of everything."

Valéria did not hide her satisfaction. The idea of their marrying had never occurred to her. Iaiá planted the seed, Estela made it flower; all that remained was the fruit, and that was precisely the difficult part, because Luís Garcia's constitution seemed to her completely averse to contracting a second marriage. But Valéria was not discouraged. *It cannot be said that he is the ideal of every bride,* she thought; *he has neither the outgoing personality nor the vigor of his earlier age; but he should make an excellent husband.* Luís Garcia had a better position now. He had obtained a promotion, and in the light of that and some extra work entrusted to him, he was able to be completely protected from the adversities of life. He had established his daughter's future and had had the furnishings of his home restored, not for his own sake, but with the intention of making things more pleasant for Iaiá.

Estela, however, imposed a condition.

"I don't want to seem like I'm throwing myself at him," she said. "That would be improper for both of us, and wouldn't be the truth."

"Not that you are throwing yourself; but who can keep me from having *guessed* that you love him?" said the widow, maliciously.

"Or that I appreciate him," added Estela. "For a good marriage nothing else is necessary."

Luís Garcia was not a little surprised when Valéria asked him a few days later if he wasn't interested in a second marriage. He smiled and shrugged his shoulders; but, since the widow insisted, he answered that it was too late for him to think of remarrying.

"Don't say that," retorted Valéria. "Iaiá is almost a grown young lady; she is going to finish school. You live alone, and, having to keep your daughter company, it is better if you give her a stepmother."

Luís Garcia shook his head resolutely.

"I have no inclination to marry," he said after a pause. "My real vocation is celibacy."

"Is that the reason you became a widower?"

"I married once, that's true, but it wasn't for love; besides, I was merely a boy."

"When I insist on something, it is difficult for me not to win," said the widow after a few moments. "Here are two people I like very much, she and you, each worthy of the other; and I feel that I should marry them, and I will. Why are you smiling with that unbelieving air?"

Since Luís Garcia didn't answer and went on smiling, Valéria rose and went to the veranda, from which one could view the grounds; then she came back in.

"Go and see your fiancée," she said.

Luís Garcia went out to the veranda; the widow pointed to Estela's and Iaiá's group.

On the grounds there was a circular garden, planted with grass, at the center of which water spouted from a fountain. Its basin was encircled by plants, whose large leaves—some of them with scarlet, other with white streaks—interrupted the monotony of the lawn. Estela had picked a few of these leaves and at Iaiá's request, had interlaced their stems, forming a garland. When Luís Garcia got to the porch window, the girl was finishing the difficult work. The wreath ready, Iaiá, who was looking at her, childishly eager, lowered her head, and Estela crowned her with the rustic garland; then she stepped back a few paces, came closer again and arranged it better. The leaves fell over her shoulders irregularly or rose over her head, and the total gave the impression of a foppish water nymph. Estela looked at her a few moments; she leaned toward her and kissed her several times. Iaiá tried to repay her for her work and affection by giving her back the garland and placing it on her head. Estela refused; but since the child insisted, stomping her foot impatiently, she gave in to her childish wish. She bent forward. Iaiá, who had climbed onto a bench, crowned her head as the other had done for her, and, her whim satisfied, jumped from the bench to the ground.

Since Valéria was speaking to Luís Garcia at that moment, the two didn't see that the girl, jumping suddenly and poorly, had fallen into the sand; they only became aware of the accident when they heard a little cry of anguish from Estela. She had run to the girl to help her get up.

The fall was of little consequence. Iaiá was trying to smile, but a pebble which lay on the ground and against which she had fallen had produced a slight scratch on her face.

"It's nothing," she was saying.

"Nothing! you hurt yourself. . . . Of all things! It's up to your father to decide. . . . Come here."

Estela took the child by the hand to the fountain; she wet her handkerchief in the water. Leaning over her, she washed the blood from her face, while Iaiá smiled spontaneously. At that moment Luís Garcia, who had come down quickly, approached the two.

"It was nothing, Daddy," said Iaiá, reading on her father's face the reason he had come. "I tried to jump off the bench and fell. It serves me right for being naughty."

Luís Garcia had spread his right hand over his daughter's head and was examining the cut, which was little more than nothing. Reassured, he reprimanded her mildly. Estela, who had interrupted the operation, concluded, saying that the matter didn't amount to much but that it could have been more serious. Luís Garcia thanked her for her care and kindness.

"Furthermore, it was my fault," said Estela, "and without justification because I am not a child. Shall we go?" she continued, taking hold of the girl's hand.

"Well, then?" the widow asked Luís Garcia as soon as he had returned.

"Let's not talk about that, unless you can perform miracles," he said dryly.

Despite the turmoil which lingered in him as a result of Estela's affectionate behavior toward Iaiá, Luís Garcia laughed the following day when he remembered the marriage proposal. When he returned there, the subject wasn't mentioned again; nor did Estela give him reason to suspect any pretensions on her part. It seemed to him that Valéria had consulted only her own private wishes.

In dealing closely with the young woman, Luís Garcia had already noticed two things: first, the restraint with which she conducted herself, without parading Valéria's friendship or falling into the motions of servitude; then, an air of sadness, which was her usual mien. He concluded that Estela must be suffering or had suffered at some time. In addition to this, he appreciated some of her moral qualities. He assumed them to be genuine, but he also assumed them to be fleeting like the charms of her face or like the flower from the field; with the difference, he would say to himself, that there is a fatal span given for charms to lose their primitive freshness and for the flower to exhale its last fragrance, while social nature has a precocious decrepitude and a beginning of corruption, which destroys in a short time all the efflorescence of the first sun.

Estela hadn't given up on the idea and was pondering a way to carry it to fruition, despite the confidence of the widow, who would tell her: "Rest easy; the net has been cast." It was precisely the idea of a net that was repugnant to Estela's simple and direct spirit. Nevertheless, each day that passed was confirming the girl's selection.

The rest was the work of Iaiá: work divided into two parts, one voluntary, the other unconscious. Voluntary because the child also, in the working silence of her brain, had constructed the project of uniting them, and had said so on more than one occasion to both of them. Unconscious, because the love which joined her to Estela was the most powerful force which changed her father. It was an intense affection, that of those two creatures; while Iaiá gave to Estela a portion of a daughter's tenderness, Estela found in the child's love an anticipation of the pleasures of motherhood. Luís Garcia witnessed this reciprocal and, so to speak, inevitable process. If Iaiá must have a stepmother, where would she find a better one? Discreet, reserved, sensible, maturer than her years, Estela had the necessary attributes for this delicate role. The widow's first hint was the main cause; but time, familiarity, the affection of the two, the necessity of providing a second mother for the child, and sooner a legitimate one than a mercenary one; finally, the certainty that this solution was not repugnant to Estela—such were the first elements of Luís Garcia's decision.

There remained only the miracle, and the miracle came. Iaiá became ill one day at Valéria's; and the illness, though neither serious nor lengthy, afforded the opportunity for Estela to manifest all the tenderness of her heart unequivocally. Luís Garcia witnessed the silent and continuous devotion with which Estela cared for the sick girl. This last spectacle disarmed him completely. Between them, marriage wasn't the same thing it usually is to others; it possessed nothing of those unutterable joys or juvenile illusions. It was an act simple and serious. And that is what Estela said to him on the day they exchanged the first vows.

"I feel that no passion blinds us, and if we marry it is because we coldly judge ourselves worthy of each other."

"A love on your part for me would be unlikely," confessed Luís Garcia. "I don't attribute it to you. As for myself, a sentiment of that nature would be equally improbable, not because you couldn't inspire it, but because I could no longer have it."

"So much the better," concluded Estela. "We are both in the same situation and we are going to begin a trip with our eyes open and our hearts at peace. It seems that in general marriages begin with love and end in respect. We are beginning with respect; it's much more secure."

Mr. Antunes consented to the marriage with the same enthusiasm with which a defendant would sanction his own execution. Not only were hopes much less modest slipping away from him, but also his son-in-law's personality was repugnant to him. He did not give in without some hesitation and struggle, hesitation in the face of the widow, struggle in relation to his daughter; but he gave in, because he had been born not to resist. He was adroit, nevertheless, in squeezing some profit from his unavoidable ills; once he had lost confidence in the efficacy of his refusal, he accepted the covenant, not only with the appearance of cordiality, but even with enthusiasm.

"The dowry tarnishes you," he wailed philosophically.

The widow was matron of honor to Estela. Her happiness was sincere, and more or less disinterested. She could almost no longer remember the danger which, two years earlier, had shaken her spirits. Jorge's letters were so free of any oppression, so exclusively military! In addition to this, her conscience was satisfied with an outcome which, in a certain way, compensated for the loss, if she had in effect caused Estela some loss. Finally, the satisfaction with which she saw her accept a marriage which Estela had incidentally suggested herself, and the happiness to which she was a witness during the early months of marriage, gave her the assurance that the young woman was already completely exempt in relation to her son. Despite Jorge's passion, Valéria had faith that time had performed its duty.

Chapter Seven

Three months after his arrival in Rio de Janeiro, Jorge had settled all of the family business. What he had inherited was enough to relieve him of having to practice law or pursue any other profession, as long as he was not ambitious and handled the use of his income wisely. He had just the qualities for that, some natural, others acquired with time. The four years of war, together with recent events, had done away with certain worries which in 1866 had been the only ones on his mind. A footloose life, elegant squandering, and seductions of youth had entirely passed.

The spectacle of war, which often engenders pride, produced in Jorge an opposite effect because he saw, besides the just glory of his country, the insoluble conflict of human affairs. For the first time he meditated; he was surprised to find in himself a fountain of ideas and sensations the diversions of bygone days hadn't provided him. Nevertheless, it cannot be said that he returned a philosopher. He was only a man, whose upright and candid conscience had survived the misgivings of an earlier period and whose spirit, seasoned by the demanding life of a long campaign, begins to penetrate a little deeper than the surface of things.

Wishing to adopt a plan for a new life, he abandoned at first all his old habits, as he felt inclined to show society only his polished rearing. At first he had the idea of establishing himself in some quiet and secluded place in the interior; but he soon changed his mind, giving in to the necessity of remaining closer to a place convenient for an overseas trip—a trip which, however, he never began.

The first three months went by rapidly; they were spent in settling the estate. The widow had left few bequests, one of them of interest to us because it favored Iaiá Garcia. In this way the widow was indirectly making Estela's husband a beneficiary. Jorge heartily approved his mother's act. He approved Estela's dowry no less, but the feeling of distress he experienced as soon as he heard about it did justice to the refinement of his heart.

Luís Garcia hurried to visit Valéria's son. The interview between these two men whom the stream of events had placed in such a delicate situation was cordial but not effusive. Jorge did not find Luís Garcia looking any older; he was the same. Neither did he find him less reserved. In the beginning, the conversation did not go beyond general facts; they talked of the war and the victories. Jorge related a few episodes, which Luís Garcia heard with interest, since he told them as though he had forgotten his own achievements.

"I can see that you're modest," observed Luís Garcia. "Fortunately we read the bulletins and the official sections."

"I did what I could," answered Jorge. "One had to conquer or be conquered. What has become of all the people I haven't seen yet?" he continued in order to change the subject.

"Everyone goes his own way. My father-in-law, I believe, has already visited you. . . ."

"He has."

"By the way, let me thank you for the kindnesses I owe your mother. . . ."

Jorge tried to interrupt him with a gesture.

"Forgive me; it is my duty," continued Luís Garcia gravely. "Even at the end, Senhora Dona Valéria wanted to show her fondness for me. She did so on two occasions, in addition to others. First, she convinced me I should marry again, something I hadn't intended. She was the main cause of the change in my life, and it happened at such a good time. She couldn't have done me a greater favor. She enhanced its value by hiding from me the token of affection she had shown my wife a few months before. She had given her a dowry, as you must know. . . ."

Jorge made an affirmative gesture.

"She felt that it wasn't enough and she left my daughter a legacy which will be her dowry. . . . She liked her very much. Not being able to thank her benefactress, allow me to thank—"

"This time you will obey me," interrupted Jorge gently.

"Yes; let's talk about my wife. I want you to know that she crowned your mother's work with dignity: she made me understand the advantages of the marriage. Soon after we were married, she suggested that I accept on my daughter's behalf the portion Valéria had given her as a sign of affection. I enjoyed listening to her because it was a mark of unselfishness, but I refused—to no avail. Finally, I gave in; it couldn't be any other way. I like telling you these things because they are rare."

Jorge showed no emotion on hearing Luís Garcia's words. He had guessed the reason for Estela's unselfishness. *That ever-present pride!* he thought. Then he thought it over and asked himself whether the girl might have confided to her husband something of what had happened between them. It was difficult to tell, and it wouldn't be correct to assume it. No woman would ever do that; Estela less than anyone else. He studied Luís Garcia's face and found it placid and still. After a few seconds of silence, he extended his hand to him.

"Will you permit me to congratulate you, then?" he asked.

"From my heart," Luís Garcia answered quickly. And after rising: "If I were in the habit of giving advice, I would tell you to get married."

"Maybe I will."

"I won't ask you about your other love; I believe you've forgotten it completely."

"Completely."

Luís Garcia shook his hand cordially and left after extending him a welcome to his home. Jorge remained pensive for a few moments. The news of Estela's dowry had caused him a certain embarrassment; the news of the gift made by the girl in behalf of her stepdaughter now produced in him a mixed feeling of admiration and resentment. He sensed a residue of hatred smoldering in the depths of the girl's heart, and in his own heart he could not keep from approving the act.

Since it was necessary to return Luís Garcia's visit, Jorge delayed fulfilling the obligation as long as he could without its being noticed. Finally one day when he learned through Mr. Antunes that the family was not at home, he went to Santa Teresa and left a calling card.

Jorge's life was then divided between his studies and society, and the latter was allotted only a minimum of time.

He studied much and planned even more. For a few weeks he outlined several projects. The first was a history of the war, which he abandoned after he encountered face-to-face the mountain of documents he would have to consult and the numerous dates he would be obliged to assemble. Then came a brochure about legal matters, and then two biographies of generals. He would no sooner write the title of the work than he would lay it aside. His impatient spirit gathered the first fruits of an idea, but otherwise he only glanced at it. Once, only once, he thought of writing a novel, which was none other than the story of his own life. After a few pages he realized that its execution did not correspond to the outline and that it never left the realm of lyrical effusion and anecdotal proportions.

During the period when he was most inclined to write his autobiography, it occurred to him to wander through the house at Tijuca, the one he had once visited with his mother and Estela, the starting point for the events which transformed his life. He wanted to see it again; perhaps there he would find a fountain of inspiration. He went; he found the place in almost the same condition. He entered, curious and at peace.

Gradually he felt that he was beginning to relive the past; the resurgence was complete when he walked onto the veranda where the first time he had found the pair of doves, solitary and forgotten. The poor birds were no longer there! They had flown away or died, like his aspirations, and so discreetly that they revealed to no one the unfortunate episode. But the walls were the same; and also unchanged were the parapet and the floor tiling. Jorge leaned against the parapet where Estela had stood before him that fateful morning with the doves. What he felt on that other occasion, although he was concerned chiefly with love, still contained a bit of youthful levity. Nevertheless, the sight of the naked and cold walls of the veranda brought back to his soul the source of somber impressions, and he again began to see the burning eyes and pallid face of the girl. It even seemed that he could hear the sound of her voice. He also seemed to see his own violence. In the midst of so many vicissitudes his conscience was still clear, but the memory made him tremble and weaken. Jorge placed his arms on the parapet again and rested his head in his hands.

"Hello there, sleepyhead! It's time for breakfast."

Jorge raised his head suddenly and looked out to the grounds from where it seemed the voice had come. Out on the lawn, twenty paces away, there was a man smiling at him, his hands behind his back, clasping a thick walking stick. Jorge felt a cold chill, as though the secret of his past had been discovered. Only after the first sensation had disappeared did he respond, smiling:

"I'm not asleep; I'm thinking about the rent."

"Are you moving out here?"

"No."

"Is the house yours?"

"Yes. Come on up."

The man climbed the six steps of the brick staircase, and entered the veranda, where Jorge had assumed the role of exclusive proprietor, looking attentively at the walls of the building.

"What are you doing around here at ten o'clock in the morning, Procópio Dias?" asked Jorge as soon as the man appeared.

"I spent the night in Tijuca. I heard that this house had been vacated and came out to see it. I didn't know it was yours. It is a little dilapidated."

"Very much so."

"Really?"

"So it seems."

Procópio Dias shook his head with a disappointed gesture.

"That's not the way a proprietor should answer," he said. "It is in my interest to find it in poor condition; it is in yours to say that it merely needs a little repair. The truth is that the condition of the house is somewhere between. Listen, if you are always willing to agree with the tenants, you'd best sell all the houses you own or you'll be ruined. So this house is yours, is it? The appearance isn't bad; there are some things that could be repaired and then it would be excellent. It's not a modern house, but it's solid. I have already seen most of it; I went down to the grounds and was examining it when you appeared on the veranda."

"Do you want it?"

"You're naive!" answered Procópio Dias, striking him good-humoredly on the shoulder. "If I admit that it isn't very dilapidated, it's because I don't want it for myself. It's too large; besides, it's too far from the center of town. If it were farther on a piece. . . ."

"But if there were some romance around here?" pondered Jorge smiling.

"Let's talk about something else," answered the other man hurriedly, flashing his eyes at him.

Procópio Dias's eyes were the color of lead with a cautious and sly expression. This man was fifty years old, fifty years that were still vigorous and prosperous. He was of medium height and build, and not too ugly; the portion of ugliness which had been his lot he covered as best he could, with the qualities he had acquired with time and social intercourse. Sometimes he would make bodily movements which produced five horizontal creases on his forehead. It was one of his ways of laughing. In addition, there was the shape of his nose, which resembled a quasi-equilateral triangle: a nose at once scornful and inquisitive.

Despite the expression in his eyes, Procópio Dias had the characteristic of appearing simple whenever it was to his advantage; it was on such occasions that he laughed with his brow. He didn't wear a beard; he shaved with the greatest of care. One could see that he was a man of means. His clothes were conservative in their cut and colors, and they were of the best fabric and the finest tailoring. That morning he was wearing a long overcoat buttoned halfway down his chest, and leaving exposed a few inches of his ornately embroidered shirt. Between the top button of his overcoat and the only one on his shirt collar a huge diamond sparkled—ostentatious and scandalous. One of the fingers on his left hand was adorned with a magnificent garnet. His walking stick had a solid gold knob with his initials engraved on top in Gothic lettering.

Jorge had met Procópio Dias in Paraguay where the latter had gone into business to triple his assets, which permitted him to rise above the twists of fortune. The two developed a relationship which was not close but of frequent mutual and enjoyable contact, and to a certain point useful to Procópio Dias, who obtained from Jorge more than one favorable reference. In spite of their frequent contacts, they were far from being close friends, and this was true not because of any exertion on the part of Procópio Dias, whose easy behavior for a long time bothered Jorge in his inexperience. Procópio Dias's interest ceased with the war, since with the war mercantile interest had also ceased. Jorge had nothing against him; when he had first met him he was going through his melancholic period.

"You still haven't responded to my suspicion," said Jorge, extending his arm to Procópio Dias.[1]

"The love affair?"

"Yes."

"There is not the slightest shadow of that, my dear friend! On the contrary . . . I think I am going to enter a monastery—it is my latest ambition."

Procópio Dias had two creeds. One of them was profit. Because of a

---

1. It is a common and widespread Latin custom for men to walk arm in arm. It is a form of courtesy and esteem.

few years of hard work and crafty cunning, he had watched his assets grow. In 1864, with truly miraculous instinct, he sensed the crisis and collapse of the banks, and withdrew the funds he had in one of them just in time. With the advent of the war he threw himself into a variety of endeavors which might triple his earnings, something he in effect accomplished by the end of 1869.

Had it not been for his second creed it is probable that only death could have liquidated Procópio Dias. Having arrived at a solid position at the age of fifty, he found himself facing another type of wealth, not inferior to the previous one: time. Now his second creed was pleasure. For him, physical pleasure was the entire destiny of the human species. He had never been base; from the early stages of life, he had reserved for himself the portion of enjoyment which was compatible with the means at hand. His philosophy had two forebears: Luculus and Solomon—not Luculus the general nor the pious Solomon, but only the sensual part of those two men, because the ever-present feminine appeal dominated him no less than the eternal desire to eat.[2] Among his business friends he was always known as a happy conqueror of weak hearts. And, contrary to others, he never gloried or prided himself in this; he preferred caution and obscurity, not out of deference to public decency, but because it was easier this way. No worldly siren would ever have had the temerity to court him on the street or simply even to smile at him; she would be wasting her time and any prospect of marriage. He enjoyed pleasure for its own sake, which is sensualism in its perfection.

Jorge knew neither the life nor the character of the other man. Procópio Dias had the worst distinction that could characterize a man without morals: he was ingratiating, affable, talked about; he had a certain vivacity and charm. He was good company for young men and women. For the former, when they asked for it, he had a coarse anecdote and a vulgar style; if this was repugnant to them, he would use different expedients. With women he was the most patient, the most servile, the most lively of men—a jewel.

"No one sees you anymore," he was saying, two hours later at

---

2. Luculus was a Roman general well known for the luxury with which he surrounded himself. Solomon was king of the Israelites (974-932 B.C.). Reference is to the Song of Solomon in the Old Testament which tells the love story of a shepherdess kidnapped by Solomon.

Jorge's lunch table in the house on Inválidos Street. "I don't know your former friends but I am sure that all of them reprimand you for this beastly life. At the theaters . . . don't you ever go to the theater?"

"Almost never."

"How about going today?"

"You tempter!" said Jorge, smiling.

That night they went to the theater. Procópio Dias was in the mood; the conversation, the meal, time itself, everything conspired to dispel the shadows of melancholy which the morning had accumulated on Jorge's brow. "Don't let yourself rot in obscurity; it is the coldest of tombs," Procópio Dias was saying at the table of a hotel where they had gone to supper. Jorge ate nothing. Despite the pleasure he derived from being with Dias, he refused to accept the courtesy of the supper from him even though he had furnished his lunch. Procópio Dias noticed this, but was not bothered by it; he lowered his head, allowed the wave of suspicion to pass, and ended up laughing. They left an hour later. The memory of Tijuca had vanished.

Jorge let himself be persuaded by the other man's advice. He abandoned the last book planned, contenting himself with having lived it. Furthermore, time was undermining the old sensation, and social life was again capturing him in its net.

Among the people whom he saw again was the same Eulália whom his mother had wanted him to marry a few years before. Eulália had not remained a spinster; she was on her honeymoon, a honeymoon which was lasting more than a year. Her marriage had been the Mosaic rod which had opened up a little fountain of tenderness in her heart.[3]

They met at a dance. Neither of them felt any reserve; since they had never arrived at the point of dealing with Valéria's projects, they were able to talk with the same immunity they had in 1866. The difference was that Eulália, who was happy, exaggerated her happiness in order to be able to display it better to Jorge and convince him that she had gained rather than lost from his refusal.

"Come over to Olinda Street," said the girl. "I want to show you my son."

Jorge went. Eulália showed him her son, a child that was the

---

3. A reference to the rod used by Moses to break open the rock from which flowed the water to quench the thirst of the children of Israel on the way to the Promised Land.

equivalent of two, so fat and energetic was he. Jorge even picked him up, but he didn't know how to cope with lace, bibs, and ribbons. Eulália, who already possessed all the maternal dexterity, took the child from his hands. "You don't understand this sort of thing," she said. And after adjusting the child's bonnet, she kissed him many times, smiled at him, talked to him, all with such grace and poetry that Jorge could scarcely imagine her thus five years before. He observed this youthful mother, elegant and natural, and felt himself seized by envy and covetousness.

This is happiness, he thought.

He returned there a few times, becoming attached to the house. He also began to receive guests. Among the visitors to his house were Estela's father, who found in Jorge the benevolence he had known in Jorge's father, the judge. Mr. Antunes was a regular guest for Sunday brunch; he always brought news of his son-in-law and daughter. He still lamented the faded illusion and found a sort of painful pleasure in speaking of Estela to the son-in-law of his ambitions. Furthermore, it was something like revenge on Luís Garcia, about whom he ventured more than one complaint. Jorge, however, listened without answering.

In mid-1871 Jorge made a trip to Minas Gerais for the purpose of kneeling at the grave of his mother, whose remains he would transfer, in due time, to one of the cemeteries of Rio de Janeiro. The trip lasted six weeks. Jorge visited a few relatives and returned at the beginning of August.

An incident upset his plans.

Chapter Eight

Arriving in Rio, Jorge received news that Luís Garcia was ill. He wasn't counting on the incident, and it left him in a predicament. He didn't want to visit him, but he could hardly keep from doing so. Luís Garcia had been a close friend of his father; Jorge himself had affection and respect for him, which was reason enough to make it advisable to perform the duty of courtesy. But, on the other hand, to go to Santa Teresa was to risk Estela's suspicion. Jorge hesitated for two long days. True, he felt a certain excitement at the idea of seeing her, an idea he tried to reject and which lingered nevertheless in his mind, latent and disguised. But the reason he gave himself was that it was convenient to do so.

He overcame his hesitation and went to Santa Teresa on the afternoon of the third day. It was not the same house; this one had slightly larger dimensions than the other one. It was new, flanked by shrubbery, and the roof tiles were still of the original color. There were two entrances—one to the living room, the door located between four windows, and another to the garden, an iron-grilled door built in the center of a little wall on top of which rested the greenery of a creeper. There Jorge found Raimundo, older than he had left him but as strong as ever. Raimundo recognized him in spite of Jorge's suntan. He opened the door for him and accompanied him happily to the back of the yard.

"My master is going to be very happy," he said as he invited him in.

"Is he better?"

"Yes, sir, he is. Look, there he is."

Raimundo pointed to a group of small trees, through whose foliage women's dresses could be seen. Jorge felt a cold wave trickle through his veins. But it passed quickly, and he took his first step as firmly as he had before López's legions.

"Who is it, Raimundo?" sang an unknown voice in the midst of the trees.

Jorge saw a girl appear who seemed to be about eighteen years old, but who was only sixteen; he recognized Luís Garcia's daughter. She didn't recognize him immediately; the effects of war had changed him. Furthermore, the few times she had seen him she hadn't paid much attention to him. Jorge was led to the chair where Luís Garcia was stretched out between two other chairs, on one of which was needle-work and on the other an open book. Luís Garcia received him pleasantly and politely; Jorge explained his delay in coming by the fact that he had been out of town. The explanation was an added courtesy; Luís Garcia thanked him for it.

"I've been very weak," he said. "I might well have been at death's door. Now I'm almost well."

Jorge had seated himself at one side of the convalescent while Iaiá, on the other side, was playing with her father's hair or patting one of his hands. Luís Garcia related the ups and downs of the illness and praised the family's devotion. Jorge spoke little, either to avoid betraying the agitation he felt on entering the house, or else not to prolong the visit and to be able to end it at the first interval of silence. After fifteen minutes he rose.

"Wait a minute," said the convalescent. "Iaiá, call your stepmother."

Iaiá rose to obey her father's request; but as she was about to lay the book in her lap on her father's knees, a step was heard in the sand, and immediately thereafter the sudden words, "Here I am."

It was Estela. Jorge's startled reaction, however imperceptible, did not escape Iaiá, and made her smile furtively; she attributed it to the suddenness. Estela appeared; but because she already knew of Jorge's presence, she was able to face him without any noticeable agitation. There was a certain hesitation between them, but it was short-lived. The girl bowed slightly and extended her hand to him. Jorge shook it.

"I haven't had the pleasure of seeing you since my return from Paraguay," he said.

"That's true," she answered. "We live very far out."

Estela approached her husband, Jorge moving aside to let her pass. "Here I am," she repeated. She had brought him a glass of gelatin. While Luís Garcia was having his convalescent's meal, Estela remained standing at his side; then she sat down and spoke to Valéria's son. Naturally she spoke to him about the campaign. He answered with composure and without affectation.

"I have already told you that he was one of the heroes," interrupted

Luís Garcia, looking at his wife; "but Dr. Jorge insists on concealing his own accomplishments—unlike Iaiá."[1]

"Is that true?" asked Jorge.

"It's true. She killed at least half of the Paraguayan army during the campaign."

Iaiá gave her father a look of delicate censure.

"You don't have to blush," said Jorge. "It's a way of being patriotic. But you can be sure there was less danger in killing the enemy from here."

"Did you kill anyone?" asked Iaiá after a moment.

"Probably. In war one has to kill or be killed. I wouldn't have minded dying, but there are times when even the most indifferent are heroes. I did what I could."

Since it was growing dark, Estela said to her husband that it was time to go in. She got up to give him her arm, but Jorge hurried to take her place. Estela went on ahead, and when Jorge entered the living room with the convalescent, she was preparing his chair, a large and ample wicker chair. Luís Garcia waited a few moments, tranquilly shifting from one foot to the other while his wife arranged the cushions.

During this short pause, Jorge looked at the girl. It was the first time he had done so deliberately. There was little difference between the Estela of 1867 and the one of 1871. She had the same pale face and the same serious eyes. Her features had not changed; her bosom retained its former gracefulness. It was only a little fuller, a difference that was not out of keeping with the rest of her figure, as she was tall.

This was Estela's physical aspect. Morally she was probably the same, but what a difference in the situation! This woman, who had sent him to serve for four years in an arduous and hard-fought campaign and whose image he had not forgotten in the midst of danger, this woman was there before him at the foot of another—happy, serene, devoted, like a biblical wife. The comparison hurt him, but his heart youthfully began reliving the hours of the past. In order to stop it, Jorge took his leave ten minutes later.

"So soon?" exclaimed Luís Garcia. "This has been a doctor's visit.

---

1. It is customary in Brazil to call anyone with higher education "doctor," and to place the "Dr." in front of the given name. It is a courteous form of address used among acquaintances.

But thank you for remembering. Our home is yours; you know that we are all very fond of you."

Jorge went home both rejoicing over and regretting the visit he had just made. He whiled away the early hours of the evening paging through ten or twelve volumes, reading two or three pages from each one. While his eyes were going over the open page, his thoughts would gradually leave and take off through an infinite expanse of vague dreams. From time to time he would return, and his eyes, which had mechanically arrived at the bottom of the page, would return to the beginning to reestablish his train of thought. As though it were the book's fault, he would exchange it for another, moving from philosophy to history, from criticism to poetry, jumping from one language to another and one century to another, with chance the only law.

The brightness of the following morning dispelled some of the cares of the night before. The first excitement was over. Jorge said to himself that it was enough to be a man, that he should forget the incident of the night before and put aside once and for all the possibility of any other. He would not repeat the visit to Luís Garcia's, and he would probably never see them again. On Ouvidor Street he ran into Procópio Dias, who said to him in an offhand manner:

"I arrived half an hour after you left."

"Where?"

"Santa Teresa. If you had delayed half an hour more, I would have run into you and we could have come down together. Have you known Luís Garcia long?"

"Since I was very young."

"I, too, but I hadn't seen him for ten years. He is the same man; better off because he married a pretty woman. Who are those people?"

"His wife was reared by my mother."

"One can see that. Oh, we talk about you a lot."

"You do?" asked Jorge with interest.

Procópio Dias looked directly at him for a moment, then smiled, wrinkling his forehead.

"A great deal," he repeated. "Luís Garcia and I engaged in a contest of praise, and if I may say so without vanity, I think I won—naturally, because I am more communicative than he is. Really, he is reserved, but the little he said he said with sincerity. The members of that family seem to admire one another very much."

Procópio Dias talked to him about Santa Teresa again the following night at a house where they dined together. He talked to him first privately and then before others. The hostess, who was a Diana of gossip and misfortune, scented some mystery between the wrinkles of Procópio Dias's forehead, and bending back the ends of the bow she subtly shot off an arrow which no one saw but which went straight to Jorge's heart.[2] The latter kept his face composed despite the shot, but inside he bled a little from irritation and fear. He felt in the depths of his conscience the warmth of an honest sentiment. Nevertheless, the opinion tended to take hold of him and probe into the ashes of his past; whether cold or warm ashes, he could not yet determine. Sure of himself, Jorge trembled in the presence of public opinion—the opinion expressed in the epigram and the anecdote, which was beginning to sound its jeering and cruel laugh.

Restless and annoyed, he left there soon after dinner. The hostess's jest continued to echo in his ear at the same time that Estela's image would appear before him in its usual manner. Already on his way up Inválidos Street, Jorge retraced his steps and went straight to a theater with the purpose of benumbing himself and forgetting more quickly. It was nine-thirty; he saw the end of a serious drama, which to him seemed light, and all of a comedy, which seemed doleful. Nevertheless, he cleared his mind of the cares of the night, and walked home unburdened and calmed. It was one o'clock in the morning when he arrived; the servant handed him a letter.

"The person who brought this letter said it was urgent."

Jorge accepted it without recognizing the handwriting on the outside. It was a woman's hand. He opened it unhurriedly, but not without curiosity. It wasn't long; it said simply this:

> Dear Doctor:
> Daddy is very ill; he asks that you do him the favor of coming to our house.
>
> Lina Garcia

"At what time did this letter come?" he asked the servant.

"At seven."

Jorge gestured in irritation and sent for a carriage. Within an hour it

---

2. Diana was goddess of the moon, the hunt, and the woodlands. Here the meaning is obviously that of "huntress."

was pulling up to Luís Garcia's door. Everything was silent. Jorge lingered a moment, uncertain as to what he should do. The danger, if there had been danger, might have passed, and the whole family might be asleep. He peeped through the door of the garden and saw a weak light through a venetian blind. The next moment he heard footsteps in the sand. It was Mr. Antunes, who had heard the carriage stop.

"My son-in-law is quite ill," said Estela's father. "He had a relapse this morning, and around eight o'clock we thought we would lose him."

Jorge went in.

Luís Garcia was prostrate; the fever burned ominously in his eyes. On either side of the bed were his wife and daughter, apparently quiet, but exercising all their moral strength to control the anguish which threatened to become tears.

"What happened?" asked Jorge, approaching the sick man.

"A small persistent fever," answered the latter.

At a signal, Estela and Iaiá left the bedroom, where only Jorge remained. In having the young man summoned, Luís Garcia was putting into practice an idea which had come to him in the heat of his fever. He had heard some words from the doctor which made him assume the probability of death; having neither friends nor relatives and not wishing to entrust his wife and daughter to his father-in-law, he was turning to one whom he thought had sufficient wisdom and the necessary influence to direct and protect them.

"Your father was a friend of my father's," he said. "I was a friend of your family's; I am much in your debt. If I die, my wife and daughter will be provided for by the inheritance because the dowry of one will do for both, since they love each other very much; but they will lose me. It is true that my father-in-law, . . . but my father-in-law has other things to keep him busy. He is old; he may fail them all of a sudden. I'd like to ask that you protect and guide them, that you be something like a mentor for the two. It isn't that they are lacking in judgment; but two women alone need counsel . . . and I . . . forgive me if I am indiscreet. Do you promise?"

Jorge promised everything in order to ease his mind, because Luís Garcia seemed excessively worried about the idea of that eternal separation. The request seemed unusual to him; he attributed it to the sick man's feverish state. He later learned that, according to the doctor, Luís Garcia's life hung upon the first critical change in the illness.

It was almost four o'clock when Jorge left. He returned at nine and found the doctor there. The crisis was expected that afternoon, and only then could it be determined whether the sick man's life was lost or saved. That is what the doctor repeated as Jorge accompanied him to the garden door.

"Nevertheless," concluded the doctor, "he has another illness which will kill him within a few months—a year or a year and a half."

"His heart?"

"Exactly."

The news worried the young man.

"Isn't this probably a medical guess?"

The doctor shook his head and left. Jorge made his way to the house, but he couldn't have taken three steps when he saw Estela coming out to meet him. She stopped in front of him.

"What did the doctor tell you?" she asked.

"He has hopes; later in the afternoon he will be able to ascertain something more."

"Is that all?"

"That's all."

"He didn't give up hope?"

"No."

Estela thought for a minute.

"Give me your word," she said.

Jorge extended his hand to her, upon which Estela let her own hand rest, cold and pale as it was.

"I'm your husband's friend," said Jorge after a few moments. "Please believe that he can count on all my devotion."

Estela seemed to awaken from a momentary stupor; she listened to the young man, withdrew her hand, and responded with a simple gesture of acquiescence. Her distraught soul had reverted to its normal attitude. Jorge watched her enter the house and remained alone a few minutes, recalling the doctor's revelation and feeling that, at the heart of the sadness that distressed him, there was something similar to a selfish and cruel sentiment.

Long hours dribbled by between hope and apprehension until the crisis came and passed, without taking with it the threatened life. The following morning the happiness surrounding the sick man was such that he understood clearly the danger he had been in and the recovery made. Neither his daughter nor his wife seemed weak from the work and vigil; they were refreshed, smiling, alert, breaking between themselves the bread of happiness as, formerly and as sisters, they had broken the bread of anguish.

During the illness and convalescence, Jorge visited them once a day; and it should be said that if for a moment there was in his heart a selfish impulse, such an impulse did not recur later. He served the sick man with unselfishness and loyalty, and the family showed its gratitude. Luís Garcia reminded the young man of the favor he had asked on the night he had sent for him, and reminded him of it, not only to thank him for his compliance, but also to explain the reason for the request. But the explanation was difficult because it revealed his aversion to his father-in-law, a man in whom he hadn't the least confidence. Despite the half words he used, Jorge understood everything.

His frequent visits became a habit. Caught up by circumstances, Jorge became accustomed to the visits, and made them more often. In the month of September, using the hot weather (which did not yet exist) as an excuse, he moved to the house he owned in Santa Teresa, which wasn't far from Luís Garcia's. There was nothing unusual about it; his mother had had the habit of spending three or four months of the year there. Furthermore, for the last few weeks he had begun to be seen less and to be less in the company of others. He could easily move to another, more secluded place.

Nevertheless, since this anticipated move to Santa Teresa might not in itself have a completely logical explanation, Jorge tried to deceive himself by gathering together the materials and jotting down on paper the first lines of a work which he would never finish, but which, in any case, justified the need for leisure. It was during the intervals of leisure that he visited Luís Garcia's house, once or twice a week. On Sundays he always had for dinner Mr. Antunes, with whom he would play a game of billiards. He tried to teach him chess, but gave up after five lessons.

"Ah! but not everyone has your talent!" exclaimed Estela's father.

Luís Garcia was a chess player. It was his and Jorge's usual pastime; on other occasions they would go for a short walk. Luís Garcia accepted in good humor these diversions which were not agitating or tiring, but mild and relaxing, such as suited him. Furthermore, they were not always fruitless recreations. Jorge better appreciated now conversations which were not merely idle talk, as the two exchanged ideas and observations. Luís Garcia was an odd type of man of scant culture; but he had natural gifts and his prolonged life of solitude had given him the habit of reflection. He would also go to Jorge's house and borrow books to read. It was late in life; he was no longer young. He had little time but ample hunger for knowledge; he threw himself into it avidly, without much method or scrupulous choice; he wanted at least to take the best from everything. And because he was a reader of good taste, one who blended reflection with impression, when he finished his reading he would think through the book, planting it, so to speak, in his mind. Though without a set method, this reading corrected some of his ideas and completed others which he possessed only by intuition.

Luís Garcia's intellectual needs thus contributed to make family life more intimate, the only exception he continued to have to his secluded life, even after marriage. For his part, Jorge had not yet failed to live up to the good opinion Luís Garcia had of his qualities, and the family saw intimacy and respect slowly develop between the two men. One night after Jorge had left Luís Garcia's house, the latter and his wife remained in the garden awhile. Luís Garcia said a few words about Valéria's son.

"It could be that I'm wrong," concluded the skeptic, "but I'm convinced he's a fine young man."

Estela didn't answer; she fixed her eyes on a dark cloud which was tarnishing the whiteness of the moon. But Iaiá, who had arrived a few moments before, shrugged her shoulders in a nervous gesture.

"It's possible," she said, "but I find him unbearable."

Chapter Nine

The new order of things disturbed Estela profoundly. Jorge's behavior on the occasion of her husband's illness did not seem to her to conceal any personal motive; but during his convalescence, and especially after it, it seemed to her that the young man's plan was to ingratiate himself with the family. To what end? Estela supposed that, after such a long time, Jorge's love for her was probably completely over, like the first fruit of a season. She did not deny him gratitude when she saw the favors he had afforded her sick husband with so much solicitude, discretion, and dignity. However, on seeing the frequency of his visits and their close friendship, she wondered if there weren't something more than simple, traditional affection. What charm could the house of a withdrawn and obscure family offer a man reared on an obviously higher social plane? His was another social level; natural inclination or future ambitions ought to carry him to another plane. This seemed an unmistakable consideration to her. She concluded that, whether conquered or contained, his love for her was again sounding a cry of revolt, and that if this was so, Jorge must be worse than he was in 1866, because at that time his feelings erupted with violence and sincerity, while now his principal aspect was pretense. His love, if indeed there had been love, was now enlightened and endowed with reason; where it had been clumsy, it was becoming cautious and subtle.

I wonder what he thinks of me? Estela asked herself. And as she asked it, Estela felt belittled and humiliated in Jorge's eyes. It was necessary to put an end to this life of reticence and doubt. Estela pondered over the way to bring to an end the close friendship of the two men—or at least, Jorge's frequent appearance at the house. She thought of asking Jorge directly, but she immediately rejected that idea, which incidentally was incompatible with her nature. Later, she thought of telling all of it to her husband.

One night during the first week of November, Estela finally decided to reveal to her husband this page from her past. She was alone in the garden and had seen the afternoon twilight fading away—it was a gray and deadened afternoon. From time to time, her thoughts would return to the past, and she would tremble all over with a strange, mysterious, and unbearable sensation. Nightfall came, and Estela's soul would also have plunged into the vague and perfidious darkness of the future, had not the crude voice of the slave come to awaken her.

"Nhanhã will get damp from the dew," said Raimundo.

Estela rose and went from there to her husband's study. Luís Garcia was working under the light of a lamp which, with the help of a lampshade, cast its beam solely on him and the papers he had before him. The rest of the room remained in semidarkness.

"What is it?" asked Luís Garcia without lifting his head.

Estela stopped on the other side of the desk. Luís Garcia raised his head and looked at her without detecting the disturbance in her features.

"What is it?" he repeated.

Seeing him absorbed in his work of devotion for her and his daughter, Estela hesitated; it seemed cruel to give him disillusionment and pain in exchange for his protection and affection. She hesitated a moment; then changed from hesitation to renunciation. Choosing silence, she restrained herself and left.

But silence in itself solved nothing. Sooner or later her husband would come to read in her face her constraint in relation to Jorge, an unexplainable uneasiness, which he might interpret negatively. It was then that the serpent taught her deception; necessity gave her Machiavellian intuition. That is, the occasion did not call for a frank and hostile attitude, but for a pleasant air, a superficial cordiality, coldly courteous, yet courteous enough. In this manner domestic peace could be insured, and that was most important. At the same time it would show the fearlessness of her heart, capable of facing all of Jorge's guile.

With time, Estela discovered that Jorge's conduct, if it was hiding a plan, didn't allow itself even to be suspected; it no longer seemed to her pretense, but abstention. He avoided her; he abstained from long conversations, especially conversations alone. He was respectful and cold.

Actually, Jorge had not abandoned any preconceived plan; he let time take care of things. He would start to take a shortcut without knowing whether it would lead to a straight road or a precipice. No worries shadowed his smiling and placid face. It could be said that after a long and arduous journey, he had attained the apex of human pleasures.

The truth is that Jorge's love had done something like divest itself of sentiment in order to embody a fixed idea. Having been born of a first youthful outburst, it had endured some years of absence. Distance had disciplined the incipient ardors, broken the impulses, slackened his amorous vigor; his love fastened to his shoulders the wings of a quiet mysticism. Nor was the change arrested here. From the heart in which it dwelt it took flight and soared to his mind, where it assumed the stability of definite resolutions. It was no longer a passion but a conviction—that is, something of a different nature. He thought often of the consequences of inheriting in a short time Luís Garcia's wife, a step that seemed to him necessary; that's what he would say to himself. Such a union would have a double purpose: reparation and redress: reparation of the evil he had done, and redress of the treatment he had received from her. Each would thus reproach the other. A marriage would absolve them both. Perhaps on an ordinary scale the debts were not equal, but Jorge had a certain spirit of equity; and he felt that if he had suffered much and for a long time, his suffering did not exceed the injury which, in his way of seeing it, had been profound.

The reprimands of conscience were not less frequent and less severe: such is the natural outcome of that kind of violent situation. In this way the most inflexible can arrive at unexplainable complacencies, and what is today repugnance is tomorrow childish hesitation. Jorge was no stranger to that customary pattern. In his own estimation he judged himself innocent because he was impassive, forgetting the law of the decalogue which prohibits not only the deed but the intention as well.

Two circumstances, nevertheless, disturbed Jorge's peace of mind before the end of that year.

One was the regularity of Procópio Dias's visits, which seemed to him to have little explanation. Procópio Dias was always received with more courteous hospitality than Jorge was. In relation to Jorge, Estela's conduct was cautious and barely amicable; Iaiá's was in some ways fearful or even hostile; but both seemed to become happy when Procópio Dias appeared at the door. Their manner was entirely different. Procópio Dias accompanied them sometimes on walks, or conversed with them for a long time, making them laugh with a spontaneity they did not have when they talked with Jorge. He obeyed the wishes of the stepmother and the whims of the stepdaughter, whatever they might be, with such great tolerance and good humor that, without knowing it, he irritated Jorge. Jorge noticed the remarks and manner of the intruder, and in time was able to allay his resentment.

He is a bachelor in need of the company of women, he said to himself.

Procópio Dias seemed to be nothing but that; a feminine atmosphere was for him a necessity; the rustle of skirts, the best music for his ears. Because of her age Iaiá acted more intimately than Estela; sometimes she even teased him, an excess her father or stepmother reprimanded, if unnecessarily. Procópio Dias neither manifested nor felt the slightest resentment; he found Iaiá witty and even played along with her.

The second circumstance that cast a shadow on Jorge's mind was precisely Iaiá Garcia's hostility.

What the devil did I do to this girl? Jorge would ask himself.

During the illness and convalescence of her father, Iaiá had treated Jorge with ample gratitude and kindness. Some time later, this attitude began to diminish, until it ceased completely and became something else: clearly, repugnance with a touch of hostility. Luís Garcia immediately noticed the difference, made all the more obvious since Estela, even if she wasn't as communicative now as she had been at first, treated Valéria's son with the affability necessary to preserve appearances. The only exception was his daughter. He didn't fail to warn her about it; he pointed out to her that Jorge was the son of a person for whom they had deep regard, and of whom she herself had recent memories; that this fact in itself should lessen her aversion if Jorge was repugnant to her. Iaiá would listen and remain silent; she would change one day, only to fall back into her former attitude.

"You're a strange one," her father said once, after repeating the admonition.

It could be a peculiarity of hers. The kind of life Iaiá had had over a long period of time had given her an exclusive love of solitude and family life. But in the present case it seemed to be a little more than that. Her facial expression when receiving Jorge was not the same as that with which she met other people. Sometimes he would arrive when she was at the piano; Iaiá would interrupt herself adroitly, sound three or four discordant chords, and would get up. If he talked to her and her stepmother, she would take part as little as possible in the dialogue and would move away cautiously. She never smiled if he said something

79

amusing or paid her a compliment; she never encouraged the adoption of any suggestion that came from him; she wouldn't read the novels he lent her. If she was invited to say what she thought about one or the other of these books, she would let the corners of her mouth droop in a gesture of indifference. She never spoke about Jorge; she appeared around him as little as she could. This constant procedure, not insulting only because she disguised it, made an impression on the mind of the young man, who could not discover its real cause, or at least not its probable one.

The true cause was nothing less than a feeling of filial jealousy. Iaiá worshipped her father above all things; this regard was the first commandment of her personal catechism. She had sought his marriage with the purpose of making his life less solitary, and also because she loved Estela. The marriage brought to the home a companion and someone to love; it did not diminish at all her share as a daughter.

However, Iaiá noticed the change that took place in her father's habits a short time after his convalescence, and especially after the latter part of September. This man, who was reserved with everyone and unrestrained only with his own family, had made an exception in favor of Jorge. Without displaying a lack of polish, which was, incidentally, incompatible with his nature, he was less reserved, more easily and consistently accessible.

It was not, however, this first observation that produced in Iaiá the marked change; it was another. Luís Garcia demonstrated personal confidence in Jorge; and the day the daughter noticed it she remembered the letter she had written to the young man on the night her father's illness had become worse, and the confidences the two shared which had never reached her ears. At that moment she felt well up in her heart the first drop of bitterness. She imagined that Jorge had come to steal something from her. She never considered whether there might be a subject which two men should discuss strictly between themselves; she supposed herself robbed of a part of her father's trust; and because she loved her father above all things, her love had the jealousies, the anguishes, the rages of another kind of love and, consequently, the same hatreds and heartaches.

The father understood all the intensity of the girl's filial affection, and his own love was no less intensive than hers; but he would say to himself philosophically, and not without sorrow, that nature would teach her another feeling, less somber but no less intense and demanding. When he pondered over this, he regarded his daughter with misty-eyed nostalgia.

At that time Iaiá possessed all the purity of a cloudless dawn. She was slender, agile, swift, with a bit of boldness; sometimes blunt, but endowed with an undulant spirit not incapable of reflection and perseverance. The portrait of the girl would be complete thus, were it not fitting to speak also of her eyes, which, if they were pure as Eve's before her sin, if they were dovelike as the Sulamite's, they also had, like those of the latter, something hidden inside which probably was not as pure.[1] When she looked a certain way, she threatened or penetrated the folds of one's conscience. But these occasions were rare. Her usual expression was another, meek or indifferent, and more childlike than that of youth. Perhaps her mouth was a little too large, but her lips were thin and energetic. In a word, those features that had been there at eleven years were now noticeable and well developed.

One afternoon Luís Garcia received an urgent request to go to the minister's house without delay. He went, leaving his wife and daughter anxious about the outcome. Jorge appeared a little later. Luís Garcia delayed a long time, and Jorge would have left had it not been for the arrival of Mr. Antunes, who revived the lagging conversation. Nine, ten, eleven o'clock struck without Luís Garcia's returning. Iaiá was impatient; she feared some sudden illness had befallen her father, perhaps an accident. It was a quarter after eleven when he entered, breathless because he had come in a hurry, having run into Raimundo, who, seeing the girl's anxiety, had gone out to find him and tell him.

Iaiá threw herself into his arms.

" 'Fraidy cat,' " said Luís Garcia, holding her head between his hands.

He sat down for a moment to rest, his left hand pressing against his heart. Soon afterwards he got up, called Jorge, and went over to one of the windows. They spoke in low tones for ten minutes. He told Jorge that he might be obliged to leave at the end of that week; it was a matter of responsibility to his office. Except for a possible change the trip was inevitable.

Iaiá wouldn't take her eyes off of either of them; she bade Jorge goodnight, extending to him her fingertips. It was the following day when Estela told her that they might be obliged to leave for some time.

---

1. The Sulamite was Solomon's beloved, exalted in the Song of Solomon.

Hearing the news, Iaiá understood the secrecy of the night before and became upset. She was the last to hear it, and the first was a stranger, an intruder—she was about to say, an enemy. No word from her father; no direct communication. *The last one!*

This exaggerated resentment was characteristic of the girl's makeup and of her almost solitary rearing. Nothing more was necessary to alienate her from Jorge; resentment took complete possession of her. If until then she had spoken to him little, the little became even less; in time it became almost nothing.

And these two forces, one of impulse, the other of repulsion, tended to collide on the path of their destinies.

Chapter Ten

In preparation for the trip Luís Garcia began to arrange some old and scattered papers. Now, four or five days later, he decided to finish the job, even though he had been relieved of that undertaking. It was New Year's Day—a beautiful, refreshing morning, with clear, blue skies. They had gone to mass at the convent chapel, then had breakfast as a family, including Mr. Antunes, who was wearing a top coat for the first time and manifested that morning a reverent aspect, or even a venerable one.

Iaiá had awakened extremely happy and lively. Mr. Antunes had taken her a bouquet of carnations, telling her that he had done so in order that she would receive other bouquets during the year. After receiving it and thanking him appropriately, the girl went and placed it in a vase on the bedroom windowsill. Mr. Antunes bade her farewell a half hour after he had had breakfast.

"Are you leaving already?"

"I'm going to play a game of billiards with Jorge," Estela's father said casually. "We'll return early."

"Is he coming for dinner?"

"I'm going to see if I can bring him."

"But . . . Daddy hasn't been advised," objected Iaiá.

"Yes, he has; it was he who authorized me to bring him. The truth is that I requested it. We owe a lot to that young man, and to his deceased father, and to his mother, Dona Valéria, God rest her soul. I'll see you later."

Iaiá remained alone and pensive for a moment; but soon afterwards she shrugged her shoulders, picked up some needlework which she had begun, and went to her father's study, where she found him with Estela.

"Good heavens!" said the girl, stopping at the door.

At the foot of the secretary was a large basket, overflowing with papers; on the desk, more papers; papers in Luís Garcia's hands, others in Estela's, some scattered over the floor. It was the accumulation of six years. Luís Garcia had the habit of keeping everything—letters, newspaper clippings in which there was something of interest, notes, and mere duplicates. Every once in a while he made an inventory and liquidated the past. It had been several years now since he had done the customary task. He had begun when he supposed he would have to leave Rio; now he was trying to finish. Estela had gone in a little before her stepdaughter; she had sat down in a low chair and was entertaining herself by singling out or picking up some pieces of old newspaper and reading some excerpt which her eyes happened to fall upon.

"What's the matter?" asked Luís Garcia the minute his daughter let out the exclamation.

"You're going to be smothered in paper," said the girl.

Luís Garcia didn't answer; he had turned his eyes to a letter in his hand which doubtless brought to mind some bitter recollection, because he smiled sadly. He read all of it, reread some portions, then made a gesture of disdain, tore it up, and threw the pieces in the wastebasket.

Iaiá went and sat on the other side, a few steps from her father.

On the desk before him was a stack of things worth keeping, a small stack; the largest portion was useless rubbish. Isn't that what the image of the past really is? Luís Garcia would sometimes open up a newspaper which had been kept avariciously for years; two checks or some marks indicated the portion which had captured his attention at the time. Now he would reread it, look for the reason for keeping it and, setting it aside, smile. The impression which had lent some interest to the writing had completely disappeared; the writing was barely recognizable. It was the same with the letters. Few escaped destruction; most of them were torn up—some in two pieces, the insignificant ones; others in thirty pieces, those which might be incriminating. Estela, who was helping him, casually picked up a letter whose handwriting on the envelope was not unknown to her.

"I know this handwriting," she said.

"Let me see."

Estela gave him the letter.

"It's Jorge's," said her husband.

He opened it and, after reading a few lines, smiled. Then he read it all the way through. When he finished, he folded it and looked at his wife; he unfolded it again, mechanically.

"I'm going to return it to him," he said after a brief pause. "He may be embarrassed at having written such things. . . ."

And he focused his eyes on the letter with an insistence that would entice the dullest curiosity. Then he turned his head around a little to where his daughter sat at a distance with her eyes lowered; he lowered his voice and said to Estela:

"Did you never learn the real reason he went to war?"

Estela became even paler than she already was; all her blood rushed to her heart, from whence not one word emanated; her response was a negative gesture. And if she was incapable of becoming any paler, she could blush, and she blushed with embarrassment. Luís Garcia saw neither the first nor the second effect of his words. He was rolling and unrolling one of the corners of the letter with his fingers. Naturally he remembered the events of those five years, the mother's and son's secrets.

"Who would ever say that after such great sacrifice . . . to what extent will boys go! How love can drive them! He liked some girl; I don't know who she was, but I suppose . . . his mother did all she could to restrain him. When she got desperate, she decided to send him south; he agreed. I was a confidant of both. Some time after sailing . . . wait . . . the date must be here . . . '67. . . . In '67 the passion was still alive; finally it seemed that the passion was only waiting for the war to end before it ended also. His ardor vanished and he put on weight. Did you never suspect anything?"

"No," murmured Estela.

Luís Garcia handed the letter to his wife, who received it trembling and cold.

"Read it, because it's interesting," he said.

Estela looked at the paper and at her husband, hesitantly, not knowing what to do or think.

"Read it; it is strange," said the latter, who had returned to the remaining papers, opening some, separating others, calm and indifferent.

Without raising her head, Estela looked at him again, obliquely, as if looking for the hidden intention on his forehead, if any there be; and her look was so hampered by apprehension and hesitancy—it was above all so sly—that she felt it herself and repented. Then she buried her eyes in the paper without reading it, without looking at a single sentence, not even a word. She didn't see the letters; she saw in the distance two doves flying and the innocence of her lips tarnished by the lips of a man; nothing more. Her hand was shaking. She steadied it on the edge of the desk; but the tremor, though scarcely noticeable, did not cease.

"Did you read it?" asked Luís Garcia, folding a newspaper he had just looked over.

Estela motioned for him to wait a moment. She was aware that enough time had elapsed for her to have read the letter twice. She made an effort, turned a page. Two or three sentences caught her eye: "The love I feel no longer knows the meaning of impatience, jealousy, or exclusivism; it is a religious faith that can live whole in many hearts. ... It came with me, despite what I heard her say on the eve of my sailing; and if it didn't grow it is because it couldn't grow. But it changed from the child that it was and became a man of wisdom." She reached the end of the letter, or pretended to have done so; she folded it and didn't dare to say anything; then she opened it again.

"What poetry, eh?" said Luís Garcia, smiling.

And the smile was so natural, so unworried, so honest, that Estela was calmed. She held the dignity and sincerity of her husband in high esteem; she couldn't imagine in him hypocrisy or such great indifference. She smiled back, but it was a smile of acquiescence, without conviction or spontaneity. Luís Garcia leaned toward her. He spoke in the same muffled voice of moments earlier; he told her of the love that Valéria had for her son and the strategy used to remove him from Rio de Janeiro.

"At that time," he said, "I don't know but that I came to repent having agreed with her; not so today. Her son was saved and recovered from his love, with position and honors to spare."

"That's true," murmured Estela, who had listened to him with restless and impatient attention.

Immediately afterwards she got up and went to the window. There she shook her head with a vigorous gesture. Perhaps opposing forces were struggling within her; or it was her past that was emerging from the shadows of time, with all its bright or dark colors, its hidden and never revealed pleasures, and at the same time its sorrows and strength. It must be this: it was the heart that was impatiently chafing at the bit of necessity and pride and demanding yet again its right to life, and it was asking for it in the name of that letter, a remote expression of a disillusioned and impossible love. Estela smothered these impulses, but they came anyway. After a few minutes she left the window and returned to her chair. Luís Garcia was reading a piece of newspaper. He didn't even raise his eyes.

Opposite them Iaiá's eyes were fixed on her stepmother. At first she had heard Jorge's name and hadn't paid much attention to it; but one or two of her father's disconnected words had aroused her curiosity. Iaiá lifted her head, then turned it sideways and heard her father's secret, despite its having been uttered in a low voice. Finally, she could no longer take her eyes off Estela. She saw her take the letter with a shaky hand, saw her become even paler; she saw her confusion and perplexity. Why the perplexity and confusion? An extinct love of Jorge's, a passion which had taken him to war, what business was that of hers? What business was that of theirs?

Iaiá looked at first with curiosity, then with surprise, until her eyes shone with wisdom and perception. The stiletto which they were hiding opened up its fine, sharp edge and extended itself until it reached the depths of Estela's conscience. It was an intense, deep aquiline look, which probed Estela's heart, heard the blood running in her veins, and penetrated her brain, which was sprinkled with thoughts that were vague, murky, and unconnected.[1] Iaiá guessed Estela's past, but she guessed even more. She strode rapidly over reality until she hit upon the possible. She guessed a relationship which preceded Estela's marriage, and which was broken against the desires of both, a relationship perhaps persisting despite time and events. All of this a simple innocence of seventeen years saw. Her crystalline and virginal thinking, not dimmed by experience, was not aware of even the first touches of womanhood. She had no idea of evil; she didn't know the vicissitudes of the heart. Like the wife in the Song of Solomon, who suddenly saw the garden gate torn down for her, Iaiá experienced in those ten minutes her moral puberty.[2] Childhood had finished; womanhood was beginning.

The impression was so profound that, despite the strength of stability there was in her constitution, Iaiá could not remain there any longer. She left and sought refuge in her bedroom. Certainly, that

---

1. The meaning of aquiline here is the same as the English colloquialism "to look with an eagle's eye."
2. Reference here is to the Shulamite in Song of Solomon, chapter 5.

intrusive love, if it existed, would afflict and prostrate the heart of a daughter, a heart crushed by affection, whose exclusive and highest form of feeling was the love that bound her to her father like an indestructible tie. Then came the affection which she had bestowed upon her stepmother, her now elected mother, an affection no less sincere and real, which now would surely weaken or even die.

Seated at the edge of her bed, her feet together and her hands clasped between her knees, her eyes fixed on the mirror before her, Iaiá mentally was struggling through her discovery. She confronted what she had just seen with previous everyday facts—that is, the coldness, the indifference, the rigid politeness of the two—and she could hardly relate one thing to the other; but at the same time she realized that she was not always present when Jorge came, or she often dodged him, and it was possible that the indifference was nothing more than a mask. Furthermore, her stepmother's agitation was significant. She looked back through time to the day of Jorge's first visit, and remembered that he had trembled on hearing Estela's voice, a circumstance which at that time seemed unimportant to her. Now she could see that such was not the case.

She spent an entire hour in that solitary pensive state, alone with suspicion and remorse—remorse also because from time to time, terrified at the spectacle of the trodden path, her soul would falter and tremble. She hated herself; but the pale picture of her stepmother would appear before her, wearing the expression she had seen on her moments before, and her conscience would make peace with malice.

Behold the result. Estela was not to blame. What was casting such a shadow on the present situation was an incident from the past, but the scene of commotion was enough to disturb the stepdaughter's spirit and to drop therein the first germs of the knowledge of evil. What if she were guilty? Perhaps the saddest effect of domestic grievances is the corruption of ingenuous hearts, impassive witnesses of what, one day, they are unaware, and only suspect, perceive, and find out the next morning: the first violation of virginity.

Agitated, Iaiá paced her room from one side to the other, desirous and at the same time apprehensive of going to Estela. Twice she got to the door and turned back. On one of those occasions, as she returned, her eyes fell upon her father's picture, which hung next to her bedstead—a simple photograph. She took it down and contemplated at length his brow, austere and pure. What! could there be on earth anyone who loved him once and didn't feel that that love would grip him for the rest of his life? So affectionate! So good! Living exclusively for his loved ones, envying nothing in other men. That's what her heart said to her as she kissed his picture with respect, with love, finally with frenzy. Great, warm tears burst from her eyes. Iaiá let them run; they mingled with her kisses. When that first explosion subsided, it subsided not to repeat itself again. Her eyes dry, Iaiá was able to reflect objectively, and the reflecting overpowered her anguish.

What transpired in that still immature but already quick brain was a decision without a plan. To clarify the spurious bond was necessary and urgent; she didn't ponder the method. Just as her innocence disguised from her the entire extent of wrong possible, thus it also hid for her the bitternesses and the obstacles of its execution. It was her heart that chose for her this role of guardian angel. A simple and undivided nature, she was going straight to her goal without the fear which experience and observation of life impart. Who knows? She wasn't acquainted with hypocrisy, but had only suspected it; perhaps she was beginning to discover it.

She had delayed a long time and it was necessary to leave the room; but because she had cried, they might be able to read the vestiges of pain on her face. Iaiá went to the lavatory, poured water into the basin, and began to bathe her eyes and face. The splashing of the water kept her from hearing someone open the door. Estela appeared suddenly.

"What have you been doing in here for such a long time?" said her stepmother, stopping at the door.

Iaiá didn't risk looking at her face; she mumbled an evasive answer and continued with what she was doing.

"What's the matter with you?" asked Estela, taking her by the arms and making her face her. "Have you been crying? . . . Yes, you have; your eyes are red. What is it? Iaiá, speak; what is it?"

"It's nothing," answered the latter, trying to smile.

"Don't lie, Iaiá."

The stepdaughter glanced in the mirror; she saw that it was useless to lie.

"It was something silly," she said.

"Some prank?"

"I wish it had been!"

Iaiá took the picture she had placed on the edge of the marble slab of the lavatory and looked at it for a few moments. Estela tried to draw her close, but her stepdaughter pulled away.

"Does it have anything to do . . . with your father?" asked the stepmother.

Iaiá gazed at her and answered:

"Yes, Mother dear; I was shaking off the dust from Daddy's picture, and I began to think . . . it was crazy . . . what if he . . . died?"

Estela reprimanded her with an interjection. Iaiá tried to continue, but Estela interrupted her impetuously:

"Hush, I said; don't think of such nonsense. Give me the picture."

"Isn't he a wonderful man?" asked Iaiá while Estela was hanging up the picture.

The stepmother's only answer was to go to her and tell her never to think of such a thing again.

"I'm not master of my thoughts," answered the girl, shrugging her shoulders.

After a few seconds of silence, Estela noticed that something was worrying her stepdaughter and told her so. Iaiá responded in the negative, but Estela insisted:

"You're not yourself, and those eyes of yours are shifting vaguely from one side to the other. Perhaps . . . who knows—"

"It's not what you're thinking," interrupted Iaiá dryly.

Then she sat down, looking out at the garden, biting her lip which was trembling, and pressing her breasts with her hand. Estela remained silent a moment; finally she shook her head benevolently and approached the girl.

"You don't trust me, Iaiá," she said, resting her hand on her shoulder. "If you did you would tell me what you are thinking about, because it's certainly something. It's not difficult to eliminate Procópio Dias; I even think it's the easiest thing. But isn't it possibly some similar line of thought? Come on now, be frank. I'm only your stepmother, and only slightly older than you; I can listen to your secrets and advise you. Where will you find a better friend than I?"

Iaiá had controlled her first feelings; she could retain the mask of tranquility completely as long as she didn't exchange it for another. She got up and said boldly:

"Very well, I am going to confide one thing to you . . . no . . . suppose . . . it's better to suppose . . . I'm embarrassed, to tell the truth. Suppose I had a school-girl romance. . . ."

"You? At thirteen!"

"At twelve and a half."

"A fine thing! You didn't begin any too late. This love naturally died out in the arms of your last doll."

"Suppose not," said Iaiá in a serious tone. "Well, if I have to marry Procópio Dias. . . ."

"Who said anything about marrying him?"

"At present it's just a joke, but if he insists, it's possible that neither you nor Daddy would reject him, and even more possible that I would allow myself to be won over in order to please everyone. But that's the very point of my secret; it's an idea that has been pursuing me for days. Should I marry one man when I love another? Can I do it? Must I do it?"

Estela trembled slightly under her stepdaughter's impassive and direct look and didn't answer immediately. Iaiá seemed to enjoy herself in the confusion of the moment, but at the same time her heart bled within because the confusion was the confirmation of her recent assumptions. The stepmother didn't have the discernment of the step-daughter; furthermore, how could she guess Iaiá's knowledge of a remote and undivulged fact? Estela didn't even consider that. The minute elapsed, and she answered calmly:

"You mustn't marry if your love can be satisfied without obstacle. If that's not the case, marriage is a simple choice of logic: sacrifice yourself."

Iaiá, who had one of her stepmother's hands between hers, suddenly released it. Estela laughed and tapped her forehead with the tip of her finger.

"That little head," she said. "In there there's a lot that needs to be weeded out. . . ."

At first Iaiá became pale. To Estela's last gesture she responded with a forced and colorless smile. As soon as Estela had left, she let herself sink into her chair and covered her face with her hands. When she left there a half hour later, she showed no sign of tears or even sadness. She wasn't happy, of course; serene, yes, of that type of serenity with which the jungle hunter prepares to face the jaguar.

Jorge came for dinner, and later in the evening Procópio Dias appeared. During dinner and throughout the evening, Iaiá impressed family and guests with the unusual change in her behavior. She was a little pale, but the brilliant light in her eyes seemed to lend to her face a portion of the coloring which was absent. She was talkative, but not playful. Her sentences were long, well thought out, and went all the way to the end without the usual interruptions and omissions. Ordinarily it seemed as if the girl thought in fragments, because it was almost impossible to have a complete and ordered conversation with her, due to her changing moods. That day it was different, as though her soul had removed its ballet costume in order to put on an everyday garment, simple, and tight, which covered her all the way to her neck. Was it better that way? Was it worse? Neither; it was a new look.

More than anyone, Jorge appreciated that change, because the girl had also changed somewhat in relation to him. That day Iaiá felt more repugnance than ever at seeing Valéria's son and even came to the point of instinctively holding back her hand. She gave in, however, and the smile with which she corrected her refusal was the first one Jorge had received from her directly. That day the girl answered him with ease, and perhaps addressed a few words to him occasionally—all of which Luís Garcia noticed and attributed to the effect of his admonishing.

Neither Luís Garcia nor Jorge could imagine that the letter of 1867 was waving its words of fire over the heads of stepmother and stepdaughter. That importunate letter, salvaged from immediate destruction, was a spark suddenly thrust on the dormant love of one and the awakening hatred of the other. Jorge was far from reading it in Iaiá's amicable face and Estela's fleeting look.

A little after ten the group dispersed. Mr. Antunes lodged that night at the house of his son-in-law. Jorge and Procópio Dias left together.

"Are you going into town at this time of night?" asked Jorge.

"Well, you haven't offered me a bed yet," said the other laughing.

"But I'm offering it now."

"I accept. I need to talk to you anyway—a serious matter."

"Isn't it probably about some supplies?"

"Man does not live by bread alone," answered Procópio Dias quickly.

"What is it about?"

"An explanation."

"About. . . ."

"We'll talk about it at the house; it's dark and the way home is treacherous."

Chapter Eleven

Once they were inside, Procópio Dias did not hurry to give or ask for the explanation. He ate first, confessing that he had acquired that custom, and Jorge was quick to oblige him. The improvised meal, composed of cold meats and two or three goblets of pure wine, left him at peace with nature. Now that he was satisfied, it was time for the explanation.

It did not come easily. Lying indolently on a sofa, Procópio Dias was smoking with sensuous pleasure and speaking cautiously, using that deliberate and quiet tone of a man who meditated while digesting his food. If some idea fluttered about within him, it was difficult to perceive it in his weary and languid look. Meanwhile, Jorge's curiosity would not permit further delay, and Procópio Dias was obliged to satisfy it when the young man, stopping in front of him, bluntly asked him to do so.

"I thought it would be easier than it actually is," he said, "particularly because in spite of the fact that we have known each other for some time, I'm not sure what your opinion of me is. Is it good?"

"Yes, it is."

"Give me your hand. Do you promise to be frank?"

"I promise."

"Which of the two women takes you to Luís Garcia's house?"

Startled, Jorge jerked his hand away quickly.

"It is obvious," remarked Procópio Dias, "it is one of them."

After the initial shock, Jorge sat down calmly, less so, however, than he pretended.

"Truthfully, your question is one of the strangest I ever expected to hear. Aren't you aware of the friendship that binds me to that house, a friendship I inherited from my family and which I am merely continuing? Which of the two! There aren't two there; there is one, only one, one . . . and. . . ."

"Isn't she the one? Isn't it Iaiá?"

Jorge made a negative gesture.

"Then please believe that you have lifted a burden from me," said Procópio Dias, settling down in the chair. "You're not my rival? Don't you have any idea? . . . any vague idea? . . . That's all I need to know . . . that's all, and it's everything."

"Do you like Iaiá?"

Procópio Dias first made an affirmative gesture. Then he stuttered over his sentiment-filled confession, but with an air of embarrassment which was half sincere and half affected, and so fitting and natural that it was difficult to know where sincerity ended and pretense began. Little by little he became inspired and hid nothing from Jorge. He confessed that Luís Garcia's daughter had completely unsettled his mind and that he was resolved to make the greatest of sacrifices in order to win her hand.

"Sometimes I supposed that you were on my heels," he concluded, "an idea that worried me because you have some unquestionable advantages over me. Then my suspicions would disappear and I would reassure myself. Today, however, I confess that my suspicion reappeared, and began to consume me; and yet it came at intervals, because at one moment it would seem to me that your object was Iaiá, and at the next that it was Estela—"

"I'm sorry," interrupted Jorge; "I have already told you all I should have, and I cannot allow you to go back to the same point. One of your suspicions is insulting to me."

"You're right; I should have thought about that," agreed Procópio Dias. "But what do you expect? One shouldn't attribute anything to the demented or to those in love. Will you forgive me? In any case, you can believe that my nature isn't so tolerant of vice that it could have made me want to hit upon a sure weakness. I'm not demanding; I know that men are governed by passions and that the strength to control them isn't common. That's the very reason one respects virtue. The day nature becomes communistic and distributes good moral qualities equally, virtue will cease to be a treasure; it will become nothing whatsoever."

"Let me speak frankly," said Jorge laughing. "I suspect that you are even less demanding than you say. It seems to me that if your suspicion of Estela had any foundation, you wouldn't listen to me with indignation."

94

"Perhaps I would have been glad."

Jorge said nothing; he only looked at his inquisitor with an air of bewilderment, at which the other smiled benevolently. There was a pause. Procópio Dias finally broke the silence:

"Perhaps I would have been glad but become angry afterwards; that is to say, the indignation of the moment would have been suppressed by the interest. Listen, doctor, let's be fair with human nature. Complete virtue is the poets' invention. It wouldn't have been handy for you to love Estela, and less still for her to return your love, because, since I intended to enter that family, I wouldn't want it to have the slightest blemish. That's the truth of the matter. But I am in love, doctor; and no matter how ridiculous such a confession may seem, no matter how unrefined I may be, the truth is that I love the stepdaughter passionately: she is constantly in my thoughts. But, if you did love the other one, what would be my first inclination? To make you an ally to my interests. If there were a secret between you, and if that secret was discovered or suspected by me, you and she would be my best allies and that girl's resistance and her father's wishes as well would work out favorably for me."

Procópio Dias uttered these words simply and with conviction. His leaden eyes seemed like doors opening upon his conscience. The expression on his face was one of frank cynicism. Jorge contemplated him for a few moments without saying a word, seemingly overwhelmed by logic. He had listened to him, amazed and pleased. Didn't such frankness indicate that Procópio Dias no longer suspected anything? Jorge smiled and replied:

"What you have just said isn't cheering news, but I'm persuaded that it is the pure truth. The only thing that amazes me is that you have so much insight and the superiority to recognize and point out the vices of human nature. . . ."

"I'm practical," retorted the other, smiling. "Rarely do I become annoyed, although I really deplore weakness or perversion. Thus, for example, I would like you no less if you had deceived me now about your feelings, because it is your duty and in your interest to deny them."

"But I beg your pardon; I've already given you my word of honor. . . ."

"You didn't give it nor did I ask for it, nor would I, because the word of honor doesn't obligate the conscience when it is given to save a matter of honor. You could give it without either sincerity or remorse. Now it would no longer be the same thing if you swore to me, because the act of swearing, of invoking the witness of a superior entity, such a thing obligates any conscience which isn't perverted."

"You're not demanding that I swear, I hope?" said Jorge.

"There remains yet a shred of doubt in my heart," replied Procópio Dias, smiling.

"Well then, I swear to you. . . ."

Procópio Dias jumped up suddenly.

"You needn't say more," he exclaimed, grasping Jorge's hands. "Now I believe; I believe completely. You're not my rival, nor are you corrupting the family I expect to become a part of. If you only knew how you have pleased me with your last words! Thank you! Now I believe. Laugh at me, laugh; I believe that such openness could have a sinister side to it—it probably has. But I assure you that if my happiness isn't complete, that is only fortune's fault, not man's. . . ."

He seated himself after these words, uttered almost without a breath. Jorge joined him in that exhilaration. Each seemed satisfied with the other. Procópio Dias confessed that Jorge was the first person to whom he had spoken of his feelings and it didn't vex him to say that, even after several months, he was able to learn nothing about the girl's heart. Sometimes he felt he was accepted; other times, and these were more numerous, he had the opposite impression.

"You of course know her and realize what a work of contradiction that little lady is," he said. "There are occasions when her familiarity with me approaches seduction. Maybe I'm exaggerating; but what am I to think of a girl who asks and insists, in a manner dramatic and filled with promises, that I go there on a certain day? I tell her I'll go; I do go. She receives me with a witticism, laughs at me, takes advantage of my complacency and perhaps of my love, because, though I have told her nothing, I feel it is natural that she might have discovered it in my eyes. If I become angry and resolve not to return there, she becomes gentle, like a dove, affectionate, soft; and my spite vanishes, and I continue my interminable journey."

"Have you never given her a hint, at least by allusion?"

"Never; I'm afraid she wouldn't let me finish."

"Don't believe it; I feel that she likes you."

"Do you *know* that?"

"No, but it is what I conclude from what you have told me. Women are sometimes fickle, and furthermore something of the child remains in her which makes her even more capricious. My thinking is this: if she has noticed and hasn't rejected you completely, it is because there still may be hope for you."

Procópio Dias couldn't express the happiness these words of Jorge brought to his spirits. His eyes shone with a strange light, then closed, while his head leaned back in a languid manner. During that momentary pause Jorge was able to analyze Procópio Dias's features, hardly appropriate to fascinate a pair of sixteen-year-old eyes, and he felt it natural that Iaiá would not feel herself caught up by blind enthusiasm. Nevertheless, it was not impossible that she return his feelings to a certain extent if reason were to remove the reins from her heart. Jorge even considered it possible that there might be in Iaiá a seed of sympathy, which would be enough to make it develop.

Entering the room which had been reserved for him, Procópio Dias was far from being sleepy; the excitement had made him alert. He went in, opened the window, and gazed about. The pungent fragrance of the plants on the estate quickened his senses even more. He was not the type of man to contemplate the stars or to philosophize about nocturnal solitude and the slumber of things; he confined himself to thinking about what he had just heard.

"He likes Estela," he murmured. "Before he swore, it might have been doubtful; the swearing makes it certain. If she doesn't like him she is making a mistake; he is an amazing young man."

Then, giving wings to his thoughts, he flew straight to Iaiá, soaring through space and tearing down walls. He examined his pristine dream, which he assumed to be quiet and pure, but which at that very hour was turbulent and already involved in ideas of evil. Procópio Dias allowed himself to move along on the whim of a passion which was ardent and sincere, a muffled and mysterious conspiracy of all the sensual forces.

The delicate and chaste image of Iaiá appeared suddenly to him one day, like a vision not dreamt of. If he were to see her in some aristocratic ballroom, he would think about her for a night, perhaps for a week, until he forgot her or substituted another for her. But what held him to Iaiá Garcia was precisely her humble birth. To possess her was to do her a favor. How many others did not attract the satyr's attention as they stepped down from some carriage or glided languidly along in a fashionable quadrille. He would see them pass or stand with their shoulders bare or wrapped with elegant cashmere, some smiling, others impassive, all of them haughty and rhythmic, and he would feel that their youth, features, and manners separated him from them; it was not difficult to erase them from his mind. Iaiá would first have to be grateful for being chosen; at least that was his conviction, and that is what most drew him to Luís Garcia's daughter.

If the girl were to realize that she would find in her husband the satisfaction of all of luxury's whims and the delight of exquisitely fine, elegant, and rare things, she would naturally give in and prefer him to someone who might give her merely love, work, and necessities. Once the idea had taken root, it grew and took over his mind completely. Iaiá became then the ever-present image before him, at one moment divine and chaste, at another ardent and sensual, because in his mind he defiled her even before possessing her.

The following day the two men awakened late and had breakfast together, without returning to the subject of the previous day. At the end of the meal Procópio Dias referred to it, saying that he had exceeded himself the night before and asking that Jorge not hold it against him, since it was all the product of a sentiment unerring in its reasonable doubts and fair in its evaluation.

"I couldn't attribute any other motive to you," responded Jorge smiling.

"Aren't you peeved at me?"

"Peeved? Suffice it to say that if your getting married depended on me, I would marry you off tomorrow."

Procópio Dias thanked him for sympathizing with his cause and for his approval, and left. Jorge dressed for the office. While he was dressing he thought about the problem of this former army supplier. They were not friends, but Procópio Dias's case interested him; he was a likeable fellow. Jorge did not inquire whether or not that regard for him sprang from fear; he naively persuaded himself of the contrary. A husband in love and opulent! Two advantages a young lady in Iaiá's condition should accept with open arms. Perhaps Procópio Dias would not be unacceptable to the girl's heart, but there remained in her some vestiges of childhood which time should erase.

"At that age a suitor is a type of doll," Jorge said, adjusting his tie. "What is necessary at all costs is to make a husband of the doll."

Arriving at the office at noon, Jorge found Mr. Antunes upset. He had slept until eleven o'clock and had arrived late at his working establishment; his boss had told him his services were no longer needed. It was a small business concern where Mr. Antunes, who knew something about accounting, had been working for some time, thanks to Jorge's recommendation.

"But have you already been fired?" inquired the latter.

"I am to settle my accounts and resign at the end of the month."

Jorge wrote a couple of lines to the employer. In the afternoon, Mr. Antunes went to Santa Teresa. Jorge was about to sit down to dinner; Mr. Antunes had already eaten but joined him.

"Come on, come on," said the young man, "I need to scold you."

Ashamed and timid, Mr. Antunes seated himself facing Jorge, who said nothing for the first few minutes. Finally Jorge spoke, reprimanding him good-naturedly. He told him that the tradesman's demands were not overbearing, and that in any case, there was nothing to be done about them unless he wanted to leave the establishment.

"That's just what I want to do," said Estela's father.

"Don't do it. One gains nothing by moving from one job to another. Besides, I can't see that arriving before ten o'clock should be a difficult thing to do. Your son-in-law has been doing that for years."

"My son-in-law! . . . my son-in-law!" said Mr. Antunes, shaking his head with a gesture of irritation.

Jorge pretended not to observe the gesture and tone of voice of Estela's father, and attempted to convert him to punctuality, a task which was beginning to become difficult, because Mr. Antunes was already beginning to experience the logical and natural consequences of a lengthy dependence. He preferred favors to work, and his age was contributing to his love of inertia and gratuitous favors. The greatest ambition which had inspired him, if fortune had allowed it to materialize, would have provided him the means with which to become old without worry. Now he had become grizzled, and his body, though agile, was beginning to gasp with inertia.

Jorge abandoned the subject in order not to embarrass his father's old protégé and ended dinner in a happy mood. When it was over he received a little note from Procópio Dias:

You can't imagine the kind of day I have had, after our conversation yesterday. I insist that I was excessive, and once again I ask you to forgive my error. Would you punish a madman? Love knows no guilt. Burn this note; at least don't show it to anyone, especially not to the person it concerns.

Jorge smiled and reread the note, then put it away in his desk and wrote this simple answer:

Once again, there is nothing to forgive. You were merely suspicious, like all jealous people; but, since you did not invent jealousy, I do not hold it against you.

Having delivered the answer, Jorge looked at Mr. Antunes, who was discreetly smoking one of the graduate's cigars.

"I heard something today," said Jorge with an air of indifference. "I heard that Iaiá is going to get married."

"Married?" repeated Mr. Antunes with a jolt. And after a moment: "It's possible. I'm the last to hear anything in that house."

"It may be nothing more than a false rumor. They didn't even tell me to whom. There is probably some boyfriend, or something like that, so people make a lot of it. But I wonder if there really is some suitor or love affair? . . ."

"Not that I know of," declared Mr. Antunes. "And let me tell you what I think. I doubt that she is thinking about such things at this time. That girl doesn't have a brain."

"Oh, my!" exclaimed Jorge, laughing.

"She really doesn't, I tell you. There it is; she belongs in a madhouse. It can't be said that it's mischief; she's not at the age for that; she's crazy. If you only knew the things she does sometimes!"

"It doesn't seem that way to me; when I see her she always seems reticent, and sometimes very serious. . . ."

"Oh well, that's because she doesn't like you."

"She doesn't like me?" asked Jorge, surprised.

"I'm not saying that she absolutely doesn't like you," Estela's father admitted. "She doesn't find much in common with you, that's what it is."

"How do you know that?"

"I once heard her father reprimand her because she had deliberately turned her back on you; she shrugged her shoulders in disdain. Her father again said that that wasn't nice, but he was getting nowhere. Iaiá looked at her fingernails with a scowl on her face, and I left because I could no longer stand either one of them."

Jorge remained pensive a few moments. It was true that Iaiá had always treated him coolly and with reserve; but, assuming that this did not mean affinity, and that she even felt some hostility toward him, he was far from attributing to her an open dislike. He didn't at all recall the gesture to which Mr. Antunes had alluded, but it was possible. Furthermore, he thought, Mr. Antunes would not be inventing it on the spur of the moment; he was no slanderer; he lacked that type of malice. But, for what reason could Luís Garcia's daughter not like him? It was the second time that Jorge had asked that question without finding a plausible answer. Immediately he remembered the night before, and observed to Estela's father that Iaiá had treated him with some cordiality the day before.

"A New Year's miracle!" explained Mr. Antunes. "I can also tell you that you have nothing to lose if she doesn't like you; it's a piece of good luck. Because when she likes someone it's enough to make one lose his patience."

"But she seems to have a good heart, and I think she loves her father very much."

"Estela also loves me."

At this point Jorge ended the conversation. His thoughts went back to Mr. Antunes's abrupt revelation. No matter how indifferent Iaiá was toward him, Jorge felt hurt by the assurance that the girl didn't like him. Why would it be? A simple aversion, or something else?

His worry disappeared the afternoon of the following day when Jorge appeared at Luís Garcia's house. It was Iaiá herself who came to open the garden gate for him, saying cheerfully: "Come in, doctor; we were expecting you." Jorge wasn't able to hide his amazement or his satisfaction. He went in and stretched out his hand to her.

"I can't," retorted the girl, displaying her own closed hand, "unless you can guess what I have here."

"It's not a star."

"No, sir; it's a horse."

At the far end of the garden was Luís Garcia, with his chessboard. Iaiá had asked for a lesson before dinner, and he had just finished giving it. She took Valéria's son over to him. For the first time she sat at their feet to watch them play; she placed her elbows on the table and rested her chin on her hands. She wanted to learn, she said, in three weeks.

"In three weeks!" repeated her father, smiling and looking at Jorge.

Of the qualities necessary for playing chess Iaiá possessed the two essential ones: a quick eye and benedictine patience—qualities precious in life itself, which is also a game of chess, with its problems and games, some won, some lost, others neither.

Chapter Twelve

Fifteen days later Procópio Dias appeared at Jorge's house, with mourning in his face and dress. Late the day before he had received news from Buenos Aires of the death of a brother, his last relative—news which obliged him to sail the following day and remain in the Rio da Prata for five or six weeks.[1] It couldn't be said that he was sad; rather, he was solemn—solemn and preoccupied. The trip to Buenos Aires had nothing to do with his brother's funeral but with the inheritance, which, though it wasn't substantial, was worth a little.

Procópio Dias offered his services to Valéria's son, who in turn offered Dias some letters of introduction should he need them. Procópio Dias accepted one. Jorge took it to him the following day. He received it with a gesture of appreciation and an almost tender manner and, after a moment of silence, said:

"I'm giving you this letter now, in person, which I was going to have a messenger deliver tomorrow."

Jorge wanted to open it. "No," pleaded the former. "Promise me you won't open it until tomorrow."

"Why not tonight?"

"Tonight would be all right; but it would be well to have the sleep and space of a night elapse between our farewell and the reading of this piece of paper. Perhaps your judgment will be different in the morning."

Jorge promised. Procópio Dias departed. The following day Jorge opened the letter and read these few words:

Be my guardian angel during my absence.

---

1. Buenos Aires, the capital and chief port of Argentina, and Montevideo, the capital and chief city of Uruguay, are on the River Plate, which runs through both countries. It is common to speak of this area of Argentina and Uruguay as the Rio da Prata region.

Why shouldn't I? he asked himself.

That afternoon he went horseback riding along the aqueduct, as was his custom, thinking seriously about the practicality of a marriage between the two. For two weeks he had had an opportunity to observe the girl's qualities, and they seemed good to him, although he also found in her something different, mysterious, or romantic, far above Procópio Dias's comprehension or sentiment. Jorge was not deceiving himself with regard to the suitor's love; he assumed it to be sincere, but he didn't attribute to it the purity of a first or second love: it was a last-minute passion, an ardent and blazing setting between the waning day and the night which would soon shadow all. Even then the alliance seemed convenient to him. Iaiá possessed the strength necessary to dominate her husband from the start; and the imprisoned titan would have at his feet, instead of a vulture pecking at his liver, a beautiful turtledove prolonging his youthful illusions.

If the impressions that Iaiá had left on him during the last few days were good, they were not, however, exempt of an otherwise passing annoyance. Once or twice Iaiá had seemed to him unusually rude, and without motive. These fits of anger, which didn't last long, were immediately compensated for by an affability which seemed livelier, noisier, perhaps a little inappropriate. On one occasion Estela said to her stepdaughter, with a reprimanding smile: "Don't bother Dr. Jorge." Jorge did not understand why that simple expression, spoken in a mild tone, produced on Iaiá's face an expression of indignation; he nevertheless remembered that it was short-lived, and that she went from singular sulkiness to her usual gaiety. "You see," remarked Estela, "you see what a child she is."

Jorge continued reflecting in this manner and on his way back he heard a voice call his name. It was Iaiá's, who was coming down from her old nurse's house. Jorge brought his horse to a halt.

"What are you thinking about?" she said.

"About you," responded the young man boldly, after ascertaining that no one could hear them.

Iaiá walked out to the street accompanied by an old man, Maria das Dores's brother.

"What are you doing around here?" continued Jorge, bending forward over the horse's neck.

"I came to visit Maria das Dores. Poor thing! She is so depressed!"

"Well. I'll tell you in a minute what's the matter; go see her."

"I've already seen her; I'm going home now. Don João is going to accompany me."

Jorge dismounted.

"Will you let me go, too?" he asked.

"All right, but just to satisfy my curiosity. I want to know what it is you were thinking about me. Shall we go, Don João?"

Jorge slipped the reins through his arm and walked along beside her; Iaiá boldly took his other arm.

"Go on, tell me everything."

"Procópio Dias sailed today."

Iaiá, who had begun walking, stopped suddenly.

"Where to?" she said.

"To the Rio da Prata; one of his brothers died in Buenos Aires."

"But without telling us good-bye!"

"Of course, it was a difficult thing for him to do, but he preferred to spare himself the pain of separation. He was with me, though, and promised that his absence would be brief. He seemed very worried about the trip, so worried that I don't know whether I should tell you that . . . that probably the pain of having to make the trip was greater than that over his brother's death. Perhaps I am doing him an injustice in saying this, but it seems that way."

"Why?" asked the girl, lifting her eyes to meet his.

"I don't know if I should tell you why," added Jorge. "And since it's not a matter of great importance—it's true that pretty girls like you are usually cruel . . . I don't know. . . . There are situations which are a little—"

"Ridiculous," concluded Iaiá.

"Ridiculous, how?"

"Yours, for example."

Jorge persisted a little. Iaiá did not seem forceful enough to make a man of society lose his poise. He smiled slightly, and retorted without irritation:

"It isn't ridiculous to be affectionate; I was trying to answer the language of your heart."

"You assumed that Procópio Dias's absence was making me lonely. . . ."

"That's right."

"What business is that of yours?"

Jorge's answer was a simple negative gesture. Withal, he was unable to get angry, because he could feel the girl's arm tremble, and looking at her from the corner of his eye, he could see she was pale and had her eyes on the ground. If the pallor and trembling were from anger he never knew it; but it was probably from exactly that, because after three or four minutes Iaiá lifted her eyes and stretched out her hand to him, saying:

"Let's declare a truce."

"I don't think we were ever at war."

"Perhaps on the eve of war."

"Through no fault of mine. . . ."

"Nor mine," hurried the girl. And tilting her little sunbonnet toward heaven: "Perhaps *he* was to blame," she said sighing.

After the sigh came a little laugh which was dry and forced but lingered even so like the sound of struck crystal. They had been walking only a few minutes, and that was enough time to awaken Jorge's curiosity and to give him the right to ask for an explanation. He asked for it in affectionate terms, inquiring why heaven was to blame for a war that should erupt between the two of them and above all what the pretext of that war could be. Iaiá thought for a moment and began to speak with her eyes lowered.

"You yourself are the reason," she said.

"I am?"

"You, my enemy who detests me. Won't you tell me what I have ever done to you?" she continued, raising her eyes suddenly. "You needn't make that gesture of surprise. I know you hate me, and no matter how much I ask myself, I don't know, I don't recall. . . . Come on, speak frankly."

"So much the better!" exclaimed Jorge. "I can see that there was a misunderstanding between us and the opportunity has arisen to clear it up. Do you want me to speak frankly? The enemy is not I; it is you. It was you, or rather, it seemed to be you. Now I understand; you were returning the dislike you supposed I felt. So much the better! Let's make peace once and for all."

Iaiá shook the hand he extended and they arrived happily at the house. Jorge tried to leave immediately, but the girl ordered Raimundo to take his horse and Jorge was compelled to remain for a few minutes. Luís Garcia was not at home. Mr. Antunes was there. Iaiá barely allowed time for the first amenities. "Come play a game with me," she said.

"In peace?"

"In peace."

Iaiá prepared the chessboard in the parlor next to the living room. Patiently, Jorge seated himself facing his opponent, adjusted the position of two chess pieces, laid aside the ones that gave him an advantage, and moved the first pawn forward.

"Go on," he said, "it's your turn."

Iaiá did not heed the invitation. She was looking at him uneasily.

"Will you give me your word of honor not to deny me what I'm about to ask?" she said after a few moments of silence.

Jorge hesitated a little.

"That depends."

"I insist. I demand it."

What can she ask of me that I cannot assure her of? thought Jorge. And he answered aloud:

"I give my word."

"Was it he that entrusted to you—"

"The sermon?" interrupted Jorge smiling. "I'll be frank: that's who it was." Iaiá lowered her eyes to the chessboard and let them wander as though she were distracted, and in a voice even lower than the one in which she had been speaking to him she asked:

"Can you keep a secret?"

"Yes," replied Jorge boldly.

"Very well," continued Iaiá, "I like him, I like him a lot; but I don't want him to know."

"Really? You aren't joking?"

"No, I'm not."

Jorge shook her hand. "Magnificent," he said happily; "that's all that's necessary. As long as you love each other, you will naturally come to. . . ."

He wasn't able to finish because the girl, getting up suddenly, moved away from the table abruptly and went to the window which led to the garden. Jorge was quite stunned. He couldn't understand what he was seeing. He leaned over the chessboard and began to move the pieces, alone, without method, mechanically. Playing thus, he could hear the sound of Iaiá's heel striking the floor tile in a precipitated and nervous movement. This lasted five minutes. Iaiá turned back inside, left the window, and approached the table. Jorge then lifted his head to her and smiled.

"Won't you tell me what I did to make you so angry?" he asked kindly.

"Nothing; it is I who was quick-tempered, maybe worse."

Jorge protested, saying that she hadn't been. "You had a reason. Won't you tell me what it was? I don't think I've treated you badly."

"No, you haven't."

"In that case the motive is within; and if I weren't afraid that you might get angry with me again, I would ask you to tell me everything— or at least something."

"What for? Let's play chess."

"It's getting dark."

"I'll have lights brought in."

The lights came; they began to play. To these two, chess couldn't offer any great interest, but even if it could, it wouldn't on that occasion. Both were distracted and preoccupied. The first game was finished in very little time, almost no time at all.

"Another game?" asked Iaiá.

"All right."

"Before we start," she said, placing the pieces on the board and without looking at Jorge, "I want to say that there is a sure way of never getting into a quarrel with me."

"How?"

"By being my confidant."

"Master of your secrets?"

"All of them."

"That's easy, but I get the best of the bargain."

"That proves what a big heart I have."

She was no longer the rash girl of a few moments back; she had spoken the last words with grace and serenity. At the same time she went on arranging the chess pieces methodically. She finished and leaned against the back of the chair.

"You haven't told me whether you would accept," she said.

Jorge hesitated a moment. Was it a joke or a serious proposition? One answers a joke with another joke; a proposition should be answered seriously. Jorge hesitated to take part of the responsibility for the girl's feelings. What would her feelings be? What projects might be awakening in that probably indomitable brain? They might be none other than thoughts of marriage to Procópio Dias, since she admitted loving him. This thought made him boldly declare that he would accept the position.

"Do you know what you're accepting?" asked Iaiá.

"I can guess."

"Shake hands on it!" she said, giving him her hand. Jorge gave his.

"In any case, it's not a matter of murder, is it?" he asked, laughing.

"No."

The second game was livelier but only on Iaiá's part. The girl laughed at times, but most of the time she concentrated all her attention on the game. When she spoke she was composed and docile. That alternate and contrasting behavior was holding Jorge's interest for the moment. What kind of woman she was—imperious like a matron, mischievous like a child, incoherent and enigmatic—was something he could not ascertain in so little time; but the enigma was arousing his attention. While she had her eyes on the board, Jorge was attempting to read her soul on her candid and smooth forehead; but he couldn't see her soul. He could see only a few strands of brown hair, which fell over her forehead and fluttered lightly in the gust of breeze which entered through the window and gave her a youthful aspect. Her delicate and pensive mouth corrected the impression her forehead gave; it was the first time he had noticed in her a strong indication of energy and tenacity.

When it was Jorge's turn, Iaiá would lean back, bend over the arms of her chair, and remain looking at him the same way he had looked at her. But in that look no curiosity sparkled; it was a veiled and lusterless light, as if alien to the outside world. Their eyes would meet thus, and the game continued to its end without further incident.

As it was about to end Estela entered the room without interrupting them. She sat down quietly at one corner of the window. The game ended just as Luís Garcia arrived.

"I lost two games, Daddy," said the girl, "but the second one only by a hair's breadth."

Jorge wanted to leave immediately afterwards; he was obliged to remain because Iaiá decided to play the piano. It was the first time Jorge had actually heard her. The girl chose a page from Meyerbeer.[2] Jorge had once confessed that he was his favorite composer.

The following day Jorge's impression was more or less complex and

---

2. A famous German opera composer (1791-1864).

perplexed. That mixture of frankness and reticence, of aggression and meekness, gave Luís Garcia's daughter a unique character all her own; it made of her an individual; but the configuration was still confused and the personality vague. Jorge felt himself simultaneously drawn forward and held back by opposing sentiments; he was curious, yet felt an aversion to penetrating the girl's character and distinguishing among the elements that constituted it. What seemed clear and definite to him was that Iaiá's first words, which had been so harsh and dry, were nothing more than an expression of disdain—the result of having assumed in him a dislike that didn't exist. And if the words themselves offended him, the explanation flattered his ego. The rest was inexplicable. Jorge resolved, nevertheless, not to speak to her of Procópio Dias anymore, in spite of her confession, which incidentally was in contrast to or diminished by the gesture which followed it.

Iaiá seemed to lose her aggressive disposition; the bonds of affability completely erased the vestiges of the old rudeness. Her soul did not become more transparent nor her character less complex, but her exquisite urbanity made tolerable the inconsistencies of her spirit and increased Jorge's interest in what there was in her of the somber and irregular. Finally, her politeness was a corrective to the tenacity with which the girl was literally appropriating Valéria's son. Jorge appreciated that circumstance above all because it made his visits to the house easier. He belonged to either the father or the daughter—often to both. Iaiá threw herself into chess with an inexplicable ardor, and since Jorge told her that she would have to read some essays on the subject, she asked him for one, and since he only had them in English, Iaiá asked him to teach her English.

"But I am a very harsh teacher," he observed.

"Your pupil is much harsher."

Estela sometimes attended the language and game lessons, two things which seemed to her incompatible with her stepdaughter's personality. The truth is that Iaiá had changed very much during those last few weeks. Estela had never imagined in her so much patience, nor such relaxed attention. Iaiá would spend from one to two hours a day memorizing the verbs and nouns of the new language, and this recent passion had the singular effect of irritating her stepmother. Jorge, on the contrary, felt in himself the joys of the pedagogue. The teacher is the intellectual father of the pupil; Jorge contemplated paternally that keen, patient, and tenacious intelligence, waited upon by the eyes of a dove and the hands of an archangel.

In mid-February they talked about Procópio Dias again, with regard to a letter that Luís Garcia had received.

"You see," said the girl, "he wrote to Daddy and not even a line to me. 'Regards to Estela and Iaiá'; that's all. Has he written you?"

"He hasn't yet."

"There's nothing like absence to make a person forget everything—that is, forget those who remain behind. Perhaps he's no longer thinking about marrying me. It was a passing fancy like all fancies; like yesterday's rain, that only splattered a little and amounted to nothing. Still, it seemed as though the whole sky were falling. Isn't that right? Isn't his love like a thunderbolt? It threatened in Rio and struck in Buenos Aires. I'll bet he comes back married. You'll see that that's all there was to it. What do you say to that? Come on; say something."

"I can't," replied Jorge. "You made me your confidant, not your counselor; I'm limiting myself to listening to you. The truth is, this position I've had has seemed like a simple sinecure until now."

"What's a sinecure?"

Jorge smiled and defined the word for her.

"It's not a sinecure," hurried Iaiá. "On the contrary, it's a very thorny business."

"I don't think so. The only secret confided until now didn't seem to me very sincere. You don't love Procópio Dias."

Iaiá frowned. "Why do you say that?"

"Because if you loved him, you would speak differently, and above all, you wouldn't speak so much. Love at this stage nourishes itself on reticence, not verbosity, and even less on such complex sentences."

"Hush!" she interrupted, striking the tips of his fingers with her grammar book. And after a pause: "If he writes to you, will you show me the letter?"

When Jorge told her that he would, Iaiá made a move to tear the volume in two pieces. Jorge asked what was the matter with her.

"I'm nervous!" answered the girl, her shoulders shaking with a chill. Then, as if to get hold of herself, she grasped one of his wrists. Jorge felt the pressure of steellike fingers; and it seemed as though other invisible fingers were also pressing against the girl's cheeks, which were as red as if they were bleeding.

Chapter Thirteen

That same night Jorge found a letter at home from Buenos Aires. Procópio Dias told him about the trip and his activities thus far, and said that he had hopes of being away only a very short while. That was one-third of the letter. The other two-thirds was expressions of feelings, homesickness, and complaints, and one name at the end, one name only, and one which was the key to his writing. Jorge read these secrets attentively, and sketched out an answer the same night. It was not easy to combine the discretion he wished to maintain in his relations with Procópio Dias, with the necessity of giving him some hope. Even though it required great effort, he drafted an appropriate answer, relating the good impressions he had—only the good ones. He didn't tell him about the doubtful ones. Above all, he did not descend to any reality, to any proper name—nothing more than a prolonged series of locutions which were as encouraging as they were vague.

The following day he did not go to Luís Garcia's house; it rained torrentially. But the next day he did, immediately after dinner. He found the family together.

"Good evening, my dear professor!" Iaiá cried out as soon as she saw him enter the room.[1]

"All this chatterbox needs is another language," said Luís Garcia, laughing.[2] "Pretty soon no one will be able to put up with her."

---

1. It is significant that "Good evening, my dear," appeared in English in Assis's original. While there is no concrete evidence to suggest that Assis spoke English fluently, it is known that he was greatly influenced by nineteenth-century English poets, Lamb in particular. He was also fond of Edgar Allan Poe, as Helen Caldwell shows in her *Brazilian Othello*. Whether he was fluent or not, Assis's knowledge and understanding of the English language must have been excellent, for his translation into Portuguese of Poe's "The Raven" is exquisite. Throughout his novels and some of his short stories he uses brief expressions in English.

2. The translation into English of "all she needs is another language" loses the original play on words which was possible in Portuguese. The word *lingua*, which I

Jorge certainly did not expect to find the girl's expression the same as two nights before when, in a nervous gesture, she had gripped his wrist. Forty-eight hours had passed, and only forty-eight minutes would have been necessary for her to compose herself. He was expecting the change. Nevertheless, he tried to read it in her eyes, and he found them as happy as the tone of voice with which she greeted him.

The lesson separated them from the others and was also the best pretext to show her Procópio Dias's letter. Iaiá saw it, sealed, and understood everything; she snatched it from Jorge's hands.

"Ah!" he said, "your gesture speaks louder than words."

"May I read it?"

"Yes."

Iaiá opened the letter and read it to herself. As she read Jorge observed her. He did not see any confusion, excitement, or happiness in her; her eyes moved slowly from one line to the next, and her firm hand turned the page. At the end, when she read her own name, she experienced a feeling of boredom and unconsciously crumpled the paper; but she immediately repented, smoothed out the letter with her hand, and returned it silently. For a few seconds, she busied herself with drawing circles with a pencil in the margin of the open page of her grammar book. Finally she raised her eyes and asked without laughing:

"Do you believe what this letter says?"

"Yes, I do; everything that is written there I have already heard by word of mouth, and with the same sincerity and warmth. Who knows? It could be this man's first love."

"The first ... the first ... ," she repeated, gritting her teeth.

"Perhaps the first," insisted Jorge, "and for a young lady I would think there would be a certain charm in being loved by a man considered to be unromantic. Procópio Dias's life has already reflected interests of a different nature. . . ."

"Have you known him for a long time?"

"Not for long; I have known him since Paraguay."

"Do you think I would do well to marry him?"

"You would do well or badly, depending upon how much you love him. That's the important point, and in my thinking, the doubtful one. I fear that you don't really love him. I have said that before."

---

have translated as *language,* could also have been translated as *tongue,* but it might have been confusing to the reader.

"I need clarifications on a few points. You must have been in love yourself at some time. . . ."

"Never."

"Never? You never had a love affair, even if only one? I don't believe it. A colonel! Never; I don't believe it; only if you swore to me. Would you swear?"

"I swear."

"On your mother's grave," she concluded, fixing on him a pair of eyes whose imperious expression contrasted with the submissive tone of her words.

Jorge hesitated a moment. He was cynical enough to utter a vague oath, but he faltered when confronted with the actual formula. He hesitated and evaded the question.

"That name epitomizes my only love precisely," he said. "I loved my mother."

Iaiá smiled with an air of doubt. Then she looked at him, moved. "I love my father," she replied. "Our hearts understand each other."

There was no need for an answer to those words; they seemed to him the condemnation of the suitor. He squeezed the hand the girl stretched out to him, and it felt cold. After a short pause, he shook his head, murmuring:

"Then, not even a shadow of hope. . . ."

"Do what you think best," said the girl after a pause. "In any case I would like to read your answer."

Jorge opened his wallet and took out the draft of the letter he intended to send Procópio Dias.

"The answer," he said, "is already written. I didn't want to destroy him, so I dropped bits of hope here and there; but I wouldn't have dared send the medicine without consulting you."

Iaiá took the folded paper, looked at it for an instant, another instant at Jorge. "Read it," he said. Iaiá did not obey: she took a pencil, and began to trace the lines of a drawing on the folded piece of paper. Since the light was striking the paper directly, Jorge wasn't able to see what it was immediately; but, facing the girl, he waited for her to give the finishing touches to her little caprice. At that moment Estela came up.

"Have you finished your lesson?" she asked.

"Now it seems it's a drawing lesson," Jorge said.

Estela placed her hand on her stepdaughter's shoulder. "It's Procópio

Dias!" she said, looking at the drawing. It was, but the drawing bordered on caricature; Procópio Dias's true proportions were exaggerated, his nose was enormously triangular, the scowls on his brow thick and endless: a comical monster. Estela smiled at the prank but reprimanded her.

"Let me see," said Jorge, when she finished.

"What for?" retorted Iaiá with indifference.

And taking the paper to the fire, she burned it. Jorge questioned her with his eyes; she faced him without becoming perturbed. Then she paged through the grammar book slowly.

"Let's continue the lesson," she said. "*I love.*[3] Go on; where were we? Here; it was here."

Estela attended the entire lesson with the patience of curiosity. She never looked at the teacher; she divided her attention between the student and the book. The lesson was long, longer than necessary, because the teacher himself was not following the text nor the reading closely. Iaiá had before her two judges, each of which was attempting to decipher from her forehead the inscription her destiny might have written there. She perceived it and was not annoyed. She moved from one verb tense to another, and from the indicative to the imperative, returning to the beginning as soon as she had come to the end, gazing at her inquisitors with a look in which all the ignorance on earth seemed to slumber.

Her tranquility was feigned. That night, having retired to her quarters, the girl gave vent to two opposing feelings. She entered her room feeling exhausted. *What am I doing?* she wondered, placing her head between her hands. She opened the venetian blinds and interrogated the heavens, but heaven gave no answer. This immense, taciturn being has eyes with which to see, but no ears with which to listen. The evening was clear and serene; millions of glittering stars seemed to be laughing at earth's myriad miseries. Two of them broke away and plunged into the darkness like the green figs in the Book of Revelation.[4] Iaiá superstitiously believed that she too would fall there, and soon. Then she closed her eyes to the great mute, and raised her thoughts to the

---

3. In the Portuguese text "I love" appeared in English.
4. In Revelation 6:13 the end of the world is predicted: "And the stars of heaven fell unto the earth, even as a fig tree casteth her untimely figs, when she is shaken of a mighty wind."

great merciful, to the heaven which one does not see but of which there is a fragment in the heart of the elements. Heaven heard and comforted her, and there she found support and strength. A voice seemed to say to her: *Continue your task; sacrifice yourself; preserve domestic peace.* Her soul thus restored, the depression passed away. When she opened her eyes again, it was not to question, but to affirm, in order to say to the night that in that fragile body there was a soul capable of stopping the wheel of destiny.

It was late when she fell asleep. When it was already daylight, she dreamed that she was walking along the edge of a precipice, and that the figure of a woman was throwing her arms around her waist and lifting her into the air like a feather. Pale, with a delirious expression and an ironic mouth, the woman was smiling with a smile that was triumphant and mean. She was murmuring some incoherent sentences which Iaiá did not understand. Iaiá called out to her in a loud voice: "Tell me you're not in love, and I shall love you as I once did!" But the woman, shaking her head in a tragic gesture and pressing her lips against Iaiá's, breathed a kiss that was as convulsive and cold as death. Iaiá felt herself faint and tumble into the abyss.

She awakened agitated and saw her stepmother looking at her at the foot of the bed. At first she closed her eyes and drew back against the wall; but immediately she came to her senses.

"I had a terrible nightmare," she said, breathing heavily. "I fell to the bottom of a precipice, pushed by two hands of iron. I'm still cold. Look at my hands. My chest is heaving. Fortunately it's over. Have you been here for very long? Was I very upset?"

"You spoke in a very loud voice."

"What did I say?"

" 'Tell me you're not in love and I shall love you as I once did.' I don't know that these words can be said from the bottom of a precipice. Dreams get mixed up."

"Perhaps. I don't remember anything else. I only remember the precipice, which fortunately was only my imagination. It's very late, isn't it?"

"Nine o'clock."

"Nine o'clock!"

Estela went to the window and, opening the venetian blind, let the sunlight in. Then she leaned there, looking out. She had come in a few moments earlier, surprised at her stepdaughter's prolonged sleep, and was about to place her hand on the girl's shoulder when she heard that sentence stammered amid great agitation—a vague and mysterious sentence, but one which embedded itself in her heart like a thorn. For her own part, Iaiá was no less uneasy. She feared that she might have said something more—a name or an exact circumstance. In any case, what her stepmother had heard was enough to make Iaiá think that the dream had flung open the doors to her conscience. Each peered at the other suspiciously and fearfully. The stepmother left the window and went over to sit on the edge of the bed. Each smiled with some effort, and neither managed to speak first. Thus passed three long minutes of restraint and mutual observation. Estela was the first to break the silence.

"Your nightmare was punishment," she said. "It was punishment for the caricature you drew yesterday. That wasn't nice. Everyone knows that Procópio Dias is welcome in our home. What will people think of us when they see how we treat people who are absent?"

Iaiá pondered for a moment.

"It was necessary," she said. "It was a way of disillusioning intentions once and for all."

"But who told you about them?"

"Dr. Jorge, who seems to be protecting him. There couldn't possibly be anyone better off than that man. All it took was for him to like me for everyone to do everything they could to approve of him and advise me not to marry anyone else. It seems to him that I—"

"Why did Dr. Jorge speak to you of this?"

"For no reason at all; he told me about it because he is Procópio Dias's friend. Didn't I once tell you that some day, if everyone persisted, I would be obliged to marry Procópio Dias? I very much fear that that's what will happen."

"No," said Estela firmly. "It won't happen that way—first of all, because I will never consent to it; then, because you love someone else. . . ."

"I do?"

"Your school love, when you were twelve and a half."

"Ah!" said Iaiá. And after a few moments she continued with a gesture of great embarrassment: "I did wrong in telling you that; please don't repeat it to anyone."

Estela didn't hear the last words. She had risen again in order to disguise the turmoil which seemed to be growing. Meanwhile, Iaiá slipped on a bathrobe and stuck her feet in her little morning slippers. When, five minutes later, her eyes met Estela's, she found them somber, like those of the figure in the nightmare; and unconsciously she looked around to see if perhaps she might have a precipice at her feet.

"Iaiá," said Estela matter-of-factly, "you're in love; you've confessed that you love someone, but I want you to tell me his name, do you hear? I insist on knowing it in order to decide what is best for you. You know that I have a mother's authority."

Iaiá felt the blood boil in her veins.

"My mother died," she retorted with equal dryness. "I am ready to obey my father."

It was all Estela could do to disguise her inner feelings. After a few moments of silence, she left.

Far from her stepdaughter, Estela gave full reign to the feelings which were shaking her. She locked herself in her husband's study; then she evoked the past to combat the present because it was the present that was threatening to engulf her. Shaken briefly by the reading of the letter of 1867, she had tried to recover her old calm; but Iaiá's interference had hindered this sincere effort. Her stepdaughter's behavior, the sudden change with regard to Jorge, all that visible and recent intimacy, had awakened in Estela's heart a feeling that spares not even the proud. Jealous or not, she had reshuffled the warm ashes and had found an ember among them. She suspected the other's rivalry, and that was all that was necessary for the cry of rebellion to make that solitary and virgin soul tremble. Her mind lost its usual serenity. Her heart began to beat with the swiftness and violence of a great fever.

It was the latent power of a repressed but intense love, like a crater accidentally sealed, locked in an ice vault; worse, it had endured the misfortune of a long confinement—the struggle between two equally formidable, indomitable, and blind forces. At one time pride had won out; now it was love, which, during its years of bondage and oppression, had developed muscles and was moving out to do battle again. Victory would constitute a catastrophe, because Estela was not endowed with the art of combining illicit passion with domestic tranquility. She would have the struggles and the first pretenses; but, overpowered, she would resort to evil.

Now in the midst of this already painful, though as yet short-lived duel, Estela heard her stepdaughter's last words, the comment which had escaped her during the turmoil of the nightmare. She was stunned when she left there, feeling her way through the shadows and turning her eyes in another direction when some bright light of reality appeared in the distance. She could not believe in the conscious and outspoken rivalry of Iaiá. It was unlikely; it would be her very shame and indictment. But those words resounded in her ears, and her step-daughter's cold, hard gesture seemed to clarify whatever was obscure in her words.

The situation in which the fatality of circumstance had placed the two women couldn't last very long. Iaiá was the more tractable of the two and also the one who had most at stake. As soon as Estela had left her alone, she came to her senses and realized that, in addition to cruelly hurting the woman who was filling her mother's role, she had lifted a tip of the veil which concealed her thoughts. Furthermore, the injury had produced the reaction of love—of the love which she felt for her and had not altogether lost, in spite of recent developments. The next day she went to her stepmother.

"I confess that I was excessive and disobedient," she said. "I shouldn't have been, but you spoke so dryly—in such a hard way. It seemed to me that you doubted me; whatever it was, it wasn't your usual manner of behavior. I have always respected you as though you were my mother; I don't deny—I could never deny—your rights, just as I am aware of your friendship. But part of the fault is yours; you have always dealt with me more like a sister than a mother. This produced some confidence, some intimacy, and that's why yesterday I forgot who we were, and treated you in a way I should not have. That's all it was; it was an excess, an imprudence, nothing more. Consult your own heart and it will tell you that that's all it was. Go ahead; ask your heart; it knows me."

Estela listened to her silently, without lowering the loftiness of her brow, but also without a disdainful or threatening expression. There was something that shone in her eyes, that was watching the other's soul from beneath lowered eyelids. Iaiá had spoken hurriedly, but not monotonously. Simplicity, timidity, ostentation—there was a little of everything in the way she expressed herself in those few seconds. The explanation was at once sincere and adroit, but the two attitudes mingled to such an extent that the adroitness was not aware of itself: it was more instinctive than calculated.

119

"What are you asking?" said Estela after a few moments. "That I forgive you? That I forget your imprudence? One is easier than the other. You're forgiven; now make me forget."

"Why not? I managed to make you love me before you knew whether I was good or bad."

"It was easy. Your mother was your mother, but she didn't love you more than I do. If you ever realized it, it wasn't yesterday; yesterday you gave in to a bad bias against stepmothers, and you erected a specter between us which, if it could talk, would condemn you, too. I'm not complaining. I've never complained about anything: when I respect someone, I forgive; when I don't, I forget. To forgive *and* forget is rare, but not impossible; it's up to you."

Overwhelmed by the tone in which her stepmother had spoken— simple and lightly touched with sadness—Iaiá gave in to a noble impulse of submission. She took her hands and kissed them. Her stepmother felt a tear on them. She did not reject this manifestation of the heart, and would have hugged her if the inflexibility of her soul had permitted it. She limited herself to contemplating her with the loving eyes of bygone days.

When they separated a few minutes later, something was saying to the consciences of each that they had not made peace but simply a truce. This conviction grew in subsequent days because each felt mutually observed. Since there was between them a tacit agreement not to disturb the household peace, Luís Garcia did not notice this new situation; Jorge, even less so. Iaiá did not alter her habits of the last few days, although she employed a little more caution. Otherwise, the relations between the two were as frequent and personal as before. On one occasion, since Jorge had been absent longer than was customary, Iaiá was a little uncommunicative; and when he asked her what was bothering her, she boldly answered that his absence had made her very sad.

"Only four days," he observed.

The first Sunday in March he came over at eleven in the morning, and found only Luís Garcia and Estela. Iaiá had gone to Maria das Dores's house. When the girl returned Jorge and Estela were in the garden, near the door to the living room; between the two was an empty chair—Luís Garcia's, who had gone in a few minutes earlier. Neither of the two was talking at that moment. Estela was snapping her nails; Jorge was stroking his forehead with the knob of his walking stick. Was it constraint or pretense? Iaiá couldn't decide which, but the aspect of the two left her pale.

The next day she went back to Maria das Dores's house; she knew about Jorge's customary walk; she wanted to see him, speak to him. The invalid was not counting on Iaiá's visit again after such a short period of time. Iaiá was with her only a few minutes, then went outside under the pretext that it was very hot, and that she wanted to breathe the fresh afternoon air. The afternoon was beautiful; the sky revealed all its hues from scarlet to opal; in the east some unusual and fine clouds colored the blue background with white.

The house stood on a small elevation; Iaiá sat down on a smooth rock which was used as a bench, and from there she took a long, circular look around the horizon. Then she lowered her eyes to the city and the sea, and this spectacle, so well known to her, took her back to the not-so-remote time when no other love had come between her father and her. In the midst of her reflections, she saw a man approach and stop in the distance. It was Jorge; he was walking with the attitude of one who is meditating. Would he pass without seeing her? She rose, saw him approach, stop again, and look in the direction of the house. She greeted him from a distance and signaled him to come up. Jorge readily obeyed.

Maria das Dores, sick with a form of paralysis, was bewildered when she saw Iaiá lead a stranger in by the hand. She questioned the girl with her eyes, and after a few moments of bashful silence, Iaiá answered with assurance.

"My fiancé is here to see you. I want you to meet him and not say anything about it to anyone, will you?"

Saying this, she brought him closer to the paralytic. The kind old woman contemplated him for a few moments, gave him some words of advice, asked him to make her foster child happy, and obtained no word or gesture of assent from him. She assumed he was moved, but he was simply astonished.

Leaving the house, they sat near the door on a rock which was sufficiently large and spacious for two.

"It was necessary to tell her that," explained Iaiá, "because I want to speak with you, and engaged couples are able to speak more freely. Besides, she's not only paralytic; she has poor eyesight; tomorrow I can substitute you without her noticing the change. Now let's talk about ourselves and that letter. . . . And before the letter, tell me, did you know I was here?"

"No, I didn't; but I didn't come all the way out here without hoping to find you. As long as you have mentioned the letter, let me explain something to you. If I haven't explained until now, it's because I hadn't wanted to return to a subject which is displeasing to you and to me."

"To you?"

"Yes, to me."

Iaiá squeezed his hand tightly.

"Go ahead," she said. "I have something serious to tell you, too, but let's hear your explanation first."

"Oh! that's not hard," hurried Jorge. "I wrote the rough draft of the letter because I felt it would please you. Do you remember that you had once spoken to me along that line? Later I doubted and told you so. Nevertheless, there was so much uncertainty and contradiction between your words and your actions that it wasn't difficult to suppose that you felt something; there are loves that begin that way, capriciously. The letter was a way of telling the suitor that his sighs might not be in vain. It was that; only that. I admit that I adopted the most passive, disinterested role possible, and I don't know if perhaps even . . . . I think you have already defined it as ridiculous. My manner may not have been serious, but my intention was affectionate; and if it deserved a smile, it also deserved a handshake. Once I had drawn up the letter, I wouldn't have sent it without showing it to you—which is what I did. But your displeasure was so eloquent that it brought me to my senses and made me recognize that the letter was too much."

"It wasn't enough."

"Did you want me to go to Buenos Aires?" asked Jorge smiling.

"Yes, if on arriving you would have said to him, 'Start thinking about something else; Iaiá doesn't love you.' "

"All I have to do to convey that is to say nothing."

"Doesn't love you," repeated the girl, "doesn't love you, doesn't love you."

"Do you really mean it this time?"

"Why are you so surprised?" retorted the girl gravely. "Don't you think it's the most natural thing in the world for a girl not to love Procópio Dias? I don't know what other men are like; I've met very few; our life is so removed from everything! But after all, Procópio Dias doesn't seem to me to be the type of man that one would die over. Yet he's dying over me. My heart forgives him! It's the most it can do. To accept him would be impossible. Have you ever looked closely at his eyes? They sometimes have a strange expression that I have never seen in Daddy's eyes nor in yours. I don't like him; I could never like him."

This time it was Jorge who squeezed her hand.

"You're right," he said. "If you don't really love him, it's all over. I'm not saying that he would make a perfect mate. He couldn't; but acceptable he was. I notice that there are differences between you and him, but what is there that time won't cure? Forget what I have told you about this, and let's agree not to speak on this subject anymore. I probably won't write anything. It is difficult to tell a man that all his hopes are in vain."

"I wonder if my peace of mind wouldn't be worth that sacrifice?"

"It's worth more than that. I'll do it."

Iaiá thought for a moment.

"No, it isn't necessary; don't tell him anything; he's sure to understand everything."

As they paused for a long moment, they noticed two or three people who were passing by below looking up with a certain air of curiosity and indiscretion. Jorge rose.

"We're attracting attention," he said; "they're sure to think we're lovers."

"Sit down," said Iaiá in an intimate tone, and she continued: "Why do you care? They'll say it's good taste on your part to love a pretty girl."

"If they were to say we were lovers, they would certainly be wrong, because I know . . . I suspect that you love someone else. I invoke my rights as your confidant to demand that you tell me the truth."

"All of it," answered Iaiá, "and this is the serious matter I wanted to speak to you about. I must ask you once again, do you respect me? Do you feel a sincere friendship for me? I doubt everything and everyone; even myself. But, after all, I need someone who will listen to me, someone to whom I can tell what I think and feel, and even what I fear, because I also fear, and there are times when I tremble without knowing why. It's true, there are times when I feel that a great unhappiness is going to befall me, and then in no time at all I think

123

exactly the opposite. I feel that the greatest happiness in the world is going to be mine, and I become as happy as a lark. I sound like a child, don't I?"

"No, like a young lady. Is it true that you're in love? With whom?"

Iaiá looked at him awhile, satisfied with the impatience she thought she could read on his brow.

"Yes and no," she said. "If you ask me whom I love, I must tell you that I don't know, that I don't love anyone. But I feel something mysterious and strange, and I don't know ... I suspect ... I don't know what it might be. Why is it that things that were not important to me before now seem interesting and I even imagine that they are speaking to me? Just a while ago, before seeing you, I was engrossed with looking at the heavens, almost without thinking, but even then curious and anxious. I was looking at the sky and the sea; my heart contracted, then expanded as though it wanted to devour everything. There are days when I wake up happy and vivacious, like a child. Daddy calls them my sunny days. There are others when I feel like breaking everything, and I don't say more than two words in the space of an hour. Those are my black days. I sometimes hear a voice speaking to me; I think it is someone and I realize that the voice is that of my own imagination. Everything is probably imagination, I think; but it's so new and so good! In any case, it seems extraordinary to me, and if it isn't madness. . . . It's true, sometimes I think I'm going mad, and on those occasions I'm afraid. Would that be it?"

"No," answered Jorge, "it's not madness. It's wisdom; it's the great wisdom of nature. This thing you feel probably isn't love, but the necessity of loving; it is the alarm your heart is sounding. Someone will come some day and the anonymous voice you normally hear will speak to you through the mouth of the man your heart points out."

Iaiá was listening to him as if bewitched but without looking at him. When Jorge finished there was a long pause between them. The girl's eyes were on the horizon, where the colors of the afternoon were fading rapidly. He was contemplating her, enthralled and even jealous. He could understand the first apprehensions of that budding heart and was telling himself that there are sensations that time takes away, never again to restore.

Iaiá awakened from her reflections.

"Frankly," she said, "aren't you laughing at me?"

"Laughing? You don't know me. One doesn't laugh at sincere

124

feelings; and it would be a very poor way to repay you for the confidence you've placed in me. Don't think of me as an ordinary person."

"Daddy speaks very well of you."

"You will learn, or perhaps you already know, that I am attracted by what is above the ordinary; you have fine traits of character. Two months ago I still didn't know you—"

"Don't flatter my vanity," interrupted Iaiá; "I prefer you to give me a good piece of advice."

"I'll give you one," said Jorge, after a brief pause. "Resist these sensations a little; your excess in them can disturb your life. It's not only your heart that speaks to you, but your imagination as well, and imagination—in addition to being a good friend—also has moments of infidelity. Allow a little of the poetic in life, but don't fall into the trap of the romantic; the romantic is perfidious. I, who am saying this to you, regret not already having that kind of sentiment in bloom; furthermore, I'm not sure that it would be to my advantage."

"What! You wouldn't be capable of loving?"

"My heart is not yet withered."

"I understand; today you would love differently. . . ."

"Differently, and as sincerely as before; a love with my eyes open."

"I think that true love, or at least the best kind, is the one that sees nothing around it and walks straight, resolute, and happy wherever the heart takes it. What good are open eyes?"

"You want to know a lot," said Jorge smiling. "It's not enough for the heart to say, 'Love this one.' It's necessary for the eyes to approve the heart's choice. Are you surprised? Hear me through. I want to protect you from some poor choice. Choose a worthy husband, a soul that understands you, that admires you, a man that is capable of honoring you; don't allow yourself to be swayed by the first pair of eyes which seem to meet yours. . . ."

Iaiá lowered her head. "I won't find any," she said. "I think this love will die with me. . . ."

This idea seemed to sadden her. Thus, on seeing that on that clear awakening there persisted a shadow of romantic superstition, Jorge became compassionate. He took her hand, saw her tremble, refuse him, and cross her arms.

"Are you afraid of me?" he said after an instant.

"Yes, I am."

Jorge grew quiet. With his cane he began to trace on the ground some reminiscences of geometry. He felt cut off, obstructed and curious, and he wished to leave there as much as it was difficult for him to do so. He couldn't quite understand her. The truth, when he was about to hit upon it, seemed unlikely. Meanwhile, Iaiá kept silent; her forehead was drooping and she was meditating. Perhaps she was meditating on the words she had just spoken, a product of the violent situation in which she herself or circumstances had placed her. It was the revolt of prudence. From time to time she would shake her head as if to rid herself of some annoying or cruel idea. On one of these occasions Jorge said gently:

"Why deny it? You are suffering. I'm not sure whether reasonably or unreasonably, but . . . you seem to be suffering a great deal."

"Oh! yes, I am!"

And this time the words were so anguished, so sincere, so much from the heart, that he gave in more to an impulse of generosity than to the desirability of not being rebuffed a second time. He took her hands and asked that she trust him completely and tell him the reason for her troubles. Perhaps he could remove them.

Iaiá lowered her head against Jorge's hands. He felt some tears which became sobs. No one was passing, but he didn't even have time to think about the possibility of a stranger. He bent over also and asked her affectionately what was troubling her. Iaiá raised her head and wiped her eyes but didn't answer.

"You don't trust me," said Jorge.

"There are things which are not done, others which are not said; some will remain between God and me," she retorted, as if she were thinking to herself. Then she looked at him and asked him to promise to say nothing about what he had just seen and heard.

"That's a promise that doesn't have to be made; it's already made. As for your secret, I don't want to violate it, but I hope that someday you will tell it yourself. I would like to know how to obtain the remainder of this confidence which you are still holding back from me."

"You're leaving already?!" exclaimed the girl, when she saw Jorge getting up.

"Haven't you noticed that night is falling? I can't stay another minute. Confidants have their limits. Listen; I'm not asking much, but I want something else. Being a confidant isn't enough; being a teacher is even less. Give me another title or job; let me be your . . . your what? Your brother."

"No," she said energetically.

Jorge turned pale as though he had just seen the depths of the girl's soul. The refusal was something more than a whim. He didn't answer; he extended his hand to her.

"When will I see you?" she asked.

"Tomorrow."

Three minutes later Jorge was on the street. Night was closing in fast. He didn't look back. If he had, he would have seen the figure of Iaiá already wrapped in the half shadows of twilight. He would have seen more: he would have seen her reflect a little and open her hand in a menacing gesture in his direction.

Iaiá went inside the invalid's house.

"What about your fiancé?" she asked.

"He's gone."

"When is the wedding?"

"I don't know the day." And after a pause: "But that it will take place is certain. Or I am not who I am."

Chapter Fourteen

As he rode home Jorge was troubled and restless; he was recalling the conversation he had just had with Luís Garcia's daughter. Fortune had confronted him with an enigma, and time was providing him with the solution; or was it the solution? The young man's mind recoiled, not trusting in reality, at least not in apparent reality. But apparent reality imposed itself on him from time to time, and Jorge reconstructed all the circumstances of those last weeks and even those of the previous months. What were Iaiá's aloofness, rudeness, and hostility if not a mask for a different feeling, the vengeance of a heart confused by the imagined disdain of another heart? This line of thinking was so in keeping with recent developments that it was difficult to find a more appropriate explanation. Immediately he reasoned that it would be absurd to attribute to the girl a superficiality and evasiveness which were incompatible with the prudence he knew her to have, despite her fits of occasional mischief.

"Impossible!" he said, shrugging his shoulder.

But that "impossible" would again descend to the regions of probability, until it climbed to the heights of certainty. Observation had shown him that Iaiá had audacity in her blood, and reason told him that unbridled love is accompanied by all kinds of imprudence and sudden impulses; that some natures are stoical, others rebellious; lastly, that there are moral situations which are intolerable and that to a candid seventeen-year-old girl it is legitimate not to distinguish between sentiment which speaks and prudence which restrains.

That was the benevolent interpretation; then came the pessimistic one. It was possible that all that daring disguised a plan—an ambitious plan which might be an attempt to exchange beauty for the advantages of a conspicuous and superior position. When that suspicion took root in his mind, Jorge did not feel his admiration or esteem diminish, since the ambition, if there was ambition, seemed to be well bred. But it was impossible to make his analysis harmonize with the tears of that afternoon, which were hot and quiet; and he couldn't believe that that near adolescent life could already possess the art of hypocrisy.

No life is so unemotional or free from the consciousness of personality that it would not suffer at least thirty minutes of insomnia in such a situation. Jorge's insomnia lasted a little longer. Mingled with his conjectures was an element of personal satisfaction. The certainty or probability that, through no deliberate act of his own, he had initiated into the mysteries of love a soul which was still young and ingenuous gave his heart a certain voluptuous pride, a sensation which in fact diminished when it occurred to him that perhaps this obscure love had already cost him tears and anxieties. He was right when he said that he wasn't an ordinary person. His early ardor had cooled; his imagination had a more limited flight; but his youthful generosity had remained intact, and with it the faculty to appreciate the pains of others.

Poor girl! he said to himself.

The following day Jorge considered carefully whether it was wise for him to continue to go to Luís Garcia's house with the usual regularity. Iaiá's moral attitude tended to become more aggravated with his continual presence; in such cases absence was an act of common sense and even of mercy. Mercy is what he told himself, and he smiled immediately afterward, a smile of embarrassed modesty. The truth is that Jorge was eager to return there. He was curious to contemplate his handiwork, now that he was discovering it or presumed to have discovered it; *if it was not that, the night had brought a shade of doubt back to him,* and he wished to verify reality definitely.

When night fell he went. Luís Garcia was a little anxious and depressed.

"Come in, doctor!" he said when he saw Valéria's son enter. "This heart of mine is my enemy." His wife was trying to lift his spirits; his daughter had a look of terror in her eyes. Jorge aided the family in comforting him. Three-quarters of an hour later the illness abated, then returned to its silent work of destruction. Luís Garcia was another person as soon as one of those crises was over. He became garrulous and gay in order that he himself might encourage his family and transmit to them the hope he was beginning to lack. Jorge did not allow himself to be fooled by the illusion. He remembered the doctor's verdict, and he sensed the forthcoming demise of the man. Iaiá did not know of the doctor's verdict, but the spectacle of her father's affliction had stunned her considerably. Apparently she did not remember the previous day's talk. One might even have thought that from time to time she did not remember that Jorge was there.

On subsequent days Jorge found her the same as she was on other days, less mischievous, however, and more a woman. At the end of a week he possessed all the elements of conviction. *She loves me!* he thought, leaving there one night. Despite the extent to which his suspicion had cautioned him, the conviction tormented Jorge's spirit, and that same night he decided not to return there—a virile resolution which lasted forty-eight hours.

A few days, three weeks to be exact, went by this way in the most enjoyable intimacy. Even if he hadn't obtained the title, Jorge actually exercised the functions of an older brother. He was a guide, a counselor, an authority. He listened to her with interest, accepted the confidence of the girl's feelings and the ambitions of a heart whose thirst seemed satisfied with the water her own hand could carry from the nearest spring along the way. At the same time he was trying to temper the romantic in her with a strong dose of reality.

During this time, no sentences like those of that afternoon came to shake Jorge's spirit; no tear fell on his hand. But, if the words didn't come, the voice was insinuating and touching sometimes; if the eyes did not weep, they shone or moved in an unusual way. Jorge pretended not to understand. Even more, he made an effort to persuade himself that he didn't understand: a useful recourse which gave him the advantage of savoring in silence the pleasure of knowing that he was loved without forfeiting the contemplation of a unique being, morally exuberant and strong, and which, above all, had for him the fascination of mystery.

At the end of those three weeks they met at the invalid's house. There was no prearrangement, but nothing was accidental. "Tomorrow I'm going to Maria das Dores's house," Iaiá said one night, as she was about to tell him good night. And on the following afternoon Jorge, whose promenades of earlier days had become less frequent, decided to go there; and his luck was such that he found the girl sitting on the same stone bench where he had spoken to her the first time.

On another occasion when Iaiá returned there, she found Jorge already there at the bedside of the sick woman. Maria das Dores was even happier with the honor of the visit than with the money he had taken her, hidden in a handkerchief of floral design. Jorge encouraged her; he told her that they would still go to the Penha that year. Iaiá stopped at the door, surprised and happy.

"Come on," said the sick woman, "come and see how your fiancé is teasing this old woman."

"Thank you," said Iaiá. "Believe me, she deserves all the consolation possible."

On the evening of that same day, when Jorge got home, a little intoxicated from the meeting, he found a letter from Procópio Dias which filled him with happiness. Procópio Dias still needed to delay about two months. Two months! That was an eternity. Jorge felt comforted with the news of such a long delay. Why would his being there matter, if she didn't love him? Jorge didn't ponder that; but Luís Garcia's daughter, when he gave her the news of the letter, asked:

"What's it to me whether he's absent or present? He or a stranger—it is one and the same."

Eternity lasted a minute; the two months flew by like a typhoon. One day, at the end of those two months, Iaiá told Valéria's son that she had finally found a husband.

"A husband?" Jorge repeated, becoming pale.

"So it seems. Don't you approve?"

"I don't even know him!"

"I don't know whether he will be my husband," continued Iaiá after a moment, "but I have found the man I love."

"It's the same thing."

"Or almost."

There was a long pause, during which Iaiá kept her eyes fastened on the young man, while his gaze rested nowhere, but wandered from one place to another. Iaiá repeated that she had found a husband.

"That's the second time you have said that," Jorge retorted, his voice shaky and irritable. "If you have found him, so much the better; you'll marry him."

"Didn't you once tell me not to let myself go with the first pair of eyes which seemed to respond to mine? Didn't you tell me that it was wise to choose a man—"

"What I said were words without meaning," replied Jorge. "One doesn't give advice to a heart in love. According to some, marriage is something made in heaven; others say that it is born of chance. Either it is destiny or a gamble. Certainly you aren't asking me to tell you what

131

the prize-winning number is? Buy a ticket and let the wheel spin. Only a few days of patience. . . . That's all."

Jorge's tension was extraordinary but did not last long. A few moments of silence were enough to ease the tension; at least his gesture did not betray his inner agitation. Pale, yes, he was pale; but if his voice wasn't firm, at least it had lost the rough edge of the first moments.

"I thought some after our conversation," he said, "and I don't wish to assume any responsibility for an act on which your life's happiness depends."

"Then, you don't like me—that's what it is," complained Iaiá.

Jorge answered with a look, and the answer, which he wished to be a simple protest, transcended that limit: it was a protest, a complaint, and perhaps a question. Iaiá lowered her eyes; a wave of color suffused her face. To Jorge she looked breathless and embarrassed for a few seconds. He didn't inquire as to the reason; he got up to leave. Iaiá held on to him by the hem of his cutaway.

"Are you denying me any help at all, then?" she asked. "After several months of a life in which I have become accustomed to listening to your advice, you refuse me now? What have I done to you?"

"Nothing."

Jorge left. *What does it matter to me whether she is in love, or marries or doesn't marry? Am I her father? her tutor?* While he spoke this way, he felt an answer within: his conscience deciphered reality for him. *Yes, you're in love,* it said to him. *You've been nothing else for the last two months; you let yourself become entangled in the invisible threads; you didn't sense that this everyday intimacy was the drop of water which was wearing away your heart. Ah! did you want to satisfy your curiosity and pull out of there without leaving something, without receiving something either? One doesn't play with an enemy; and that's what she was, and will continue to be, because you are definitely caught.*

Jorge shrugged his shoulders at that persistent and true voice. He tried to find refuge in sleep. Sleep fled from him completely. Then he smoked, walked over the grounds; he exhausted his body in order to better put his spirit to sleep. But the moon, which was casting a shadow on the fountain, showed him first a hut in Santa Teresa, then a veranda in Tijuca, as if they were both sides of the coin of his heart, the whole story of the life he had lived until that time. The difference between these two phases was that now disillusionment would not take him to war, nor would it leave him as desperate as it had earlier. No. The following morning Jorge awakened a little shaken but not entirely depressed. He felt some kind of moral oppression, a desire to know who the preferred adversary was. Would he deserve her? And what if he did deserve her? Jorge had first and superior rights; since he loved her, he was excluding all the rest. He thought about it so much that he caught a glimpse of reality; he asked himself if the girl's declaration might not, on the other hand, be a stratagem. It could be: he had seen her blush, lower her head, and remain shy and touched for some time. That thought relieved his mind a little, and he wasn't slow in transferring to fact what had been a conjecture of hope. He recalled all of Iaiá's actions, her words, the circumstances and terms of reconciliation, the tears without motive, the patience, the interest, her pleasure in talking with him; finally, that mysterious something which indicates to one soul another's preference for it. When this idea gradually penetrated his heart, Jorge recognized that he had been impetuous. He wanted to write her but hesitated; he wanted to return there but decided to the contrary.

If it's a trick, he thought, *it will be her punishment; if she really loves another, why should I go there?*

This was what he thought; he thought further. The only thing he didn't think about was Estela.

Iaiá was unable to control herself. After seven days of not seeing him, she decided to go to the place where she had met Valéria's son on more than one occasion.

"It's going to rain," said Luís Garcia. "Postpone your visit until tomorrow."

Iaiá insisted on her decision. "It's a passing cloud," she said. "When the moon comes out you'll see how the weather clears up."

She was restless, worried, and extremely nervous; she paid no attention to her father's second remark. Her father was telling her that there was no need to disobey in order to fulfill a whim. Since he repeated the remark, Iaiá didn't dare to answer. But Estela, who was quietly observing the advice of one and the resistance of the other, said to her stepdaughter, smiling:

"Go on; your father will let you go."

Iaiá was about to thank her for her intervention; but when the eyes of the two women met, each stopped for a long moment. A few minutes later the girl arrived at Maria das Dores's house and sent

Raimundo away. The door was open; she went in. From the room where she waited she heard Jorge's voice in another room in the interior of the house.

"Don't forget; you are to give this to her when she comes. Don't send it to her house; it's a book."

Iaiá went in.

"Weren't you expecting me?" she asked.

"No; that's why I was leaving you this book," answered Jorge, taking the package away from the old woman and giving it to the girl. "It's a novel; I think I told you about it once."

Iaiá took the book from him, opened it, and paged through it impatiently as though she were sure she was going to find a marked page. There was a marked page; the mark was a note. She opened it. This is what it said:

> You once bestowed a title on me which I hoped would come to be true. Tell me if I was wrong—if heaven has chosen another man for you, or if my heart may still hope. It won't cost you much; a simple word costs little.

While she read these lines quickly and read them again, Jorge withdrew to the front room. The letter was of the kind that does not permit the author's presence. Such letters require the fascination which absence provides; they are, so to speak, cryptic expressions which the imagination completes and amplifies. Jorge was going to leave when he heard the sound of Iaiá's steps; he delayed to await the answer. The girl stopped in front of him, and between the two there was a moment of silence and hesitation.

"Blind man!" said Iaiá finally, extending her hands to him with an air of simplicity and confidence.

Jorge took them in his, and the language which the soul didn't wish to entrust to the man's lips, they conveyed through their eyes for a few minutes. Jorge finally asked her: "Is it true? Do you love me?" Iaiá put her arms around his neck and lowered her head in a gesture of submission. Jorge leaned forward also, and on the strands of her hair which fell over her forehead, he placed the purest and most fleeting of kisses. Upon contact of those lips, Iaiá blushed and trembled all over. But she didn't pull away, she didn't withdraw her arms, she allowed herself to remain submissive and happy.

134

Homer relates that Venus, descending upon the battlefield between the Greeks and Trojans, emerged wounded and bleeding.[1] Iaiá's fate was that of the Homeric goddess: placing herself between Jorge and Estela, she emerged with a wounded heart. In the space of a few months, during the labor of patience and struggle, of violence and pretense upon which she had converged all her moral strength, she didn't suspect that in conquering Jorge, she might be conquering herself. She wanted to be a barrier between the past and the present without thinking about the difficulty of the plan, nor its possible consequences. Above all, she didn't think about the moral effect of her action. What could she know about such things? Her mistrust might even admit of the persistence of love in her stepmother's heart, but she attributed to her no more than an aspiration or silent yearning; that was all she knew. It was to combat this silent enemy that she threw into the field of battle that portion of shrewdness which nature had given her, her facial charms, and her spiritual acumen.

Iaiá walked through the doorway and left; she needed some air, space, light; her soul coveted an immense bath of blue and gold, and the afternoon awaited her clothed in its most beautiful, celestial shades. Jorge accompanied her; his feelings were sincere and strong, but less intense, less extravagant than Iaiá's, whose eyes seemed to be saying to everything that surrounded her, from the setting sun to the last blade of grass: "Look, see the marriage of my heart; this is my beloved."

When it was almost nightfall, Raimundo came for her. Jorge accompanied her. Iaiá thought to trace with a hairpin Jorge's name and the date on the moss which covered the aqueduct; since she insisted, Jorge wrote down her name also. Raimundo smiled lightly. On the way they spoke about the present and the future; and during a pause they touched lightly upon the past.

"You know, I am a little unhappy," said Iaiá. Jorge questioned her with his eyes. "It's true, just a whim," she continued. "I wish that you had never liked anyone else, and it's quite possible that this isn't your first love."

---

1. Reference here is to the passage in Homer's *Iliad,* in which Aphrodite, or Venus, comes to the aid of her son Aeneas, who had been wounded. While she crosses the field of battle with Aeneas in her arms, Aphrodite is wounded by Diomedes. Iris, who is as swift as the wind, removes her from the field of battle. Aphrodite is then taken into the fold of her mother, who reminds her that she was created for the battles of love, not those of war.

"No, it isn't," answered Jorge after a moment of thought. "I loved once, a long time ago; but the past is over."

"Are you certain it's over?"

"What a child you are! What girl is there that has never feared a love of the past which began and was over before she was loved in return? That the new love be sincere and faithful, that is what one should ask and require. As for the past, it's like the dead; one prays for them when one prays."

"I'm afraid of souls from the other world," Iaiá replied, smiling.

Iaiá was very talkative that night, and through the following days she spoke so openly of what filled her life that Estela understood everything that was going on between her stepdaughter and Jorge. There are some attachments, no matter how true, which are preceded by many counterfeits. Before the soul realizes it, it has exhausted its innocence in base sensations. Iaiá was ignorant of everything. She hadn't learned to read love slowly and carefully; she had learned it at one blow. Her heart was intact; its awakening was sudden but limpid and gleaming. Amid the intoxication which the new feeling produced in her, she didn't ponder its possible consequences. She didn't ask herself if it was true that in her stepmother's heart there was a longing or a silent hope, and whether this could become the root of unending hatreds and domestic dissensions. She didn't question the future. Strange phenomenon! The memory of her father was for an instant forgotten; love's egotism consumed her.

Chapter Fifteen

Estela's forehead didn't reveal the sadness of one vanquished. Love lingered in her heart like an unwelcome guest, and the spectacle of those last months had only aggravated it. But Estela's moral strength subjugated it. The struggle had been long, violent, and cruel; her awareness of what was right and her own self-respect won out in the end. It was perhaps not difficult to perceive beneath the serenity of her face the exhaustion which great moral tempests leave behind. No one saw the tempests.

Nevertheless, on the day the love between the two became evident to her, Estela felt a wave of anger surge in her heart, a strong and sudden wave. This time Iaiá's penetrating look was unable to read deep in her stepmother's soul; and perhaps that diminished Iaiá's suspicion when she saw Estela contemplate the situation born of her only effort without irritation or depression.

Meanwhile, the illness which was undermining Luís Garcia's existence worsened around that time, and he was compelled to ask for a few months off from work. The doctor was summoned, and he recognized that the illness was nearing its culmination, and with it, the man's life. He didn't tell Luís Garcia's family, but he didn't hide it from Jorge when Jorge asked him directly.

"He will die," he said. "The illness has consumed him slowly, but surely. He may live two or three months."

Jorge was stunned. Developments had taken such a turn that now he was pleading for Luís Garcia's life. Who would have said it a few years before? Not only would he himself suffer with the man's death, but he would have to see Iaiá suffer, whose filial devotion he had witnessed. He even feared that the blow might be fatal to her. He said nothing, feigning tranquility and indifference; but he felt that the events designated him to protect the family, and he was determined to assume that role when the time came.

Estela was no less apprehensive than she had been during the previous illness, but this time she did not ask Jorge about it, although she had seen him speak to the doctor. Of late her silence was more frequent and routine. She seemed disinterested in everything except her husband. She suspected the seriousness of his illness, questioned the doctor, and was given words of hope.

"I am not asking you for false hope," said Estela; "I am asking that you tell me the whole truth."

"The truth will sound cruel."

"Is he lost?" she asked in a muffled voice.

The doctor's silence was a confirmation of what she had asked. Estela felt the blood drain from her, but she didn't shed one tear. She was able to reflect on the danger of such evidence of trouble being seen and controlled herself. When she was alone she gave vent to her anguish: she faced the catastrophe and thought about the consequences of the death and about the uncertain future that awaited her within a few days. The future brought her to the present and the present took her to the past. Life had only afforded her minimal happiness and maximum pain. It was not love which had led her to marriage, but convenience and logic. In marriage she had found feelings of esteem, mutual respect, and the gentleness of domestic relationships. Nevertheless, that fire—whose intensity does not last but which is as blazing as the sun of the first days, a necessary precursor to the restful afternoon and tranquil night—that fire, that fusion of two lives, that expansive ardor, condition of her moral nature, Estela had not experienced. Either destiny or pride deprived her of finding in marriage the sanctity of love. Well, if something could compensate for this loss, this thing that was missing, it was the long duration of certain, though lukewarm, happiness; it was like becoming old under the monotony of a horizon without either sunshine or storm. Destiny denied her any compensation.

Estela had no one with whom to share her sadness, her father least of all. Widowhood would leave her without a family. That idea brought to mind another: that of expediting her stepdaughter's marriage so that no moral bond would survive her husband. One night, when Luís Garcia had fallen asleep, Estela hinted to her stepdaughter that her father's condition was serious. Iaiá became pale. Jorge gestured his disapproval.

"It isn't a mild illness, to be sure," he said, "but that doesn't mean that one should—"

138

"Everything must be considered," retorted Estela. "As I see it, to be prepared for a tragedy is not to cause it to happen. Iaiá knows how much her father loves her; it would be very helpful for him to be able to bless her. Come on, now," she continued, taking a hand of each in hers, "why don't you two get married?"

Momentarily embarrassed, neither of them consented or refused. Iaiá looked at her stepmother, amazed.

"Silence is a way of answering," she continued. "You mean that you agree with me, don't you? In that case there are three of us to do the easiest thing in the world, which is to marry two creatures who love each other. . . . Why don't you ask for her hand tomorrow? The marriage can take place within a few days, 'a la capuchin' . . . it's simple. . . ."[1]

Iaiá had finally emerged from the first moment of stupefaction. "But is Daddy's condition really serious?" she asked.

"All of us are in a serious condition, even though we are enjoying good health," answered Estela. "This house may collapse some day. His illness is serious; it's his heart—"

"You're right," Jorge intervened; "we can do everything in a few days, two weeks, three at the most."

Jorge was not a little surprised by Estela's intervention. Knowing how she felt, he admired her moral impassivity which either forgot or pretended to forget. Then he examined his conscience; he felt that the love which dominated him now, though it was deep, was not violent; it didn't burn in his heart. He compared himself now to what he had been, and this comparison at first was not annoying; rather it was a lesson and a philosophy. Mentally he smiled. Was he the same man? In bygone days he had resigned himself to tragic solutions; now, with equal sincerity, he was giving his heart to another woman. On this one's brow he had barely dared to drop a timid and chaste kiss, he, the author of that scene in Tijuca. He was not the same man. Despite his present detachment, Jorge experienced a bit of past nostalgia; he smiled without bitterness, but with a melancholic aftertaste.

That pride is even greater than I thought, he said.

The following day Procópio Dias awakened him at home.

"When did you arrive?" asked Jorge.

"Yesterday afternoon. This is the first visit I have made. It took me

---

1. *A la capuchin:* modestly, simply.

longer to get here than I wished; but at last I'm here. . . . I'm here, and thinner than before. You're the one who looks fatter."

Procópio Dias spoke at length about Argentine politics and Buenos Aires magistracy; he also spoke a little about the women of the Plate area. From time to time he would pause a moment as if to allow the other to slip in something of a less foreign nature. Jorge, however, spoke little, and without much interest. His constraint became visible when Procópio Dias questioned him about Luís Garcia's family; he answered without enthusiasm. Procópio Dias gazed attentively at him for a few moments; the creases in his brow deepened extraordinarily.

"And what about Iaiá?" he asked. "Does it seem to you, then, that there is no hope?"

He paused. Jorge filled the pause with a smile that was pale but sufficiently clear. Procópio Dias began to sense the truth, but his facial expression did not betray that impression. After a long silence, he began to laugh in a good humor.

"Do you want me to tell you something?" he asked. "I want you to know that I have returned cured. When I think about my sickness I'm ashamed; it's true—I'm ashamed of the spectacle I caused. I am too mature for grand chivalry. The sickness lingered for a while. I recovered with the change of climate; love, at least at my age, is a kind of beriberi. You must have laughed at me; it's only fair, because I do so myself now."

Jorge protested with a simple gesture. But Procópio Dias was speaking with such ease, laughing with such frankness, that his explanation gave to the conversation the spurt of life which it tended to be losing. Jorge grew more expansive, more jovial. He didn't entrust him with the new situation, but the secret seemed to unfold from his eyelids and from the corners of his mouth. This happiness was a sigh of relief to his conscience, as he felt a little guilty in the presence of the man whose trust had been the origin of his recent love. His was also the satisfaction of not having been able to bring about a union with Luís Garcia's daughter, an undesirable and unnatural partnership whose result would have been to give the young lady long bitterness without the assurance of deliverance.

When Procópio Dias left there, he left feeling suspicious of the way things were. *But what about the other girl?* he was asking himself. He shrugged his shoulders but felt no more relieved. He was already feeling a little impatient and annoyed. His forehead was darkened by a cloud. Later a sudden, though feeble, flash of light cleared it up; it was a reverberation of hope. Perhaps he had judged prematurely: it was possible to attribute Jorge's reserve, not to personal reasons, but to a way of interpreting social etiquette. Who could tell? He may have regretted promising so much. That reflection refreshed his spirit without freeing it of its corrupting effects. It was necessary to learn the truth. That same day he went to Santa Teresa.

Luís Garcia had given his daughter's hand that very morning. When Procópio Dias entered, she was beside her father, and he was contemplating her with love and devotion—twice as intensely because death would separate them. He was recalling the time when he and she were heaven and earth to each other; and he asked nature if it was fair to superimpose a strange tie upon the original one, and nature answered him that, not only was it fair, but even necessary. Then her father became happy over the happiness of his daughter, whose egotism had taught him self-denial. If she should love someone else, what else could he do but give in? As for the fiancé, he deserved all the father's approbation—he was the only stranger who had penetrated a little farther into his intimate circle; a loving person, well liked and well off. He could give the young girl, in addition to happiness, all of the social advantages including the most lasting and the most diverting ones. And this obscure, weary, and skeptical man relished the good luck his daughter would find on the carousel of life—something he had never coveted.

It took Procópio Dias only one night to learn of the situation. Despite his assertions, which Jorge accepted as sincere, Jorge had tried to disguise the truth. If Procópio Dias had never seen the girl again, it is possible that time would have smothered his passion. But he did see her, and he thought her more beautiful than when he had left her.

"And what about the other girl?" he asked.

This time the question stuck; it brought an idea with it, one in the face of which even Procópio Dias hesitated. This idea was to poison his recent affection at its very root, no less than if he had denounced the stepmother to the stepdaughter. If there were anything that could lessen the perversion of such a step, it was the persuasion he had that he would be telling the truth. He really believed in the secret love of the two; with a little effort he could cause it to be assumed that the marriage of Luís Garcia's daughter was the stepmother's suggestion. He himself felt that such a union would be right, convenient, and conciliatory.

"Rascal! Two-timer!" said Procópio Dias in a muffled voice.

The opportunity arose. A little irritated with Procópio Dias's assiduity and with the confidence which seemed to be reborn in him, Iaiá decided to tell him frankly that she was about to get married. Procópio Dias became pale. He had assumed as only probable that which was already definite. He gazed at her at length. The extinction of hope did not mean the extinction of his desire; on the contrary, it tormented and incited it. His eyes then mirrored two different expressions: the first involuntary, the same as the one with which the two old men of Israel peeked at the daughter of Helcias, an earthy and evil look; the second a voluntary one, not of complaint, not of pleading, but of pity.[2] The evil idea again began to burn in his mind.

"I didn't know," he said after a short pause. "To whom?"

"To Dr. Jorge."

"Ah!"

Procópio Dias smiled blandly, and again looked at her with pity. "Poor girl!" he murmured between his teeth. Iaiá stared at him gravely; then she smiled and asked with a bit of irony:

"Don't you approve of the choice?"

"The choice is excellent," he said, "but there are circumstances which make the best extremely bad. Listen to me. You know that I have loved you; you assume perhaps that I do not any longer and you are mistaken; I love you as I did the first day. The idea of marrying you did occur to me; I gave up that idea, but the feeling remained. That perhaps will diminish in your thinking the sincerity of my words; but I am responding to the voice of my conscience without counting on your approval."

He paused.

"Go on, finish," said the girl.

"There are things an inexperienced heart cannot understand, things that perhaps it should not be told. Do you want some advice? Don't

---

2. In Daniel 13 Susanna, the daughter of Helcias, causes two old judges, moved by her beauty, to go berserk with passion (cf. King James Version). The Authorized and other versions do not contain this chapter. According to Helen Caldwell, the Susanna story in its older editions formed a part of the Apocrypha, but today it does not appear at all.

accept this marriage; break your engagement, not to marry me, but break it."

Iaiá became pale. Procopio Dias, astounded at his own courage, realized that he had gone too far in those few words, but it was too late to explain them with any appearance of truth. As though he were carrying on an internal dialogue, he shook his head, or curled the corner of a lip, while his eyes, lost in space, had the vitreous aspect of intense concentration. Iaiá looked at him, shaken and confused: she didn't know what to think; she either couldn't or didn't want to understand. Finally, gathering all her strength, she boldly asked for what reason she should break her wedding plans.

"Whatever the reason," he said, "I do not advise you to accept the proposal immediately as final. Think, before making up your mind; the responsibility as well as the advantage will be yours. My advice is that you break it off. Because many times marriage is . . . is a mask, a. . . . Your fiancé loves someone else. . . . What's wrong?"

Iaiá had become pale. Terror, indignation, faintness—her soul went through all these states; she even felt them simultaneously, without finding so much as a word of reply or protest. The accusation had annihilated her. Nor was Procópio Dias able to understand the reason for so great and sudden an effect. The effect frightened him in a way, and in another way appalled him. Some fiber in him had remained intact in the midst of the moral decomposition of all his being, and it was enough to resent the blow which he himself had struck.

"Another . . . what other?" stuttered Iaiá, grasping one of his arms.

Procópio Dias shook his head solemnly, as if to say that he could go no further. This gesture was followed by a long silence, during which the girl was able to overcome her initial agitation and to reflect upon what she should understand.

"He loves someone else?" she asked. "Whoever this rival may be, the young man is now mine; and it is logical that he must love me more than her, since he has chosen to marry me. . . ."

Despite the firmness which she endeavored to give her words, they came with difficulty, and her voice seemed to be dying in her throat. Procópio Dias realized that her emotions were barely under control, and that the venom had penetrated below the surface. It was the first time he had ever seen this painful aspect in her. Before sailing he had known her as a capricious girl; upon returning he found her a reflective woman. On this occasion, the pain, though hidden, made her all the more charming, in a way. In effect, Iaiá's face reflected the condition of her heart; her eyes did not respond to the effort she was making to conceal her feelings.

"If you prefer, forget my advice," he said, "and don't misunderstand me if I gave you a scare. Perhaps the scare is over. It doesn't matter. Please believe that there are impossible marriages, marriages that are destined to . . . to, I don't know what . . . to nothing perhaps . . . or to something very serious, very serious."

"Shut up!" the girl screamed at the top of her voice.

Procópio Dias continued:

"One more word," he said. "You are sure to attribute the warning I gave you to spite. It's true: there is a great deal of spite in me. Why should I speak to you if I didn't have a personal motive? This man betrayed me; I had entrusted my love to him; he took advantage of that trust; he let himself be loved in my place. I'm not complaining about you. You didn't owe me anything—a little sympathy, perhaps. In the future you may also owe me a little gratitude."

Procópio Dias left immediately after these words. He was satisfied. As long as he was able to formulate in one or two rationalizations the hidden feelings that had caused him to act, he found in them the justification of everything he had just said. It was a duel: he had received a blow on the shoulder and was returning one to the heart, a more accurate and probably more deadly one. And if it wasn't a duel, it was ambush for ambush—the right of reprisal.

Prostrate from the blow she had just received, Iaiá didn't even have tears of desperation nor of indignation. There are silent pains, as there are mute angers. The suspicion—which time should completely destroy, and which her love for Jorge was already causing to become problematic—that evil suspicion was reemerging and becoming as fixed as a few months before, when it tore from Iaiá the first tears of womanhood. She could not believe that Jorge's love was not sincere; it was . . . or it seemed so, at least. But it was not her heart that told her of the existence of another love; it was a strange voice that accused him: a new circumstance, which caused the previous doubt to reappear to the point of giving it all the marks of reality. Iaiá found herself thrown again into the vast and dark space of her old cogitations, abandoned, destitute of all human protection. All that remained for her was to doubt and tremble, until she found in the flexibility of her own spirit the strength that could not succumb to any outside influence.

Her stepmother came to her half an hour after Procópio Dias left. Just before, her husband had been through such a siege of suffering that Estela had actually come to fear the final blow; now he was prostrate. Estela came to her stepdaughter with an uncertain step and a frightened look. Iaiá didn't see the change, nor did she hear the first words which Estela spoke about her father. All she did was look on, while her heart seemed to want to leap from her bosom.

"Iaiá, go see your father; your father is very sick today."

Seeing that the girl didn't move, Estela threw her arm around her waist. "Come on," she said. Iaiá trembled all over; then, shoving her hands against Estela's shoulders, she pushed her violently toward the door.

"Iaiá!" cried her stepmother.

Her stepdaughter turned and, placing her finger on her lips, silenced her.

Her confused and absentminded look seemed more like one of madness than of indignation. Estela was stunned.

Luís Garcia was the tie that was still able to keep these two creatures united, now that they were antagonistic to each other. His life was necessary to both of them. One of them placed in him all the hopes of a naive heart; the other one gave him only that last portion which doesn't abandon the needy. There were truces, but they were somber and violent. The two didn't speak to each other; they didn't exchange even one look in Luís Garcia's absence; in front of him, they were as before. As a matter of fact, this intolerable situation seemed permanent.

Jorge noticed it. In the beginning he felt that he was the cause of an occurrence which he could not decipher and which was necessarily serious. Iaiá, nevertheless, controlled herself in relation to him. If the wind had swayed her soul, it soon righted itself. She was tender and warm toward him, and impatient to bring the marriage to fruition. Only one thought motivated her: to seize that man, to draw him to her, to dominate him afterwards, to obliterate once and for all the ties that bound him to her stepmother's heart.

The wedding was set for a Saturday, but early in the week the family decided to defer it until a better occasion. Luís Garcia grew worse rapidly. His illness entered its last stage.

Iaiá saw the Saturday sun die sadly, and she didn't see Sunday's rise any more promisingly. She hadn't thought about her father's death yet, but something made her heart tremble. Jorge's presence gave her comfort and encouragement, since he himself was feeling apprehensive about the immediate outcome of her father's illness.

Slow and unpredictable at first, the sickness had a rapid and inflexible ending. After a few days, death was declared imminent. Estela, although she was prepared for the blow, was barely able to cope with the first shock. Iaiá acted as if she were deranged. Her father had been her first and continuous love. For a number of years she had known no other world, no other affection, no other family except that solemn and tender man, whose eyes protected and enlightened her. At first she couldn't believe the sad news. But the reality opened her eyes, and it was then that her soul tried to rip off its bonds and fly ahead to await him in the immense, blue vastness, so that they might undertake the final trip together. She didn't cry at first. The pain had held back her tears; but they came soon after and she exchanged them for silence, smothering her sobs, writhing in the solitude of her bedroom.

Luís Garcia reiterated to Jorge the request he had once made of him in relation to his family, but now Estela was restricting it.

"I ask you not to abandon my loved ones. I know I am dying and I want to be sure that I leave behind little nostalgia. You're going to marry my daughter; nothing worries me in this respect. But Estela, who is not Iaiá's real mother, or rather who is her mother by affection, is going to be alone, and I wouldn't wish to die with the idea that I am leaving her unhappy. Promise me that you will never abandon her?"

Jorge promised. Estela, who was present, tried to reassure her husband and asked him not to speak so much. Luís Garcia paid no attention; he praised his wife's virtues, her dedication, her zeal, the affection she had for him.

"I tell you that I have been happy," he concluded. "My soul was already old when hers was joined to it, and nevertheless . . . yes, my soul was rejuvenated a little—"

"You have already spoken too much," interrupted Estela. "Rest. I don't want you to talk anymore."

Luís Garcia further asked his wife and daughter to continue to love each other as they had until then. He had spoken excessively; he became weary. From then on death swallowed up its victim little by little. That evening was more cruel than the previous ones; the entire next day was one of anguish for the two women. On the morning of the following day his agony, which lasted a few hours, began.

On seeing him die, the two women remained prostrate for a long time. It was the first time they had looked upon death. Neither of them had ever seen a human creature pass away, and the first one whom they were seeing bid life farewell represented years of tender and deep affection and the strongest spiritual tie that linked one to the other. During that solemn moment, they embraced each other without thinking. The pain impelled them with its iron hand, and stepmother and stepdaughter mingled their noble, sad, and fruitless tears.

Standing at the foot of the bed with a pained expression, Jorge observed the suffering of the two women, without either being able or wanting to help them. As for Raimundo, he was not able to see his master pass away; he ran out to the garden, where he remained sitting on the ground for a long time, his greying head between his knees, shaken by the violence of his sobs.

Chapter Sixteen

Luís Garcia's death presented another complication. The first two months having passed, Jorge intended to have the wedding with little public ceremony as a simple act of domestic concern, rather necessary because of the situation the two young women were in. Mr. Antunes had gone to live with them, and now he was the natural head of the family; but Jorge had not forgotten that Luís Garcia had little confidence in the person of his father-in-law. Furthermore, he had placed Jorge directly in charge of the household. Now it was his duty to legalize and honor the dying man's wishes.

But if this seemed to him clear and necessary, he didn't, under these circumstances, even dare to suggest it to his fiancée, and for two reasons. The first was the natural consideration he felt for the suffering of the daughter, whom he could hurt even more by bringing up the matter of marriage again so soon. The second was the coolness and silence with which the latter had been treating him since her father's death. The difference was unmistakable and inexplicable. But good will can explain anything, and Jorge attributed the new attitude on the part of the girl to the deep blow her loss had dealt her. He knew all about Iaiá's filial devotion; he was a witness to her constant adoration, which seemed to look at life as though it never ended.

The idea of going to Estela passed through his mind only briefly; he rejected it without effort. He limited himself to waiting, and he went there as often as his position as fiancé allowed. He would go at night, not every night; he would spend one or two hours and engage in light and often uninteresting conversation. The memory of the deceased weighed upon all three, but particularly upon the two women. Mr. Antunes took part in these intimate conversations, and it was he who made an effort to restore their lost cheerfulness; he interspersed some witty remarks, which were heard with indifference when not with irritation. Even though Jorge's marriage to Estela's stepdaughter had

148

been settled, he nurtured the hope that something would dissolve it, and upon that uncertainty he was betting his entire fortune.

One night Jorge directly suggested to Iaiá the need to expedite the marriage.

"Since the ceremony will not be a public one," he said, "we won't be giving anyone anything to talk about, if there *is* anything to talk about—"

"Do you want my answer right now?" interrupted Iaiá.

"It might as well be now."

Estela, who was present, approved Jorge's observation. "It would be convenient to decide as soon as possible," she said. "Nothing is gained by letting any more time elapse uselessly."

"Uselessly?" repeated Iaiá, looking up at the ceiling.

"Of course. . . ."

Iaiá lowered her eyes to the two: she gazed at them one at a time, seriously, for a long while. Then she retorted in a sharp tone: "At least allow me the time to mourn my father's death!"

Jorge offered a few words of affection; Estela neither protested nor answered back; she rose silently and left them. The silence was long. Jorge did not take his fiancée's plea wrongly; he attributed it to a feeling of filial grief, which was stronger in her than any other feeling.

"Iaiá," he said, "no one is denying you the right to mourn your father's death; if we insist, it is for the good of the family. Your father asked me to look after his own, and I should like to be able to do it, not as a stranger, but as a relative; for this reason I thought of the convenience of carrying out the marriage as soon as possible. But if you feel that it can be put off. . . ."

"It can."

"Until when?"

"Until someday."

"What day?"

"Easter Saturday, for example."

"Let's be serious," said Jorge.

"Serious? Not until Doomsday."

Jorge frowned. "What do you mean by that? Are you going back on your vow? Whatever the case, I should have the right to know the reason; there must be some reason . . . ?"

Iaiá had risen, taken him by the hand and led him to the window. The discomfiture was visible in her features; her eyes shone with impatience, while her words seemed fearful and recalcitrant. Astonished by what he was seeing and curious about what she would tell him, Jorge didn't even think about attempting to quiet her. If he took her hands it was an instinctive move; but when he felt them icy and trembling, he became terrified.

"What's wrong, Iaiá? You're suffering; come now, speak. Tell me about it. Do you no longer love me?"

"No longer love you!" the girl said emphatically, casting her eyes to the heavens as if invoking them as a witness to the sincerity of her heart. But immediately afterwards she repented and returned to a restrained mood: "I loved you; whether much or little isn't important, but I loved you. You were the first person who made my heart beat in a different way from the way it used to beat; you were the first person to speak refreshing words to me which did me good. . . ."

Jorge threw his arm around her waist and drew her close to him. "You're right," he said, "I shall repeat those words for the rest of our lives. Be kind, and above all be frank. Why should you deny what is obvious? I know you still love me. . . ."

"I?" said the girl, disentangling herself from his arms. "I loathe you."

Jorge smiled. "Why so?" he asked. But the girl's gesture immediately erased the smile that was forming on his lips. Iaiá had pressed her hands to her bosom as if she were trying to contain the impulses of her heart; her eyes sparkled with extraordinary brilliance. Breathless for a few moments, she was unable to articulate even one word. When she finally spoke she said simply:

"What reason is there for us to get married now?" And after a pause: "I am jealous of the past, and you have already loved someone. Just as I was going to give myself to you with my heart innocent of any previous love, so I wished that you had never loved anyone else. What is your heart to me? A surplus left over from someone else; perhaps not even that; even that surplus doesn't belong to me. Let's leave things as they are and each of us follow his own path."

Iaiá refused any further explanation, which was, at any rate, unnecessary; her words were self-explanatory. Jorge left there distraught and confused. The reason for the refusal, to be truthful, was too childish or whimsical; never had a bride-to-be been jealous of a bygone attachment. Thus Iaiá's allusion was neither vague nor without founda-

150

tion but pointed straight to Estela. Could that be it? Jorge didn't want to believe it, yet he could scarcely doubt it.

The following day, after he had finished lunch, Estela's father approached Jorge.

"Iaiá sends you this," he said, taking a letter from his pocket.

Jorge received it eagerly and opened it. He read only these words:

I cannot be your wife; forget me and be happy.

He turned pale; he read the letter again without understanding it, since it was no more than the written and dry formula that Iaiá had given him the night before. But between the resentment and the outpourings of a moment of discouragement and that implication, there was an abyss. The letter contained the mark of a definite resolution, which he had not found or wanted to find in the girl's verbal declarations.

"Did Iaiá give you this just now?"

"Before lunch," answered Mr. Antunes, whose expression revealed that he was making every effort to read in Jorge's face a few of the traces of the drama he supposed was going on there.

"Don't you think Iaiá has been sad lately?" asked Jorge after a minute.

"Her father's death has saddened her considerably."

Jorge went from there to his office; Mr. Antunes accompanied him. The young man's preoccupation was like a benevolent rain to the hopes of Estela's father, all of which seemed to be reviving again. Since the latter spoke of his daughter with the astute verbosity of a suitor, Jorge considered an idea which at first seemed absurd to him, but which he favored more and more. A suspicion that Iaiá's behavior was an act of revenge by Estela, a kind of belated vengeance, pierced his heart. The inexplicable part of the letter could justify to a certain point that suspicion which, though without foundation or semblance of truth, eventually encountered no resistance in his conscience.

Two hours later Jorge was writing these few words to Luís Garcia's widow.

Iaiá sent me the enclosed envelope a while ago. I would appreciate an explanation.

Iaiá's letter had been written that morning after a night of agitation and struggle. Nor was it the only one she had written. She had written another, less laconic, to Procópio Dias. Since her father's death, that man had gone there on three occasions without exchanging with the girl as much as one word about the strange confidence he had betrayed earlier. They were half-hour visits, no more. During that brief lapse of time Procópio Dias did not once vary from the somewhat morose air of gravity which he had adopted. He was not the easygoing man of times past, but neither was he a desperate and pallid poet; he remained somewhere between the two. Events seemed to dictate to him a discreet absence; but, in addition to the fact that he had neither sensitivity nor scruples, there emerged in him a hope, the tenacious hope of the greedy. He did not whisper it to the girl nor did he flaunt it openly in his eyes, in his composure, in his gestures—all of which seemed impregnated with the submission of a disenchanted and passive soul. Iaiá treated him with more constant kindness now; and even though the idea of marrying him never entered her head, she was not averse to that resigned and mute passion.

After letting her decision be known, Iaiá felt that she should give him the final word, freeing herself of the solemn promise. It was not without many a lonely tear that she did it. The poor child loved Valéria's son with the innocence of an almost adolescent heart, and only then was she able to measure the scope which his heart had attained over her. But two circumstances compelled her to act: the first was Procópio Dias's revelation, a confirmation of her suspicions; the second was the spectacle which occurred before her that evening, just after she had taken leave of her fiancé. Knowing that her stepmother was in her father's study, she went there and peeked through the keyhole. She saw her sitting with her head lowered toward the floor, her hair undone, but undone violently, as if she had plunged her hands into it in a moment of depression, so that her hair fell in large waves upon her shoulders with the disorder of the sinful woman in the Gospels. Iaiá could not look at her without her eyes becoming moist.

"Let them get married!" said the girl resolutely.

Freeing herself of her promise, Iaiá reflected that she would be left alone, and that, without question, she needed some kind of support; it was then that she thought of Procópio Dias. She did not confront the idea without distaste; acceptable as someone to converse with, Procópio Dias was not pleasing to her for a conjugal life. She couldn't love him, and, once determined to accept him, she immediately began to detest him. So what? He could be a husband; she did not require any other virtues. The letter she wrote to him was not dashed off; it was written and rewritten. The definitive text instructed him to come there without delay in order to speak to her of a matter which was of mutual interest to them. This, and nothing more than a tear which dropped from her eyelashes on to the paper like a protest against what was written on it.

Raimundo, who had been summoned to deliver the letter, accepted it after some hesitation. He looked at the paper and at the young girl. Then he shook his head with an air of doubt. Iaiá pretended not to notice, but the black man's gesture made an impression on her. She was about to leave; Raimundo detained her, saying:

"Iaiá will forgive me . . . this letter . . . Raimundo doesn't like to speak to that man."

"Don't speak; all you need to do is leave the letter at his house."

Raimundo didn't insist. He accompanied the daughter of his former master with his eyes, shaking his head with the same air as before. Then he looked at the letter as if he wanted to guess what was in it. It was not only a premonition, but also a conclusion from what he had been seeing those last weeks. They had given him the news of the wedding; it had been discussed every day before Luís Garcia's death. With the latter dead, all allusion to the plan, which seemed as though it should have been executed within a short time, ceased. The old servant's heart told him that that letter was something more than an inconsequential message. He wanted to take it to Estela; but he rejected that solution because it seemed like disloyalty. Ten minutes later he left in the direction of Procópio Dias's house.

In the meantime both Jorge's and Iaiá's notes had reached Estela's hands. The widow couldn't believe what she read. Her stepdaughter's letter was an act of insubordination, inexplicable in its essence and form; and if that letter astounded her, Jorge's made her tremble. The disillusioned fiancé was appealing to Estela for intervention. His first love was now his confidante, to whom he was writing without nostalgia, without remorse, perhaps without hesitation.

"Stepmother!" concluded Estela with bitterness; and lifting her eyes from the paper to the mirror which hung from the wall before her, she silently contemplated her still-youthful graces. Iaiá entered at that moment. Her stepmother called her to her side, and showing her the note Iaiá had written her fiancé, she asked her what was the meaning of it all. The stepdaughter remained silent for a few moments, but her resolution gave her strength and tranquility.

"It means what's written there," she answered. "I can't marry Dr. Jorge."

"Why not?"

"I can't."

"Why?" repeated Estela with authority.

"I love someone else."

"I don't believe it; you must surely have another reason."

"What reason?"

"None which makes any sense," the stepmother quickly retorted, "but some reason there must be other than the one you have given. The step you have taken is serious; it isn't proper for an obedient girl; it is tantamount to discourtesy. Never mind; everything can be explained; explain this letter to me."

Iaiá did not obey her stepmother's command, and in order to take from her refusal any offensive aspect, she maintained an air of modesty and resignation. Estela herself did not give up. She made Iaiá see that only a serious reason could justify such an act, and that it was necessary to explain it to her bridegroom; she reminded her finally of the esteem there had been between Jorge and her father. At that point Iaiá trembled all over and gazed at her stepmother with eyes which were unlike those of a few moments before. It seemed to her a sacrilege to have her father's name evoked. She couldn't contain herself. She took one step and interrupted Estela coldly.

"I can't marry him because you love him."

Estela, who was then seated, jumped up suddenly upon hearing that abrupt and unexpected explanation. Her pale face, which seemed even whiter against her widow's attire, became flushed. It could have been confusion or indignation. For a relatively long pause Iaiá did not take her eyes off her stepmother. Like searchlights they were trying to examine, at the supreme moment, all the intricacies of Estela's conscience and all the byways of her past. She said nothing in order to better be able to enjoy the blow she had just dealt Estela; it was the interest accruing from her sacrifice. But Estela sat down in a moment and was the first to break the silence.

"You're crazy," she said, calmly. "Whoever put such an idea in your head?"

"Let's not try to discover now who, or what it was that made me guess the truth," answered Iaiá. "It is enough to know. Suffice it to say that I decided to break off the marriage, that I sent word to Dr. Jorge, and that perhaps within a few days another person will ask you for my hand."

These words completely upset the widow. Astonished and irritated, she walked around the room, trying to contain the explosion of her feelings. Iaiá went to her, spoke to her with kindness and submission.

"Don't be angry, *mamaezinha*.[1] If I didn't tell you earlier what I have just told you, I was certain you would approve, or that you would at least forgive me. The man I am speaking of loves me, and you yourself did not reject the idea of seeing me married to him."

"You're not to blame for the indiscretion you've committed," said Estela, "because before this you had lost your senses. Come here. You have just made an absurd statement and it is necessary for you to explain it. 'Because I love him'? " she continued after a few moments. "What do you mean by that?"

Iaiá lowered her head.

"Speak!"

"I'll say nothing; I have explained enough. If he loves me the way I believe he does, it is his happiness that I give him—I won't say at the expense of my own, because that would be to throw in his face my sacrifice—but at the expense of an illusion, and nothing more. Don't think I think ill of you; I can't dislike someone who has or had some affection for me and who took my mother's place so nobly. If I didn't love you, I probably wouldn't have done what I did."

While her stepdaughter was speaking, Estela had lowered her forehead and was pensive, an attitude she remained in for a while.

"You can see that I was right," said Iaiá. "Your silence confirms my suspicion."

"I!" exclaimed Estela, trembling. "You understand nothing about feelings; you don't know the heart. Love him? I? No. It's not possible!"

"Perhaps not, but what's done is done."

Her stepmother tried to stop her but was unable to; Iaiá left without saying any more. Estela remained shocked, confused, and even afraid. Iaiá's words echoed in her ears, not like a sound from without, but like the cry of her own conscience. She conquered her own weakness, reacting rapidly as the circumstances and the very necessity of her

---

1. The diminutive of *mamae,* or mother, used in an endearing, loving way.

nature demanded. She did not have time to ponder the manner in which her stepdaughter had come to suspect a feeling which she had repressed in her heart. It was urgently necessary to repair the harm done by the girl's imprudence. Estela prepared to answer Jorge's letter immediately, and she didn't yet know clearly what she would say to him. She tried first to call Raimundo. Seeing that he didn't answer, she went to Iaiá.

"Raimundo has gone to take Procópio Dias a letter of mine," the latter answered.

Estela fell back into a chair. For the first time a cruel idea flashed through her mind, the idea that Iaiá's suspicion might be more than a simple conjecture. The look she gave the girl burned with indignation. She covered her eyes hurriedly, not in order to cry, but to escape Iaiá's look. Estela's look caused her stepdaughter's conviction to falter for a moment; her wrath seemed sincere and even excessive; but the gesture that followed was gentler and erased Iaiá's first impression. She thought she saw in her stepmother's attitude an involuntary confession, an expression of weakness and desperation like that of a person who catches a glimpse of her own happiness and judges that she must sacrifice it for that of another.

Iaiá was generous. She walked over to her, knelt, and rested her arms in her lap, trembling with emotion. With her hands she moved Estela's away and gazed at her eyes, which were somber.

"It was rash, I confess it," she said. "I should have consulted you before doing what I did. But I feared opposition from you, and I don't want to disgrace you. I am younger than you; if I had to console myself, I would do so in a hurry. But I don't have to; I wasn't in love. I gave in to a whim, and I don't feel the slightest pain in bidding it farewell. Come, forgive me; and rest assured that I will not love you any less than I have until now."

She rose and tried to kiss her stepmother. Estela instinctively pulled her head back; it was a gesture of rejection which Iaiá's innocent and pure disposition soon threw off. Was it fair to assume so much pretense in one so unsophisticated and of such tender age? Estela concluded that her stepdaughter's action came, not from an insulting supposition, but from an unselfish impulse. Whatever the basis for her suspicion, her stepdaughter's behavior had the earmarks of candor and good faith; thinking thus, Estela felt relieved. She was not generous—that is, she possessed only that cold and proud generosity which is born of vanity.

But she was not insensitive, and the girl's unselfishness touched her heart deeply. She leaned toward her, took her face in her hands and gazed at her with a look both serious and maternal.

"I forgive you," she said finally, "because you don't know what you've done. Your intention is what saves you from my anger—or rather, my disdain. If you want to measure accurately the depth of the abyss you have just created, know that you have injured me, thinking you were doing me a favor, and that the outcome of your mistake may perhaps draw bitter and useless tears from you. Your punishment will be that only I will dry your tears. Are you listening? Only I."

Having said this, she released her stepdaughter's head with an abrupt gesture, one in which there was even yet a little irritation. Iaiá was pale. She sensed in the dry and cold words of her stepmother a breath of sincere indignation; and her soul sank even more than her body, which, unable to sustain itself, sought support on the nearest piece of furniture it could find. The doubt which had earlier crossed the girl's mind now began to invade it. Iaiá looked at Estela with the most piercing of looks; she accompanied her from one side to the other, because her stepmother had begun to pace the floor and to reflect immediately after the words she had spoken. If the widow was sincere, Iaiá had just accomplished her own undoing; that is what she was thinking. In the midst of the moral stupor into which this supposition had thrown her, Iaiá found herself between two desires, ill defined but completely opposed to one another. She wanted and didn't want to be mistaken; she aspired to a reconciliation of her heart and her conscience. She recalled the initial hour of suspicion—that fateful morning when Estela read Jorge's letter—and remembered her stepmother's gesture, her trembling, her ashen pallor, her pronounced symptoms of worry, of fear, or of remorse. Could she have been mistaken? Was it not evident that they had loved each other, that they were still in love at that time? And, if that were the case, was it not possible that Estela still loved *him* at least?

Iaiá held to that conclusion, even though it confirmed the ruin of her hopes; her conclusion, however, was contradicted by her stepmother's impassivity. Estela had already recovered from the agitation of the first moment. After a few minutes of reflection, she stopped in front of her stepdaughter. It was difficult to detect in her quiet attitude, in her role as serious and dignified matron, anything that resembled the anxiety, triumph, or humiliation of a rival. Iaiá remained facing her, looking unflinchingly at her. The aspect of Estela's manner that appeared in her face was so cold, so indifferent, that it could barely be related to the sentiment Iaiá was attributing to her. That was what Iaiá thought she saw with her acutely penetrating eyes. And in the midst of that contrast between her present aspect and the past revelation, Iaiá ended up not knowing with certainty where the truth lay and was at the point of begging her for it on bended knee.

At that moment they were in Luís Garcia's study in front of the desk where the deceased man had found, among other papers, the letter which had given rise to Iaiá's conjectures. There had been no change either in the number or arrangement of the pieces of furniture. Only the light was different, because on that day it had been bright and clear, filtered through an atmosphere as serene as the life of that family had been before, while today the light was dim, darkened by the clouds of a rainy and dreary sky. During the long pause that ensued, the only sound that was heard was the patter of the rain on the leaves in the garden and the ticktock of a wall clock.

"Listen," Estela said finally, "if you have some reason to believe that I love this man, I will have to reveal to you the truth of things."

Estela opened two or three little drawers in the desk, and after some search among the bundles of letters she found there, she took one out, opened it, and handed it to her stepdaughter. Iaiá accepted it, her hands trembling with curiosity. She read all of it; it must have been the same as the one her father had shown her stepmother.

"That girl was you?" she whispered as if she still expected a negative reply.

"It was I."

Iaiá let herself slip back into a low chair, the same one Estela had been sitting on when she had listened to her husband's revelation.

"You see?" said Estela. "It was for my sake that he made the sacrifice of going to war, with no hope of being rewarded nor of being able to someday count on my gratitude. He went to war, fought, and suffered, true to the sentiment that had taken him there, to the point of believing it to be eternal. Eternal! You know how long that eternity of a few years lasted. It is a cruel thing to hear, my dear, but there is nothing in this world that is eternal—nothing, nothing. The deepest of passions dies in time. A man sacrifices his leisure, risks his life, incurs the displeasure of his mother, rebels and seeks out death, and this violent and extraordinary passion ends up at the doors of a simple love affair, between two cups of tea—"

"Did you never love him?" interrupted Iaiá, sensing the quiver and the resentment with which her stepmother had pronounced those last words.

"There existed between us a great chasm, very broad," said Estela. "I was humble and obscure, he distinguished and esteemed, a difference which might have disappeared if nature had given me a different type of heart. I took the full measure of the distance which separated us and decided simply to avoid it. It was then that he departed; in my heart I approved of it. Perhaps I did not deny him a bit of silent compassion, but that was all. Marriage between us was impossible, even though everyone worked to that end. Yes, it was impossible because I would have considered it a type of favor and I hold myself in very high regard. My father had already noticed some manifestations of pride in me as a child. How can you expect that I, with such feelings, could marry a man who was socially superior? I would have had to possess another nature. I found all the joys of marriage at your father's feet. We didn't marry for love. It was a choice of the mind, and for that reason it was right. We had no illusions; we were able to be happy without disenchantment. Your father's feelings were not the same as mine; he was more timid than proud. Whatever the reason may have been for his withdrawal from the world, that he felt that way was sufficient to make me happy. Thus we lived some years in isolation without knowing any bitterness, which is what there is at the bottom of life, without the necessity of having to resort to pretense. . . . I'm lying; I have felt a need to pretend since Jorge returned; it was necessary. One day your father showed me that letter and mentioned to me the secret love which is discussed in it. You can imagine whether or not I was able to listen calmly.

"But with the exception of that event, what else could disturb my soul? I never saw doors opening for me as a favor; no hand ever shook mine out of condescension. I have never known humiliating courtesy nor friendliness without warmth. My name never served as pasture for the natural curiosity of my husband's friends. 'Who is she?' 'Where did she come from?' No one ever asked me where I came from, isn't that right? Did you ask me who I was? No, you didn't. You loved me as you had loved your mother, and I loved you as if you had been my

159

daughter. And all that was necessary for that to be possible was for us to stretch out our arms; neither of us had to ask questions."

"No, we didn't," cried Iaiá. Touched, she grasped Estela's hands.

"Now you can see that I was, and am, a kind of wild animal that prefers the moor to the garden. I didn't feel flattered with the passion I inspired; I rejected a husband perhaps worthy of any woman's ambitions. Was that what you wanted to know? Well, there you have my story, the story of that letter, which we can now destroy. . . ."

Estela picked up the letter and tore it slowly into small pieces while her stepdaughter pondered over the revelations she had just heard. The stepmother threw the fragments of paper into the wastebasket.

"What remains is to make amends and to get married," said Estela, giving her words a light tone.

"I don't know," whispered Iaiá. "What you have told me is serious: that there are no lasting feelings. It seems that after such a great passion, any other probably won't last long."

"Why not? Now, you're not going to want a love that will cause him to leave for war; that would be a disaster. But it is in your hands to see to it that he loves you always and deeply."

Iaiá thought for a moment.

"Swear to me that you don't love him!"

Estela frowned, then showed her the note Jorge had written her earlier and whose text would erase any doubt the girl might have with regard to her fiancé. It was an evasion in order to avoid either confessing or lying to her. The first time she had denied her love it was more the outburst of a heart which wanted to deceive itself; now she preferred to remain silent. The certainty of Jorge's exemption was of greater import than that of Estela. For the first time Iaiá's soul breathed easily. The respect she had for her stepmother, and a little retrospective jealousy which was gnawing at her as she thought about that passion which had been so violent and disillusioning, were hindering the girl from any other manifestation. When she was alone, she felt relieved of the suspicion which had oppressed her for many months; but the wind which blew the shadows away burned some of its blossoms which were blooming in the warmth of the early sun. Her happiness had an aftertaste of disappointment and humiliation; her heart trembled with fear.

When she was most absorbed in this contrast of sensations, she saw Raimundo come through the garden gate.

Chapter Seventeen

Iaiá went to meet Raimundo.

"Did you deliver it?"

"No, I didn't," said the black man.

Iaiá remained motionless for a few moments. Raimundo took the letter from his pocket and held it in his hands without daring to raise his eyes; finally he did raise them and said firmly:

"I didn't think it was right for you to write to that man, who is neither your father nor your fiancé, so I came back to speak to Mistress Estela."

"Give it to me," said the girl abruptly. "You don't need to."

Raimundo gave her the letter and shook his grizzled head, as if he wanted to deny the years which weighed upon it and retrogress to the time when Iaiá was merely a child—mischievous and nothing more. His resolution had cost him dearly; three times he had approached Procópio Dias's door in order to obey his former master's daughter, and three times he had hesitated, until foreboding won out in him—something which pounded in his heart, as he told Estela when he related everything to her.

Estela did not hold herself back any longer. In the letter she wrote to Jorge, she said that her stepdaughter was only a romantic, distrustful, and inquisitive girl; she wanted to break off the marriage because she felt that she was not loved as deeply as she loved.

"Iaiá adores you," concluded Estela, "and she doesn't feel adored. Come and throw yourself at the foot of the altar, and you will find in me the most compassionate *sacristã*."[1]

Iaiá heard about the letter when it was already too late to offer any objection. Her first impulse was to thank her stepmother for her pious

---

1. A *sacristã* is a laywoman or nun responsible for the maintenance of the sacristy.

deceit; but her soul, stung by a remnant of jealousy, quickly repressed the impulse, and the girl's only response was a gesture of timidity and long silence. After that she listened to Estela without either bitterness or impatience, alert to the slightest hesitation which might halt her speech or the slightest shadow of bitterness which might obscure her vision. The truth is that her stepmother's tenderness and the recent gaiety of her manner were characterized by an unfamiliar and violent air, and this excess caused the stepdaughter to reflect.

Meanwhile, Estela's letter reached the hands of Jorge, who had read it twice in order to understand it. The explanation had the defect of being a little subtle; but Jorge's mind always kept a door open for the unusual. Furthermore, any favorable explanation was a good one, and this one had the advantage of flattering his ego in addition to being logical, considering his fiancée's restless and quick temperament. He read the letter without relating the text to the signature, without observing that the latter belonged to the *sacristã* around whose shoulders he had once wished to place the priestly vestments.

That same night he went to the home of his fiancée, who received him with neither joy nor humiliation, but rather a little laconically and meditatively. Neither of them alluded to the recent events; but Estela did, with much relevance and tact. Nevertheless, since the widow's explanation did not correspond exactly to the actual facts, the situation remained unclear and vague, and perhaps it even emphasized the reciprocal shyness that was present. The belief that Iaiá insisted upon more intensity of feeling on his part had not inspired in Jorge any theatrical exhibition, but had resulted in instilling in him greater tenderness and increased the vitality of the feeling which is the unselfish side of egotism—the happiness of making someone else happy.

"Let's set the wedding for this week," said Estela one Sunday night.

"Not yet," answered her stepdaughter.

Even though she had seen the storm which had darkened over her head die out, Iaiá could still observe on the setting side a specter, and on the rising side a possibility. These two ominous points appearing on the scene were ruining the celestial beauty of the heavens and making them heavy and threatening. The mystery of the future was joining the mystery of the past; both were capable of consuming the present, and she was afraid of being crushed between the two. The intimacy of family life terrified her. What could a marriage be for her if she were forced to enter it with that permanent threat before her eyes, the old

162

seed of love, which the first breeze of spring could cause to take root and grow again? She believed in her stepmother's present immunity and in Jorge's complete recovery, but what about the future? Estela's beauty was still far from declining, and Iaiá's modesty caused her to believe that, even upon its decline, it would be superior to her own.

One night Mr. Antunes brought a letter to his daughter, who read it in silence.

"Look at this," Estela said to her stepdaughter, handing her the letter.

Iaiá read it. It was two full pages, written from top to bottom and in an unknown hand. An old schoolmate of Estela's from northern São Paulo state was accepting Estela's offer to direct the educational establishment she had recently founded.

"You can see why you must get married as soon as possible," said Estela, as soon as her stepdaughter had finished reading.

Iaiá felt tears come to her eyes and threw herself into her stepmother's arms. Her outpouring was sincere; affection, recognition, and admiration were there also. But precisely because it was sincere, it should have annoyed the stepmother, if anything could yet annoy her. Estela smiled, a smile that meant, "I know very well that you no longer need me." Nevertheless, she uttered no word at all.

"What does this mean?" asked Estela's father, who knew nothing of the letter, and consequently did not understand anything about the girl's outburst.

Estela showed him the letter. Her father didn't need to read it to the end; the first page had made everything clear. His eyes were going from the paper to his daughter, and from his daughter to the paper, without his lips daring to formulate any complaint or censure.

"I'm not saying you should obey me," he mumbled, "but it seems you could have consulted me. . . ."

"I was certain of your approval," answered Estela. "Or do you think I did wrong?"

"You have never done the best thing in anything," her father said sadly. And taking her hands, "So young! so pretty!"

The date for the wedding was definitely set that night. Since Estela had declared that she would serve as matron of honor herself, Iaiá tried cautiously to dissuade her. The moral assistance of the widow was also not desired by the groom. But Estela pretended not to understand. The role of acolyte which she had given herself, she performed with loyalty and dignity. She wanted to go all the way It was the best way to show herself immune and superior. Jorge felt annoyed and at the same time enraptured as he observed the simplicity and diligence which the widow manifested in her attitude. Iaiá felt only admiration and gratitude. She was now certain that the past was of little consequence and that the future would be of no consequence whatsoever. The marriage was going to separate them, reconciling them.

With the two married, Estela prepared to leave on her journey despite her father's resistance, which was tenacious and adroit. He would remain. He was too tired for long trips! The difference in climate, the absence of relatives and friends, the necessity of not allowing his job to slip away were motives of great import for his not risking leaving Rio.

"Will you at least promise to come to see me from time to time?" asked Mr. Antunes, feeling a sincere tear trickling down his face.

Estela replied that she would; she then asked that he accept a monthly allowance from her. Her father refused, touched. "You are worth a great deal," he exclaimed. The tone in which he enunciated these words gave his daughter hope.

"You could be worth more than I," she said.

Then she told him about Jorge's love and all about the Tijuca episode, the original cause of the events narrated in this book. She showed him with fervor and with eloquence that, in refusing to acquiesce in Jorge's love, she had sacrificed some advantages for the sake of her own dignity, a sacrifice which was even more significant because she was in love with Valéria's son at that time. What was she now asking of her father? Little, yet much: she was asking that he accompany her, that he cease the life of subordination and servitude in which he had lived until that time. It was a way of showing respect for her and for himself. Her father listened to her, astounded.

"You actually loved him!" he exclaimed. "You didn't hate him? You loved each other? And only now do I learn about it. . . . I'm right when I say you are cruel. You have never felt sorry for me in my old age. . . . He is so good! so worthy! And what if he had died because of you? Wouldn't you feel remorse? Wouldn't your heart ache when you heard that such a well-born young man who loved you . . . yes, he loved you very much, and you loved him too. . . . and only today!"

Estela closed her eyes in order not to see her father. Not even this refuge remained to her now in her loneliness. She realized that she must count only on herself now, and she faced the future serenely. She left. Her father bade her farewell with despair, and this time his pain was unselfish and genuine. Jorge quickly consoled him. There was no change in their relationship, and Mr. Antunes continued to find in Jorge's home the same protection and cordiality as ever. If the marriage was a threat to his life, he absolved them of that, and shared with them infinite solicitude. Once again an ever-present companion at meals, he again became the confidant. When he was not there, the hours of leisure which his limited work left him were employed in the sessions of the jury, in the halls of the Chamber of Deputies, or at the tables of the *Carceler*.[2] No longer having the aspiration of a profitable alliance, he became a devotee of the lottery. It was he who secretly gave Iaiá news of Estela.

The former found untold happiness in marriage. Society did not deny her affection and respect. If, before she married, Iaiá already knew the rudiments of elegance, she quickly learned its development and rules; she acquainted herself with all the refinements of society with the speed of a sagacious and penetrating spirit. Not a single cloud from the past appeared to darken the brow of either of them; no one came between them. From time to time Iaiá would write to Estela, who answered her regularly and in the most genuine family style. Ever so often the stepdaughter would send a gift to her stepmother, who returned the favor at the first opportunity. As for their meeting, it was unlikely; Estela put all her time into her new profession.

Procópio Dias witnessed the death of his last hopes with a philosophy he was not aware he had in himself. Naturally he suffered a few days of spite, but his spite ended when his love did. The truth is that the coveted marriage aroused in him the desire not to die a bachelor, and with one opportunity lost, he tried to see to it that he had others available. In the end, he returned to the order of celibacy.

Two or three times he ran into Iaiá and her husband. The last time was at an evening party. He played omber with Jorge, and escorted his wife to her carriage, not without casting a furtive look at its step, where Iaiá had placed a foot that was tired of waltzing.[3]

---

2. The Chamber of Deputies is equivalent in the Brazilian government to the United States' House of Representatives. The *Carceler* was a well-known and popular restaurant in Rio during the last quarter of the nineteenth century.

3. Omber is a card game.

One year after Luís Garcia's death, Iaiá went to the cemetery with her husband to place a memorial wreath on her father's grave. Another wreath had been placed there, with a ribbon upon which were written the following words: "To my husband." Iaiá kissed the simple dedication with ardor, as she would have kissed her stepmother if she had appeared at that moment. The widow's sentiment was sincere.

Something, at least, is salvaged from the shipwreck of illusions.